BEAUTI

FUL

PLACE

THE BEAUTI FUL PLACE

LEE GOWAN

Thistledown
Press

F
GOW

Thistledown Press Ltd.
P.O. Box 30105 Westview
Saskatoon, SK S7L 7M6
www.thistledownpress.com

Library and Archives Canada Cataloguing in Publication

Title: The beautiful place / Lee Gowan.
Names: Gowan, Lee, 1961- author.
Identifiers: Canadiana 20210185155 | ISBN 9781771872089 (softcover)
Classification: LCC PS8563.O882 B43 2021 | DDC C813/.54—dc23

Cover design: Alison Hahn, Hahn Studio
Interior design: Marijke Friesen
Author photo: Marion Voysey
Printed and bound in Canada

Thistledown Press gratefully acknowledges the financial assistance of The Canada Council for the Arts, SK Arts, and the government of Canada for its publishing program.

For Ranjini George, my compassionate one,
and for Riley, Rohan, Sarisha, and Adam.

Beauty is only
        the first touch of terror
                we can still bear
and it awes us so much
        because it so coolly
                disdains to destroy us.

RAINER MARIA RILKE

November 1, 2012

I address this to you, Mary Abraham, because you told me how you had met Jesus in a dream and walked with him to a desert well, and in another dream met Buddha under a tree by a river and sat before him and shared a bowl of rice, and being that you are the only person I know who knows gods personally, I thought you could pass along this message. Either Buddha or Christ is fine. Whoever you happen to see first.

You shared your divine meetings with me the first and only time we met, in my office at Argyle, where I'd worked for twenty-five years. Marjorie, our receptionist, showed you to my door and, when she introduced you, I stood. You wore a saffron cotton *salwar kameez* (not a sari, you later corrected me) with matching *dupatta,* and tiny silver buttons that plunged between your breasts. "Joseph Abraham is one of your clients," you said. You did not ask.

"No, I'm sorry," I said, realizing that you must be Mr. Abraham's daughter. "Not my client. You need to talk to one of my colleagues. Marjorie, is Sid in the office?"

Marjorie shook her head, knowing that I already knew the answer. "He's out all day."

Following company protocol, we were doing our best to deflect you. In our business, it is generally advisable to avoid dealings with the family of a client, as the family interests are not well aligned with the interests of the client or of Argyle.

You produced something from your bag, approached my desk, and held it up much closer to my eyes than was necessary. It was my business card.

"I discovered this in Mr. Abraham's things. You have met him."

"That's right, I have, but I'm only the sales manager. Mr. Abraham is not my personal client. You should make an appointment to talk to Sid—Mr. Hedges. Marjorie would be glad to help you."

You put the card back into your bag, also saffron, but silk with silver beadwork that shimmered in the fluorescent light. You shook your head, your long black hair swaying with the motion of your frustration, and you said, "I would be pleased to talk to you." I smiled and nodded. It did not appear you were prepared to leave. I did not want you to leave. I offered you a chair and Marjorie raised her eyebrows and closed my office door.

You went on to tell me how you had talked to Buddha, talked to Jesus. Wise men and women had explained to you that only a person too shallow to understand the power and the glory of dreams would fail to understand that you had really met these men. And now you had dreamed of me and wanted to talk to me.

One of these men is not like the others.

I am half a century old and worked the last half of my life for Sid and for Argyle. Now that they've let me go, I don't know who I am. I wake in the morning and miss the subway ride to work that I once hated more than anything. This morning, after I finished my coffee and a bowl of granola and yogurt, I went down to the cramped storage room under the stairs and shifted things until I found one of the cardboard boxes I've carried through my life's many transitions since the 1980s. I was searching for the remainders of my previous life in Saskatchewan and Vancouver. There in a banker's box were photos of Denise, my ex, and Sheena, my elder daughter, and I discovered my old journal and some of my fiction and poetry.

When I dug to the bottom, I found what I was looking for: the gun my famous grandfather gave me. A Browning Hi-Power in its holster, exactly where I'd placed it so many years before. It's a nine-millimetre, his Second World War service pistol, manufactured right here in Toronto by John Inglis and Company, and the magazine holds up to thirteen shells. I also discovered a box of ammunition. At least three decades old. Do bullets have an expiry date? They've been stored in damp basements over the years, so perhaps I have not kept my powder dry. My grandfather taught me how to clean the weapon, but I hadn't done it in at least twenty years. I disassembled it on the basement coffee table and polished and oiled the parts with lubricant I'd bought for my hair clippers. Once I had it back together, I slid in a single shell.

My cell phone rang.

I set the gun down on the coffee table.

My daughter Sheena. My girl was up and calling me at seven in the morning, Pacific Standard Time. Unusual, to say the least. I wondered if her mother had died.

"Hi! You're up early. Just thinking of you."

"Really?"

"Yeah. In fact, I was just looking at a photo of you. When you were six. Wearing a princess dress. You're posed like someone about to take over the world."

"I do like to pose."

"You did. Let me see your face. I'll show you."

"Oh, god! Okay."

Sheena appeared before me, sideways on the screen. She was still in bed, her smoky-brown hair, the colour of her mother's, spilling over her pillow, her eyes still swollen from sleep, as if it were I who had called too early and woken her. I could see every wrinkle in her white sheets. Still none on her face. No makeup to cover her freckles. She needed no make-up. She propped herself up on one arm before she spoke.

"Where are you? You're not at work?"

"I'm in the basement. Looking at pictures of you. Here."

I held the photo before the phone and waited. No response. I took the photo away and looked at her empty face. Apparently there was no joy in seeing her younger self.

"Looks like I was channelling the goddess."

"It does. How are you?"

"Fine. I got your birthday present. Thanks."

"You're most welcome. You haven't already read it?"

She shook her head. "No. Haven't. I don't read men. Especially not straight white men."

"Oh." This was something new and, I understood immediately, designed entirely to crush me into something so small I might easily be discarded. A man, the privileged gender. A white man, the privileged race. A straight white man, the privileged sexual orientation. Her tiny father, this privileged specimen, there before her on her tiny screen, had sent her a cheap and stupid gift to commemorate her birthday.

"Edward Albee was gay," I said.

She flinched with a flash of interest before shrugging.

"Gay man writes about straight couple. Brave and exciting. I was hoping for a cheque. You usually send a cheque."

"Things are a bit tight at the moment."

"Tight? Really? What a coincidence. They're a bit tight here too. Mom said to call you."

"How is your mother?"

"Fine. She fell and broke her wrist. They had to put in a pin."

"Unfortunate. That's what comes of not drinking your milk. If *you* don't drink your milk you'll end up with osteoporosis like her."

She let her head drop back to her pillow and rolled her eyes before closing them.

"Thanks, Dad. She doesn't have osteoporosis. Yet."

"Early onset. You're welcome. How much do you need?"

"A quarter million."

"Ah! A quarter million. That's what you were expecting in your birthday card? You're buying a house?"

"In Vancouver? Wouldn't get you a garage. I'm moving to New York City. I got a fifty-thousand US fellowship to go to Parson's to do my master's. I start next fall."

"Well … congratulations! That's wonderful!"

There was a pause as we studied one another, one of her finely plucked eyebrows raised in an ironic way. She was analyzing my reaction. I was trying to communicate my pride in the way I held my jaw.

"Thanks. But it's not enough. And I won't be able to work on a student visa down there. I've been advised not to fuck around with under-the-table stuff. They'll actually kick you out if they catch you. 'Damned foreigners stealing our jobs.' Mom says she'll split the cost with you."

"She will? Very generous. Where will she get the money?"

"She says she'll sell the house if she has to."

"And buy a garage to live in? I thought you were doing well. You won that juried show last summer. What's wrong with Vancouver?"

"What isn't? It's the edge of the earth, Dad. It's nowhere at all. How can I expect anyone who matters to see my work here?"

"There's no one that matters in Vancouver? What about your mentor, Professor Taylor?"

"She told me to move to New York."

That silenced me a full ten seconds. Dr. Theodora Taylor is very close to my daughter, so what does it mean if she's sending her off to New York City? But, of course, it's clear what it means: she thinks my girl has talent. Her great-grandfather's blood in her veins. Philip Bentley left her his talent and left me his gun. If she were able to escape Canada, maybe she'd have a chance to make an actual living as an artist. Maybe she'd have a chance to write her name on history's wall instead of being a mostly forgotten provincial figure. Like her great-grandfather.

"I see," I finally said. "Well, the thing is, I lost my job."

"You what?"

"I lost my job."

She raised her head off the pillow and looked me in the eye. "You quit?"

"No! I was … let go."

"Fuck! Sid fired you?"

I nodded.

"Fuck!"

"Have you talked to Arabella lately?"

Arabella, Sid's daughter, lives in Vancouver and was a childhood playmate of Sheena.

"Of course not. She hasn't starved herself to death yet?"

"Not that I'm aware of. I thought maybe you or your mother might be in touch with her."

"Not a chance. Talking to her makes me want to kill myself. Fuck! So what does this mean? What are you saying? You've got nothing for me? After all these years you must have some sort of settlement?"

I didn't tell her that Beth and my debt on the line of credit would swallow the entire amount, but she could probably see it in my eyes.

"I'll do what I can. But Manhattan? Do you know what it must cost to go to school in Manhattan?"

"Yes, I know! That's why I'm up at seven-fucking-o'clock-in-the-morning calling you."

Tears formed in her despondent brown eyes (even on the tiny screen I could recognize this in the way her face contorted as it had when she was a child) and, embarrassed, she blinked them back. I reached out to touch her, but there was only the machine there before me. We looked into the image of one another's eyes for a few painful moments.

"I'll do what I can. I'll do what I can."

My pension fund and retirement savings plan intruded into my consciousness, not for the first time today. That large pile of money I'd accumulated for my old age, a heap of paper that amounts to my only accomplishment in life. Not even a heap of paper—just some figures on statements. Nearly a million dollars. Approaching the one and all those zeros. A figure that used to designate great wealth, but now wouldn't buy a single house on this block. My last will and testament directed a quarter of it to Sheena, a quarter of it to my younger daughter, Julia, and half of it to my wife, Beth. Enough for everyone, I thought, knowing Beth would not agree.

"Okay," Sheena interrupted my numerical musings. "I'm sorry he fired you. Shitty as hell. You must want to kill him."

I shrugged, raising my trigger finger to indicate my assent to this imaginary violence.

We talked a little longer on the way to goodbye.

I hung up. The gun still rested there on the coffee table. I picked it up.

The infinite eternal math. All those ones and zeros.

I put the barrel between my lips, taste the metal and sulphur with my tongue, and pull the trigger. Easy as pie.

November 2, 2012: The Day of the Dead

I confess, Mary Abraham, that I have not managed to finish the job quite yet. I'm a coward. Afraid that when I act, I will finally meet your friends, gods you've walked and sat with, and I will be faced with their terrible judgement. Or yours. I'm really more afraid of you, for surely only a goddess keeps company with gods?

I will try to put a positive spin on my delay by arguing that I am still in the midst of debating my paternal duties. I can't help thinking of my much younger daughter, Julia, the one who, it might be argued, will benefit somewhat less from the solution offered by Philip Bentley's service pistol.

Last night after hiding the gun under my dresser—last night after dinner, I was drinking a glass of red wine on the couch while Julia slouched at the other end reading, and our kitten, Cleopatra, named by Julia, caught the smell of something she fancied and started licking my fingertips with her sandpaper tongue. Unable to resist the enjoyment of the physical contact, I let her. Who would not allow himself to be licked by Cleopatra?

Julia noticed and looked up from her book to watch.

"She's giving you a disease that will kill you. But not for a hundred years."

It took the breath from me: my ten-year-old daughter was also contemplating my mortality.

"That's good. I'll be a hundred and fifty by then. I'll be ready to go."

"And I'm going to die of it too." She reached out to pet the carrier kitten, allowing her to lick her fingers. "At the same time. In a hundred years."

"But you'll only be a hundred and ten."

Julia grinned, revealing the gap where she was missing a tooth on the right side of her smile.

"That's okay. I don't want to live without you, Dad."

When her pale blue eyes returned to her book, I studied the top of her head, the part in her feathery blonde hair, and I thought that I had not wasted my life completely. I had made something perfect.

Sheena is perfect too, in all her messy imperfect ways. The various and sundry drugs and the hatred for the male half of the human species and the sex with an endless stream of women her mother has made sure to inform me of, all of it little more (in my privileged mind) than a romanticized attempt to sear on the brand of a bona fide artistic identity to her actual work. Superficial and disappointing, but who was ever perfect at twenty-three? At ten, Julia is still young enough to be perfect.

Julia is a twin. Her mother, Beth, as I bragged to you that day in my office when you asked about her photo on my desk, is a relatively famous Canadian television star. She was out of my league, but she picked me; had given up on actors for partners, and saw me as a responsible alternative. I would make a reasonably suitable father for the child she'd decided to have before it was too late to have a child. It was her next big role and she meant to play it well. I was not ugly. I had a steady job and no substance abuse issues.

When the doctor told us there were twins, Beth was ecstatic: she was obviously excelling at this mothering thing. We went out for dinner to celebrate, decided there was no need to rush into a wedding, and I got very drunk. It was more than I'd planned. Two would outnumber Sheena and be twice as expensive as one. I was still hanging onto the fantasy of someday quitting my Argyle job and becoming a full-time writer. The next day Beth nursed me through my hangover, making me a strawberry milkshake and reassuring me that the four of us would make the happiest of families. Sheena would love being an older sister.

Julia's sister passed away next to her in the womb when they were only five and a half months beyond quickening. The placenta wasn't rich enough, the doctor said. I felt responsible: that I had somehow wished her away. Beth also felt responsible. The stronger fetus was too much competition for the weaker, the doctor said. We never told Julia this detail, not wanting her to feel responsible for the death of her sister.

The doctor worried that the twin might strike back and that septicemia from the tiny corpse might kill Julia. And Beth. There was no way to remove the corpse from the womb without endangering Julia. It was too soon for her to be born. Beth was hospitalized for more than three months and I visited her daily, going straight from Argyle to her bedside, then home to my bed to sleep. She was released on day passes from time to time, but came home only for a few nights over that span. They wanted to keep a close eye on her. Wan and swollen, she felt lonely and guilty and depressed, unable to let go of the fear that it was her fault one daughter had died. She had worked too hard. She had not eaten the right foods, not taken the right vitamins, had drunk that glass of wine. She did her best to hide her depression and was known by the nurses for her high spirits and wicked sense of humour: "What do a nearsighted gynecologist and a puppy have in common? Wet nose." They encouraged her to spend time with the other grieving mothers on the ward—they usually recognized her from television. Thus she was given the job of supporting these other suffering women who were not so lucky as her to still have a surviving fetus. She could not feel lucky, or, if she did, she felt guilty for feeling lucky. Her actor friends visited, some trying to make her feel better by telling her that it was a blessing: twins would have been too much for her to handle. All of this only increased Beth's burden, her guilty stew.

I really have no idea, I must confess, of what exactly Beth felt. My failure, not hers.

Thank God for universal health care. If Julia had been conceived in the United States of America we could not have afforded to keep her alive. My former boss Sid would argue, without specifically referring to Julia or any of the other children he wishes to erase, that theirs was the proper state of things: that Canada's liberal health care policy allowed inferior genes to survive and spread our national inferiority.

At eight months, according to plan, they induced labour with an oxytocin drip. If the labour didn't take, they would do a caesarean. We paced up and down the hallways of the maternity ward, Beth pushing the stand with the drip bag of oxytocin that flowed through a plastic tube and into her arm. She was walking because this was supposed to encourage labour. We stopped at the window to the neo-natal unit to watch the babies through the glass, as Beth had done almost every day of the last seventy-five.

"Thelma will be there the next time we come," I said. Our joke, when we were still expecting them both, had been to call them *Thelma and Louise*.

"Julia," she corrected me, "will probably be there," and she repeated the phrase one doctor had used: "There is now a high probability of her successful delivery."

The labour did not take and the next evening, a Thursday, the operating theatre was booked for nine o'clock. Before Beth was wheeled away to be prepped and given the morphine epidural, she made me promise not to look when Louise was being born. Being *removed*. I promised that I would not, though I couldn't help imagining the tiny corpse, a mummified husk still attached to her by the umbilical cord. In the locker room where the doctors prepared themselves, I put on green scrubs and gloves, booties over my shoes, and a bonnet to cover my hair. The last time I'd been a spectator in an operating room had been cryonics surgery: the removal of a patient's head for storage in The Beautiful Place. Sid insisted that all of the salesmen witness the procedure. While awaiting the removal of the mummified Louise, I could not help remembering the sound the saw had made.

My lost daughter. How perfect might she have been if she had been born?

The nurses set up a drape so Beth wouldn't be able to watch herself being cut into. Beth joked with the doctor about how he'd better not leave her with a nasty scar, and he promised to make the incision where it would be hidden by her bikini.

"I'll never wear a bikini again."

"Of course you will."

"You really think so, Doctor?

"There's no rush. I'm relaxed. I feel confident it will be a work of art."

He might have passed for a Hollywood artist, the young doctor, with his chiseled features and his nine o'clock shadow: what was revealed of them above his surgical mask. He claimed he was a fan of Beth's cancelled television series.

"I can't imagine ever wearing a bikini again. Can you imagine me in a bikini, honey?"

There was a slight slurring in her voice that suggested she was stoned. And then I wondered if it was the epidural.

"I've seen you in a bikini. How could I ever get *that* image out of my mind?"

"But that was before. Look at me now. Can you imagine this body in a bikini?"

"You'll get your old body back," I murmured reassuringly. I was standing above her, looking down into her eyes, massaging her temples the way she liked. A tangled wisp of hair the colour of ripened wheat straw had escaped from her bonnet and I tucked it back inside.

"I don't want my old body. I want a brand new young and perfect body."

"I'll do my best," the doctor said with a wink for me. Beth, behind the drape, could not see his face. Peering over the drape, I watched him make the incision. Beth reminded me again not to watch Louise's removal. The incision was a thin red line on her pale skin. Watching the scalpel cut into Beth while she was speaking to me was not quite real even though it was happening: the invasion of her numb body, the vulnerability of her skin. Our daughter had not even made it into the world. Someday Beth would be gone and so would I. The doctor glanced up at me.

"All right. You want to look away now?"

He was giving me the choice, and I realized that I wanted to look. I wanted to see my lost daughter, to have some image of her in order to know her in some way. To be able to speak to her in dreams. But Beth had ordered me not to look. I ducked my head behind the drape, gazing straight into the shocking blue of her eyes.

"You didn't look, did you?"

I shook my head.

"Every time I looked at you, I'd see that image in your eyes."

"I promise I didn't look."

I heard the doctor and the nurses moving around, the tinkle of instruments being dropped into trays as they dealt with the corpse of our daughter. There was not even an identifying smell. At last the doctor said, "All right. We're ready for the baby."

I straightened and watched as he reached inside Beth and pulled out a tiny red squirming thing coated in chalky vernix.

Mr. Bentley, meet your daughter, Julia. She balled her fists in terror or anger or agony or frustration or some emotion I was and am too old to comprehend. She opened her mouth and wailed.

"What's happening? Is she okay?" asked Beth, a little breathless with joy.

The doctor handed Julia to the nurse, who put a gloved finger into her mouth to make sure her airway was clear, and Julia cried out again, a thin piercing scream. The doctor snipped the umbilical cord. Beth began to weep.

"I want to see her. I want to see her. I want to see her." They brought her around to show her to her mother, all the while dressing her squirming body in a gown and a doll's tuque because the room was cold. She was tiny enough to lie stretched out in my hand. Seeing the chips of fingernails on the ends of her clenching fingers, I reached out to let her grasp my finger, but the nurse shook her head and backed away.

"Bacteria," she said apologetically.

"She's so small," Beth said. "How'd such an itsy-bitsy thing make me blow up like a balloon?"

"She's beautiful," I said.

—

The recovery room was much warmer than the operating room. Julia, a month premature, had been taken away to the neonatal ward and put in a closed box incubator on another floor.

"She's not beautiful," Beth said. "All greasy and bloody. She looks like a live roast." Her sense of humour could at times be more than a little dark, the darkness signalling some light had flicked ablaze inside of her. Perhaps the morphine dose had been increased once the operation was over. Beth seemed even more stoned than before, and ecstatically joyful; happier than I'd ever seen her before or since.

"She is beautiful. You're beautiful." I kissed her forehead and she grabbed me by the ears and kissed me back, pulling me down to her lips so that she didn't have to lift her head off the gurney.

"I have never been so happy in my life," she said when she released me—and anyone could have seen it was true.

I recall that moment as if we were floating in a perfect iridescent bubble. It was just me and Beth and our baby, Julia, who was elsewhere being looked after by others more capable than us, by machines of loving grace, and there was nothing to worry about in all the world. I was beginning a second life, erasing all my past failures, and this time around everything was going to be perfect. Vancouver erased by Toronto just as Saskatchewan had been erased by Vancouver. Beth replacing Denise. No more mistakes.

And then a doctor walked into the room in his scrubs, and the bubble burst.

"Congratulations, Beautiful," the doctor said.

It was actually Beth's ex-boyfriend Tony. The scrubs were stolen from a role he'd had in a CBC medical drama.

"How did you get in here?" I asked, looking around for Security.

"I know a lovely lady who nurses here and she gave me detailed directions. You just have to act like you belong and no one looks twice."

"Oh, Tony! Only you would dare!" Beth said, delighted, reaching up for him. "Kiss me. I'm stoned. You wouldn't believe how stoned I am. I feel like there's ants crawling all over me, but I don't care."

"Just like the old days. What will you wear to all tomorrow's parties? A hospital gown, of course. Only you could make a hospital gown look sexy," Tony said, leaning in to kiss her fully on the lips.

He looked up and noticed the murder in my eyes. He stepped away from Beth, took me in his arms, and squeezed. "Congratulations! You're a very lucky man."

—

When we first met, Beth was still doing some acting—had been cast in a prominent Toronto theatre company's production of *Who's Afraid of Virginia Woolf*. She was Honey, and I thought she did an excellent job, but the reviewer in *The Globe and Mail* ignored her performance completely (mostly gushed on about the amazing interpretations of two has-been Hollywood stars who played the lead roles) except for some disparaging comment about her recently cancelled television series, *The Trials of Trudy*. Beth always insisted that she never read reviews and I never mentioned *that* review to her, hoping she hadn't read it, but I later wondered whether it might have been at least one of the causes of her abrupt decision never to act again. She insisted she was giving up pretending to be other people to fully inhabit her new role as mother.

Though I went to a dozen performances of *Who's Afraid of Virginia Woolf*, my most haunting memory of Beth on the stage wasn't from that play, but from another production she was doing at exactly the same time—the only other I ever saw her in. This one was based on a Canadian novel, and was only performed a half dozen times. The play was a little boring, but I went back for each unique iteration. The reviewers did not find it boring and were considerably more appreciative of Beth than the *Globe and Mail* reviewer had been. She was incredible. She was sensational. She was "herself and yet something beyond herself." She was "the very heart of a woman, exposed and terrifyingly vulnerable."

There wasn't much of a story. It was one of those experimental pieces. The actors barely interacted. There were four of them, two men and two women, including Beth and her ex, Tony. The four sat on a row of stools near the front of the stage delivering their lines directly to the audience. A spotlight shone on whomever happened to be speaking, leaving the others in darkness for the duration of that particular monologue, except in rare instances when there was actually some exchange between them, when two or three or all four of them might be revealed simultaneously.

A piece of Beth in this role caught in my mind like a stylus stuck in a vinyl groove and repeated through the years, over and over and over again, to this very day. It wasn't anything she said. Most of her lines had to do with her doomed love affair with the man sitting in the dark on the stool next to her—the man played by Tony—but there isn't a single word that has stayed in my head. What did stick was the image of her in a skimpy red chemise, perched alone in the spotlight on that simple stool, her legs crossed, her left foot on the lower rung, her hands clasped on her knee. Everyone looking at *her*, Beth: the halo of her hair shining in the spotlight, her bedroom eyes, red full lips, the hollow of her collarbone, the birthmark at the top of her left breast. The audience gazed at her up there in the radiance, enraptured. And I knew that later that evening Beth would go back to her apartment with me, and we would make love not quite the same way as we had made love a few hours ago, before I had driven her down to the theatre. Our love was that new—we were still performing it three times a day and never repeating ourselves.

But beyond that image of her sitting on the stool, talking to me in the darkness, the part of the memory that haunts me was my urge to answer her. One evening a feeling overcame me that I needed to say something back to her, to let her and everyone in the audience and on the stage know that she was really talking to me. Only me. I wanted to get to my feet and shout something—I wasn't sure what. Just something that would remind her I was there, sitting in the dark, watching and admiring and loving her. I could feel myself beginning to rise, so that I had to force myself back into my seat and listen, just listen, looking at her up there, sheathed, barely, in red silk.

—

I met Beth at a house party in the west end of Toronto on February 2, 1996, which meteorological records show as the coldest Toronto day of the last decade of the last millennium. Groundhog Day, St. Brigid's Day, James Joyce's birthday, Imbolc: pagan festival of the pregnant Earth Mother, huddled under snow, preparing to burst into flower. It had been reported that Wiarton Willie had not seen his shadow and therefore winter would soon be over. Punxsutawney Phil, on the other hand, *had* seen his shadow and it would be six weeks before spring arrived. The contradiction amused me, indicating, I believed, the absurdity of all manner of faith.

I beg your pardon, Mary Abraham.

I was in Toronto for an international morticians' conference (Argyle salesmen are wise to nurture their relationships with those in the death industry) and I ended up at the party with a couple of colleagues, Mike and Tina, who were having a secret relationship that everyone knew about except me. My marriage to Sheena's mother Denise had recently ended after I'd discovered I was afflicted with crab lice and she accused me of having an affair before confessing that she had fucked a twenty-one-year-old Brazilian sailor she'd met in a Vancouver dance club and that, at the same time, she was in love with a sixty-five-year-old visual artist from Regina who also, very likely, had been afflicted with the young Brazilian sailor's vermin. Denise had taken up painting to fill her days, and ended up taking up with the instructor, an abstract expressionist who had once met Clement Greenberg and went on to base an entire career around a single reference the critic had made to his work.

I felt betrayed and lonely and was nurturing a crush on Tina, so I'd asked her if she wanted to go for a drink; feeling sorry for me, she invited me along on her date with Mike. We went for Vietnamese in Chinatown and then to a screening of a new print of Blade Runner at the Art Gallery of Ontario. Afterwards Tina wanted to meet some friends at a house party and Mike and I agreed to tag along. It was the birthday party of a young director and mostly film and television people were there: Tina had been a film producer before she started selling for Argyle.

The party was so crowded that I never managed to get beyond the front hallway, where a couple of Tina's friends happened to be standing, drinking scotch, when we arrived. Tina introduced Mike and me to her friends and promptly disappeared deeper into the party. We made small talk, drinking whisky from plastic cups.

I felt tired and out of place. Where had Tina gone? What was the point of an Argyle salesman hanging around with people so young they believed they were immortal? I was still only in my mid thirties, but that party made me feel old. I had my cell phone out and was about to call a cab when Beth appeared. She wore a red stetson, blue silk cowboy shirt with pearl buttons, black jeans, and white rhinestone-studded boots. She cradled a glass of red wine in her right hand as if she were warming brandy with her palm.

I recognized her immediately: *Trudy*. It was definitely Trudy from *The Trials of Trudy*, a sitcom filmed in Toronto but set in Manhattan, about a beautiful young lawyer and single mother trying to climb the corporate ladder, raise her little boy, and find love. I hadn't seen the show but recognized her from the commercials—the blonde hair, slightly freckled skin, and ironic twist to her blood red lips that warned you of danger at the same time as her eyes invited you in. TV Trudy looked me up and down and said, "Oh, this is where the adults are hiding."

"Adults?"

"Haven't you noticed?" Trudy asked in a stage whisper. "There's no one over five foot six or twenty-two at this party. Except out here in the porch." She looked around at the blank

walls and the rows of winter boots by the door. "Front vestibule. What are you doing hiding in the front vestibule?"

I felt like the television was talking to me and did not
respond.

Trudy / Beth knew one of Tina's friends, and Tina's friend
introduced Beth Adams as a writer and actor, mentioning
that she was just about to appear in a production of *Who's
Afraid of Virginia Woolf* but making no mention of *The Trials
of Trudy,* which had been cancelled a year or two before.
Something about this omission suggested it would be better
to leave the curtain down on *The Trials of Trudy.* I asked her
what she wrote. She glanced to both sides before leaning in
close to my ear (I smelled her perfume, some hint of pepper
and cloves or cardamom) and whispered that she was a kind
of ghostwriter, penning bestselling books for a well-known
Canadian television personality. Her breath smelled of cigarettes and whisky, which I found somehow erotic even though
(or perhaps because) I don't smoke. "But his fans believe he
writes the stories himself," she continued. "They're mostly
women, and they think he portrays women so sensitively. So,
no one can know it's really my writing. But that's okay. I'm
paid well to keep the secret." I blurted a single spontaneous
guess at the identity of the well-known Canadian, wondering
if it might just be the talk show host Peter Winston, who'd
published a series of bestselling books.

Trudy—Beth—nodded sadly and said, "Now I'm going to
have to kill you."

Unfortunately for both of us, she allowed me to live.

—

Two days later I walked into my hotel room after the banquet and keynote address at the morticians' conference and saw the red message light flashing on the phone. I was flying back to Saskatchewan the next morning, back to the draughty house I'd rented across the street from the courthouse in Broken Head, and I thought the message might be from Sheena. Or maybe it was Denise who wanted to talk to me. She'd grown tired of the pale cadaver of an artist, her lover, and wanted me back.

At the same time, I realized these hopes were not the least bit credible. Sheena, only seven, would have called me on my cell phone if she'd wanted to talk to me. So would Denise. The message was probably the front desk calling to confirm my morning check-out.

It was a woman's voice. She said her name was Beth Adams. With all the whirl of unfamiliar faces at the conference it took a few moments for my mind to focus on that face: *Trudy*. Or, what did she just say her name was? Beth. She said she'd really enjoyed talking to me and wondered if I might like to get together for a drink. She left her number.

I was shocked. We did have a nice chat at the party, but it had never occurred to me that there was any possibility I would ever see Beth again. Except in a rerun on television. I had already turned her into one of those stories of brushes with fame that I was looking forward to telling Sheena. Despite what I would later recognize as her obvious interest in me, it would never have occurred to me to ask her out for a drink. Aside from being the same species, we had nothing in common. I'd always been hopeless at reading the signals women sent my way. Tina was with Mike. For some inexplicable reason, Beth was interested.

I hadn't even asked for her phone number, a fact which always bothered her, as it forced *her* to track *me* down. She'd called Tina and found out where I was staying.

Her attitude toward cryonics also blinded me. Scepticism was something I'd become accustomed to, of course, but it set up a complex set of impediments in my mind. My livelihood was cryonics, but the sad fact was I did not believe in cryonics and, therefore, I immediately felt very uncomfortable when anyone showed anything like contempt for cryonics. It left no space for me to hide my hypocrisy. At the party she'd tried teasing me as, apparently, she'd often done with Tina—"So, how are things in refrigeration? Must be tough finding clients on days like today, when you could just lay them out in the garage?"—and she was embarrassed when I could only respond with a deer-in-the-headlights look.

"Oh? I'm being rude," she had said. "I'm sorry."

"No, no," I'd protested, but couldn't think what else to say. At least I hadn't responded with a self-righteous defence of the science, trotting out *vitrification* and *nanotechnology* and other phrases borrowed from marketing brochures.

Whatever the reason, her phone call took me completely by surprise. I immediately called Tina on her cell: she was getting into a cab with Mike, heading home after the keynote.

"You know your friend, Beth, we met at the party?"

"Yes?"

"She called me."

"Yes?"

"She asked me out."

The line crackled for a moment.

"Yes."

"What's she like?"

During the ensuing silence I heard Mike giving Tina's address to the taxi driver. Mike was from Halifax. He covered the entire east coast. I covered all of Saskatchewan and Manitoba and Northern Ontario. Tina covered Southern Ontario. Derek was Alberta, Elsie was British Columbia, and Michel was Quebec. Sid had dubbed us The Super Six.

"Beth is very nice," Tina said in a girlish saccharine voice she only used with clients. There was another silence. "She has a beautiful apartment."

I called Beth five minutes later and got her machine; imagined my voice talking hollowly in her beautiful apartment. With an embarrassing sense of urgency I said I was delighted she'd called and I'd really enjoyed talking to her too and I'd love to go for a drink, but I was flying back to Saskatchewan the next morning, so unfortunately it didn't look like we'd be able to get together, but if she did happen to get the message in the next hour I was still up and wouldn't mind at all going for a drink, though I couldn't stay out too late or I'd be a zombie tomorrow.

I'd already undressed by the flickering glow of the television when the phone rang. It was Beth. She apologized for calling so late, but she'd been out at a meeting and had just come home and heard my message and wondered if there was any chance I'd still like to go for that drink. I said I'd be delighted, before remembering I'd used that word in my message. I never used that word. Who exactly was I pretending to be? I said it would be a pleasure to have a drink with her.

"Great. I promise I won't keep you out too late." She didn't mention zombies; suggested a place on College in Little Italy and we agreed to meet there in half an hour.

I struggled back into my clothes and surveyed myself in the mirror. My shirt was wrinkled and I only had the single pressed one I'd saved for the flight the next morning, but I took off the wrinkled one and put on the fresh shirt and my suit jacket, black wool overcoat (ten per cent cashmere), and black leather gloves, before rushing downstairs and climbing into a cab. I was only a couple of minutes late reaching the restaurant and was relieved to see that Beth hadn't yet arrived.

Twenty minutes later there was still no sign of her. When she was thirty minutes late, I began to imagine she wasn't coming, and wondered how long I should wait. It wasn't anger I felt, but a bewildered sense of shame for being so foolish as to have believed that such a beautiful woman would actually put up with being seen with me in that bar. I was the only person in the room who was alone, and it wasn't a large room, so there was no doubt that everyone noticed me sitting there by myself. I surveyed the curlicues of the plaster mouldings and sculpted ceiling as though studying them was my reason for coming. A man at the next table in a purple velour jacket had a sharp, cruel, laugh that skewered me every time it erupted.

And then through the window I saw her directly in front of the restaurant, stepping from a yellow cab. Exhaust plumed from the idling car, wafting sluggishly in the bitter cold, but the yellow paint was so cheerful and welcoming that I caught myself smiling in the reflection in the window. Her foot extended out the door and Beth Adams emerged looking hurried and a bit upset. She wore a long overcoat and, despite the temperature, a dress that couldn't be seen: her lovely calves were visible above a pair of spiked heels. Women do this in Canada: wear their dresses and heels as if to spite the ice and snow. I raised my right hand to signal my presence, but she didn't see me through the glass, was too focussed on something in the direction of her feet. She paused, staring down with an expression of horror. She hadn't closed the door to the cab. All at once she got back inside, slammed the door between us, and said something to the cab driver. I could barely make her out through the night and the two layers of glass separating us. The cab drove away.

I sat staring into my own reflected eyes, seeing a man who appeared to have taken a severe blow to the head. It was as though I'd re-experienced my entire broken marriage in that moment as I'd watched her burst from the cab only to retreat immediately back inside and drive off into the frigid night. The anticipation and the rejection managed to encompass it all: the sudden realization that there was nothing desirable about me.

The man in purple velour put a hand on his companion's shoulder and squeezed. I recognized something authentic in that squeeze that made me focus on their conversation in an attempt to distract myself. His back was to me and so I didn't hear what he said, but I did hear his companion's response: "Stage four. Too late for radiation and surgery's not an option because it's both lungs. Everywhere. They'll try chemo but they say it'll only give me a few extra months." The man in purple velour let his hand slip from the shoulder. "A few months is something. It'll have to do."

The dying man looked up and caught me staring at him.

"Excuse me," he said. "Would you like to join us?"

I shook my head. "I'm sorry?"

"Are you?" asked the man. "I had the impression you were eavesdropping on our conversation. Is that what you're sorry about?" The other man had turned, dazed, to see who his friend was talking to.

I stood and teetered, a bit dizzy, the few feet to their table.

"I am sorry. I really am sorry. I did overhear. I didn't mean to. I was just … waiting for someone. I'm so sorry. You must be in shock." The man nodded, looking pleased that someone had diagnosed this fact.

"It's okay," the man said, a little embarrassed now that he'd made such a scene, waving a hand to dismiss the whole thing.

"No, it's an unforgiveable intrusion. I assure you, it wasn't intentional."

"I believe you. I appreciate the apology."

I nodded. "God bless you," I said. I had no idea where this came from, but suddenly it came out of my mouth.

The man gave me a look as if he were finally recognizing the face in a mirror that had puzzled him. He sprang to his feet and embraced me. At first I thought the man was weeping, but he was only taking very deep breaths. The man in purple velour watched with a helpless expression. Seconds passed, the man still clinging to me. I would have held him longer but my cell phone rang and the man took this as a signal to release his grip and take a step back. I answered the phone.

"It's Beth," the voice said.

Both men were still watching me, listening, as though there were some possibility the call might be for them. I held up my hand, rigid, gave a regal sort of wave and turned away from them, walking back to my table.

"I'm sorry I'm so late. You'll never believe what happened. I was all the way there, to where you are, and when I was getting out of the cab I noticed I had a long tear in my stocking. I know it's stupid, but I knew it would drive me crazy and I wouldn't enjoy myself, so I'm on my way back to change my stockings and I'll be there in a few minutes. Half an hour at most."

An hour later, she arrived.

The most striking feature of Beth, even more striking than her dangerous blue eyes and red lips, is her hair, which at that time reached most of the way to her waist, and in its meticulous shimmering waves managed to convey both her practiced composure and a hint of the volcano that lurked beneath. She liked to run her fingers through the mane with one hand, like a young girl petting a horse, while she held a cigarette with the other. (We had met in a millennium when it was still legal to smoke in public places). We talked mostly about relationships: I elaborated considerably on my broken marriage. Beth was fascinated with Sheena. I told her about Denise's new relationship with the decaying artist she had left me for, painting myself as the martyr.

"You've never had an affair?" she asked.

I coughed. She went on to tell me about something that particularly shamed her. Years before, during *Trials of Trudy*, after a serious fight with the boyfriend she lived with at the time, she'd fallen into bed with a guest star on the show,

Tony Lee-Knight. The next morning she went back to her boyfriend, her co-star on the show, and confessed the whole thing. She felt good about that at least. Coming clean.

Once she'd told me, I confessed I'd had more than one affair. Well, not really affairs. Like the experience she'd described, they didn't amount to more than one night stands. Can you really call that sort of random and unsatisfying fumbling an affair? But, at any rate, I was suitably ashamed. In fact, ashamed enough to speculate that the whole dismal failure of my marriage might have been entirely my own fault. Unlike Beth, I hadn't come clean until I'd found out about Denise's affair with the artist. My pitiful revenge. I asked Beth if her boyfriend had actually been pleased to know about her deed. Surely the telling hadn't washed her clean in his eyes?

"No. He hit me. He almost broke my arm. We never really recovered. At some point the damage gets so deep it's impossible to fix." She shrugged, and flipped the cascade of her hair back over her left shoulder. "But I'm still glad I told him. That's important to me. The truth. That's when I started my relationship with Tony. But that's another sad story."

On that first date we were already attempting to give each other important lessons about ourselves, and we were listening and not listening, our eyes and ears both open and closed. Mostly we wanted to touch, but neither of us was ready to acknowledge this yearning. We were superstitious and aware that touching too soon might make our meeting part of the random and unsatisfying behaviour we were testifying to as a means of sharing some kind of intimacy that would serve to replace the intimacy we really wanted to share. She drank red wine, I drank manhattans.

I was still feeling confused about why she'd be interested enough in a salesman from Saskatchewan to want to have a drink with him, when she smiled, lovingly stroked her hair, and said, "Did you know your grandfather well?"

For a moment I could not speak. Tina must have told her my grandfather was Philip Bentley. It was the only thing about me that interested Tina. That, and the fact I had actually succeeded in selling cryonics to farmers. A hollow sensation exploded in my chest like an umbrella opening and I felt myself fading away right in front of her. Trudy. Beth. She didn't even see me. I was nothing but my name. I imagined her repeating it, her lips vaginal in their sensuousness. *Bentley, Bentley, Bentley.* She was having a drink with a Bentley and they drank manhattans.

"I didn't know him at all when I was growing up. In fact, for a long time I didn't even know he *was* my grandfather." I fished the cherry from my drink and swallowed it. "You're a fan of his work?"

For the first time, she looked uncomfortable.

"Not exactly. I mean … I respect his work, but it's really not my thing. It's a bit dated." She looked at me nervously, apologetically, trying to judge my reaction to this observation. "Kind of Group of Sevenish? Which is great if you like that kind of thing. I prefer abstract. Rothko. Newman. De Kooning." My mind was suddenly overwhelmed by the image of the face of Denise's corpse lover. "I just think formalism didn't really survive the twentieth century. It can't feel fresh. Too overripe to have any real life left. At the same time, I really respect the importance of your grandfather's work in what it did to push the boundaries at the time, and how it influenced a lot of really important painters in Canada." I nodded, but didn't offer anything to help her out of the hole she was digging. She grinned and shrugged. "I'm more interested in photography. How could formalism in painting compete with photography? How could you not know he was your grandfather?"

"My father didn't want me to know. Did you study visual art?"

"No, no, not at all. I'm just … interested in it. I'm no expert by any means."

"But you know what you like."

She watched me fade away until she could see the wall behind me and she began to worry that she was there all alone. She was too beautiful to know how to be alone.

"I honestly do respect his work a great deal. The Main Street series is amazing. In its way. For its time. No one would deny that."

"Oh, but people do. People hate it. One critic said that he was responsible more than any other single person for Canadian art's reputation of being boring. I guess that would make him important. In a way. For his time."

"I didn't say his work was boring. I don't think Canadian art is boring. Why didn't your father want you to know he was your grandfather?"

"Because he abandoned my grandmother and my father. He ran away to become a famous painter."

"But wasn't that because he was gay?"

I had been worrying the cherry pit with my tongue. I took it from my mouth and placed it in her ashtray.

"I don't really want to discuss my grandfather. I don't know all that much about him. You probably know more than I do. You'd be better off to buy a book than talk to me. Someone just published a new biography, I heard."

Beth leaned back in her chair, her eyes on my hands, and for a moment I had to look at the table between us, until I realized that the reason I had to look away was because she was seeing me. I lifted my chin and met her eyes.

"You have beautiful hands," she said. "I wanted to have a drink with you because I wanted to hear you talk about your daughter some more. I love the way you talk about your daughter. I'd love to meet her. And I wanted to see if your hands were as beautiful as I remembered them being."

I was blushing.

The man with the purple jacket and his friend rose to leave, both nodding politely in my direction as they pulled on their overcoats and gloves. I excused myself and went over to shake the man's hand, squeeze his shoulder, wish him well. He thanked me, sincerely, his friend in velour looking at the door.

"You know a lot of people in Toronto?" Beth said when I returned. I explained what I'd accidentally overheard. She leaned forward, her eyes widening as I described the man embracing me. She was smoking a cigarette, and though the mention of lung cancer didn't make her butt it out, she moved the filter away from her lips.

"You gave him your business card?"

"No."

"Why didn't you give him your card?"

I thought she was making fun of my job again. I looked at the table and told her it wouldn't have been appropriate. I had a policy of never offering services unless solicited.

"It would be appropriate," she said. "He's facing oblivion. You offer a solution."

"A possible solution," I said. "For those who are interested in the possibility. If he's interested, he'll contact us."

She took a deep drag on her cigarette and tapped it on the ashtray, burying my cherry pit.

"Oh, that's interesting. I respect that approach. But what if he isn't aware of the possibility? Tina would have given him her card."

I studied her eyes and the way she pressed her lips together, trying to see if she was mocking me, but what I saw was entirely genuine. Or perhaps that's all I was willing to find in those blue eyes.

"You're probably right. Have you seen Tina do that?"

Beth shrugged.

"She did it to me. I'm one of Tina's clients. But, now that I think about it, I honestly prefer your approach."

—

That was oh so long ago. If we had turned that day to see our future selves sitting at the next table, we would not have recognized the unhappy couple.

We went to an appointment with our marriage counsellor this afternoon. The doctor would not like that title—has important letters after his name. We had not seen him in a while, but Beth thought it might be time again to subject ourselves to the excruciating methods of this trained scientist of the human mind.

The doctor's office is on Queen East above a health food store, just a block from Lake Ontario and a few blocks from our home. As I pulled open the door for her, I imagined my-self bolting in the direction of the water for a peaceful stroll on the boardwalk, beneath the naked November oaks. I had not even settled in my chair when Beth began her furious ex-position of the shock and awe of my firing and the financial burden this will cause her, and my supposed blaming of her for the firing, and the main issue: my alleged dalliance with you, Mary Abraham, a client's daughter, the real cause of my termination. She might have been a witness in a court-room testifying to my terrible overwhelming guilt, sitting rod-straight in the chair she'd chosen: the one closest to the doctor's desk. My chair, as always, was the one by the win-dow. Otherwise my chair and hers were exactly alike, white and modern, and overly comfortable despite their severe appearance. Our identical chairs were separated by a little table with a potted plant. I thought about the chairs in order to avoid focussing on Beth, who had been all day rehears-ing what she would say and had whipped herself into such a frenzy that she was visibly shaking. I stared at the potted plant, which had tiny white flowers (presumably to match the chairs), until I detected a long silence and realized that I was expected to speak.

"Yes, I lost my job. As Beth says, my firing was related to this woman, Mary Abraham—to the fact that Beth would not allow me to meet with her. That's a rule we made here in this office, under your guidance, Doctor: that I need Beth's permission to meet people for coffee. So that she feels safe. And so I asked for permission and was not given permission and so I did not meet with Mary Abraham." I spoke to the window, making it clear it was the doctor's fault I had lost my job. The sound of a streetcar squealing past interrupted me for a moment, thereby forcing me to make a dramatic pause. It is a small room, our dear doctor's office, not unlike my former office at Argyle, except for the degrees decorating the wall above the doctor's desk and my office's lack of gratuitously comfortable chairs. My office had a better view. "It was an agreement we made right here. *I* made. Therefore, I take full responsibility. My firing was my fault alone. I have not and do not blame Beth."

"Agreed to what?" Beth asked. "You could have met her in your office. We didn't agree to anything that would not allow you to meet clients in your office."

"Mary Abraham was not a client. She is the daughter of one of Sid's clients and she didn't want to meet in the office. Our business contradicted her faith and beliefs, and so she emailed to ask to meet outside the office. And so, according to the terms we agreed to, right here in this office, I asked you if it was okay to meet her outside my office, for coffee, and you said it wasn't. Which was your prerogative. You did not feel safe."

"She asked *you* for coffee?" Beth asked, using a dramatic intonation that has become all too familiar: she was being Trudy from *The Trials of Trudy*. "Are you sure it wasn't *you* who asked *her* out for coffee?"

I looked from Beth to the silent doctor, both awaiting my response. This is generally his tactic: give us a forum to flail away at one another while he looks on, only now and then interjecting with some vague reference to some vague plan of his that will suddenly somehow be revealed to us and make us well and happy. His major dogma is that running a marriage is like running a small business.

"No. I did not ask her. She asked me for coffee."

Beth dove for her purse, ripped open the clasp, and produced a sheet of neatly folded paper that she handed to the doctor.

"Liar!" She was facing the doctor when she shouted, so for a moment it seemed she was calling *him* a liar. "Here's his email to her. I went onto his computer and found it and printed it off. I just had to know if he was lying again."

Busted. Guilty as charged. Trudy's courtroom triumph. The music rises into a baroque crescendo. The villain on the stand opens his mouth but cannot speak.

The doctor waved the piece of paper away, making it clear that he was a man too principled to stoop to reading private emails.

"Is this true? Were you lying about the woman inviting you for coffee? Did you invite her?"

"No!" I protested.

Beth shook the piece of paper in my face.

"I can't remember. If I made the invitation it was only because she'd already made it clear that she didn't want to meet in the office. I did meet her in the office once, the only time I met her, before her father died, and at that time she made it clear she doesn't believe in what we do there. She wanted to meet on neutral ground."

"It's here in black and white," Beth said. "You invited her."

The doctor nodded, stroking the cleft in his chin and smiling faintly.

"And do you recall that you *also* both agreed that you would no longer lie to one another under any circumstances, and if either of you broke that agreement, you both agreed that this marriage would be over."

"That's right!" Beth cried.

"So that being the case," Dr. Mengele continued, "there's really nothing to do but continue these sessions as a means to resolving your separation in the healthiest way possible. We need to deal with your grief and all the implications that your living apart will have for your daughter."

Numbness spread through me: blood congealing in my veins. It felt as though my skull had been battered by some blunt metal object. I saw an image of my grandfather's gun discharging into my head.

"Her father was a client. It was to be a business meeting and *we did not in fact meet.* We did not even meet. Which is why I was fired."

Beth was weeping, but what could I, the liar, the betrayer, possibly do to comfort her? Only the doctor, her ally, could calm her now. Out on the street, the bell of the Queen car rang its way past.

"Liar," Beth repeated, shaking her head mournfully, tragically, and I saw an image of her on that stool in her red silk. I was thus transposed into the loathsome character Tony always played.

"I really don't see where this is getting us…" the doctor said before I interrupted him.

"Me neither. Good-bye."

I struggled to my feet, wavering, dizzy, so that I almost collapsed, but caught my balance by placing a hand on the pale cream of the approaching wall and stumbled toward the door.

"Sit down, Mr. Bentley. We need to talk about this. Please take your seat. You can't run away from this. You've lost your job and now you've lost your marriage, but you have a daughter who needs to be made to feel her world isn't falling apart."

I closed the office door, gently, behind me. In the reception area, I couldn't help but notice that one of the other offices was for a family law lawyer and wondered if Dr. Mengele had some sort of kickback arrangement with his solicitor neighbour.

By the time I got to the street there was no streetcar in sight.

I picked up Julia from daycare and still got home before Beth, so I started dinner and had it almost ready by the time she arrived. She looked in on me at my kitchen preparations, said not a word, then went into her office and shut the door. When I called them for dinner, Julia came in five minutes and Beth in ten.

"I think Robert Winthrop likes me," Julia broke the silence. Beth did not seem to hear: stared into her plate, willing the pasta to rise to her mouth.

"Why do you think so?" I asked.

"I don't know." Julia sucked in a noodle and wiped her lips with her sleeve. "He said so."

"Could be," I said.

—

I have no idea why she is so insecure about other women. As you well know, Mary Abraham, there is nothing between us. I barely know you. I met you only that once in my office. We did not share coffee. I have never been unfaithful to Beth.

She doubts this, imagines numerous liaisons with numerous women based on the one night stands I confessed had happened during my first marriage, and she insists that even if none of these recent imagined affairs have actually occurred that I have been unfaithful in my mind. Emotionally unfaithful.

Okay. But even though the first anniversary of the last time we made love is about to pass, even when I do imagine other women in that way, something inside me unfailingly leads me back to imagining Beth on one particular evening not long after we first met, back in 1996. I'd come to Toronto on the pretext of a business meeting, but really to see her. That was just before Argyle was bought by the California venture capital company.

Even as I was boarding the flight in Saskatoon, I was beginning to feel ill. I only barely managed to struggle through Pearson Airport, huddle into a limousine, and make it to my hotel room before I was heaving my entire being into the toilet bowl. It was a nasty flu, so powerful I could hold nothing down for two full days, sleeping almost all of that time, the room darkened, the whole world unaware of my existence, except the maid who I sent away each day after she'd cleaned the washroom. She wore a pair of blue rubber gloves.

"You need doctor?" she asked in an accent I couldn't place. Cambodian? A survivor of the killing fields now cleaning my viral toilet? Did she consider this progress? Obviously.

"I'm okay. I'll be fine. Just need sleep."

When I finally got enough strength to call Beth and let her know I was in the city, she came carrying supplies: cold medicines and juices and hot soup that I refused to eat. She urged me to call Sheena, only seven years old at that time, and tell her that I was okay. I did. It had not occurred to me that Sheena might be worried or miss me, and when I talked to her, after a tense few words with her mother, she was distracted by friends she had over and it did not sound as though she missed me at all.

"She's okay?" Beth said when I'd hung up the phone.

I nodded, smiled weakly, thanked her again for coming.

"Daddy's okay?"

She crawled into the bed to nurse me, felt my fever, my weak quivering limbs, and the next thing I knew she was making love to me. It is this image that I keep returning to as I am relieving myself of pent-up sexual energy: Beth straddling me, breasts swaying, hips rocking rhythmically so that I appear and disappear inside of her, mouth opening wide as she comes.

I apologize for sharing this image with you, Mary Abraham, but I want you to know that I still desire my wife. It is she who no longer desires me.

I did not mess up this marriage in the same way I damaged the first. There is a contrast between the two that creates a tension and an aesthetic pleasure. I'm no artist like my grandfather, the great Philip Bentley. The modest work I tried to create—no masterpiece—is a life itself, a life I strove to live in a way my daughters might admire, despite my mistakes. I am aware that I've made mistakes, but there is a subtle contrast between my two marriages that I believe has beauty.

November 3, 2012 3:30 a.m.

I'm about to chop off the head of your father, Mr. Joseph Abraham. He kneels before me, his neck on the scarred wooden block. I look away, embarrassed by the intimacy of his posture (crouched on his knees, hands clasped behind his back at the base of his spine in a sort of unorthodox prayer) and I notice I am wearing blue scrubs and that the axe is leaning there against the wall of the operating theatre, the handle smeared darkly with blood.

Impatient axe.

The feeling of an axe waiting is unlike anything I've experienced before. The blade glares at me and smiles an empty smile. Your father senses my hesitation, straightens to his knees, and squints up at me.

"I'm ready," he says. "Please make sure my wife is well looked after …"

—

I woke up sweating.

In your email you said your frozen father had come with a message for you, Mary Abraham: that he wished to be buried and that it was your duty to get him underground. Now he has come with a message to me. A message about your mother. Why would he come to me?

After the dream I lay there in bed, contemplating the ceiling, the blemish below where the racoon clawed through the roof a few years back and the rain got in. I had climbed up into the attic to find the mother and three babies nested in a low spot where the joists meet wall. When I moved the beam of my flashlight across them, the mother bared her teeth and hissed. I considered if there was any way I might tidily exterminate the entire family (carbon monoxide, arrows, bludgeon, axe) but instead opted for the socially acceptable alternative and phoned a pest control professional. He came and trapped them to release somewhere not too far away. I'm sure they were back in someone else's attic a couple of days later. Job security for pest control professionals. Dad would have taken care of them. But that's not how they do things these days. Not in the city anyway.

Now I finally have the time to fix that stain on the ceiling. A little drywall mud, some primer and paint. Could I actually do it? Or would I only make a terrible mess? "We should have had it done the same time they were fixing the roof," Beth said, "but you were saving pennies." Now finally my frugality has seen its justification. Now she will be glad of those pennies.

After lying there more than an hour, seeing your father over and over again looking up to tell me he is ready for the axe, listening to Beth's nostril whistling as she hugged a pillow between her knees, I finally slipped out of bed, careful not to wake her or to startle Julia when I passed her bedroom door, and teetered my way downstairs. I heated myself an

Ovaltine in the microwave and ensconced myself here at the dining room table, in the morbid glow of my grandfather's painting.

It's not really your father in the dream. It's me, telling myself to bring down the axe on my own neck and reassuring myself that when I do Beth will be well looked after. Not just the girls. If I weren't such a coward it would already be done. Sheena needs her future. Julia will be fine. Stupid of me to hide the gun under the dresser. I could do it right now instead of sitting here drinking Ovaltine.

My older brother killed himself when I was seventeen. He took a .22 rifle out to the barn, sat down in a shallow feed trough, cradling the rifle between his knees, looked down the barrel and pulled the trigger. Mom found him still sitting in the wooden trough, a hole between his eyes.

These many years later I sit here trying to imagine what he was thinking as he walked out to the barn with that rifle and sat. He was always braver than me, never the least bit afraid of dying. Once he rode a horse over a railroad bridge near our home: we called it the trestle. Another time he drove the blue pickup truck over and down what was essentially a cliff. One of those prairie cliffs.

But Julia. But Sheena. Is it worth it? My old friend Sid long ago convinced me of the emptiness of pursuing the dream of being an artist. He used to tease me about my grandfather. Where did painting get him? Dead. Forgotten. Frozen stiff and stored away in The Beautiful Place, where he was recently joined by the head of your father. My grandfather and Sid's wife Arabella Wiseman checked in the same day over twenty-five years ago, Mr. Joseph Abraham not even thirty days ago, but it all amounts to the same thing. Time is plastic. Elastic. Flies when you're in a coma; stops when you die. That does sound pleasant. I could use the rest.

Even if you are any good at writing, Sid once told me, *better than the average human being* (he said this while his eyes mocked me that I was not), *before we know it machines will be writing stories and novels and poems and screenplays superior to any possible human effort.* All the world of literature, every language, every great story ever told, has by now, presumably, been inputted by Google into their endless machine mind, and soon you'll only need to push the proper keys to ask for the story or novel or screenplay or poem you wish produced and the machine will spit it out a moment later. Judging by that movie Beth and I went to see last month, the latest Oscar favourite, it's already happening. The screen was badly blurred by robotic fingerprints.

With machines creating art, we humans are left free of all purpose (the very definition of art: beauty without function) and I am left scratching away here in my last Christmas journal at these humanly inferior sentences to myself. It only makes you wonder all the more why people like your father and my grandfather have had themselves frozen in a longshot gamble at eternal life. To do what in that eternity? Watch the movies and read the books the machines write for them? Push another button and the machine will read the words to you in the exact voice of your mother reading you a bedtime story.

That's what I need right now: Mom to read me back to sleep. She used to every night, read to me and my brother, even after I could read myself. Thornton W. Burgess. Those animals in the woods and all their anthropomorphic doings. I've read that Buddhists believe the enlightened soul, as it approaches the death of the body, is like a child jumping into the lap of his mother. Is that so, Mary Abraham?

In a way, I suppose, the machine will become Grandmother Abraham: the nanobots that will eventually be injected into your father to repair his diseased and vitrified flesh will be the mothering saviours that give him rebirth in the perfect land of the future.

Personally, I'd just as soon be dead. Buddha had it right: what he wanted was death.

Why would your father want me to look after your mother? I met him only a few times and our relationship was entirely professional. He was not even my client. I tried to convince him that whole-body preservation might be preferable, but he was price sensitive, so I quickly gave that up. I met you just that once in my office, six months ago. You were a little embarrassed, but proud too, when you told me of meeting God in your dreams. More than one god. I have a feeling you believe in them all, every last god, while I can't seem to believe in anything at all. You really met them, your teachers told you. Dreams can be as real as life, more real than life. Life is only a dream. You had a passion in your voice that I've seldom heard. You insisted that you did not normally tell anyone about your nocturnal visitations with the divine; it was only because you had found my business card and then the night before you had dreamed of me and you knew immediately my importance to you, that you needed to talk to me, and so you had come to plead your case.

I was embarrassed for you, the way one is always embarrassed when talking to the delusional about their delusions. But in my job, selling an immortality that I do not even believe in, I was used to that.

I waited, wanting to hear your story of your dream of me just as much as I wanted to know what it was like to meet a god. My desk between us. My old desk. Instead you repeated that Joseph Abraham must not go ahead with the procedure. You called him that, Joseph Abraham, as though you were speaking of a client. He must not pay to have himself decapitated, you said. To do so would endanger his soul. He had been raised a Christian; had lost faith and lost track of his soul, but his soul, you insisted, had not lost track of him.

I had to disagree with you, while justifying it to myself by doubting your motives.

It's his choice, I said. It's his money. It's up to him. The catch being the usual one: that if he chose immortality his money would come to his future self (and Argyle) instead of to his children.

Amen.

I have to admit that I even enjoyed sharing my harsh truth. You made a claim of knowing God and I put you in your place. I got the better of you. Though deep inside I was ashamed. I already knew that you would get the best of me in the end. I failed to appease you and thus unleashed the beast that would devour me.

You're the straw that broke the camel's back. I couldn't pass through the eye of the needle.

When I told Beth about you, she was immediately suspicious.

Dreamt of Christ and Buddha, dreamt of me.

Tired.

Let me leap into the lap of my mother and take her withered breast between my lips.

Good night, good night, good night, Ophelia said.

November 4, 2012

I had left Saskatchewan for Vancouver on New Year's Day, 1986. Took the Greyhound that absurdly cold winter afternoon. I was twenty-three, the same age as Sheena is now. Life on the farm did not appeal to me and my father's disappointment weighed heavily on us both. I was the remaining son, so I was expected to take over the farm. Since high school there had been five years of long silent meals, utensils scraping plates, my mother pointing out goldfinches that flew by, the deer in the garden eating the corn, me and my dad raising our heads to look out the window at the wildlife, but never speaking.

I went to Vancouver to search for my grandfather. A tiny story in the arts and entertainment section of the Regina newspaper told me that Saskatchewan-born artist Philip Bentley had recently moved to Vancouver from Montreal— this tiny spark finally got me moving. I had never met the man, but it felt as though my entire life was defined, through my father, in opposition to the *somewhat* notable bisexual painter who had fathered my father and then abandoned him and my grandmother. My father had devoted his life to farming (against his mother's wishes) at least partly in rebellion against his absent father, and he expected me, as proof of my worth and my manhood, to step into his boots and take over the farm he'd sacrificed so much for (losing three fingers to a throwing chain in the Alberta oilfield, where he'd worked for years to save the money to buy the land). Though I don't remember my father ever once directly acknowledging the existence of my grandfather (I got my information on him from my grandmother, Old Mrs. Bentley), he had always taken every opportunity to point out, with the one remaining finger on his right hand, the uselessness of a picture hanging on a wall. Our own walls were decorated with wooden plaques bearing edifying homilies: *May the road rise to meet you/ and may the wind be always at your back; Today is the tomorrow/ you worried about yesterday/ and all is well; Yea, though I walk through the valley of the shadow of death, I will fear no evil, 'cause I'm the meanest SOB in the valley.*

Still, my grandmother liked to say that my father was his father's son. This could be seen most easily in the way he, even while avoiding adorning his home with pictures, had instead done a significant bit of decorating with dead birds. I'd come home on the school bus on a winter afternoon to find him at the kitchen table, skinning out an owl or shaping the body of one out of wood shavings (which are called *tow*) wrapped with cotton string. He had special tools: for example, a tiny grapefruit spoon with jagged teeth that he used for scraping brains from a bird's skull.

He tried to teach me, but I had neither the talent nor the patience and so found yet another way to disappoint the man. I did like to look at the birds: the carnage of the golden eagle killing the pheasant above the calmness of the songbirds and rooster, preserved behind glass in a diorama on the north wall of our living room.

When it came to farming, I was as useless as a picture hanging on a wall, and my father, suspecting this might be weakness inherited from my grandfather, set about to shame me into action. Physical violence was never used as a teaching tool in the Bentley household. There *was* violence in my father, but it was contained, controlled, like everything else about him. Guilt and humiliation did the job efficiently and without visible scars. "If a person could believe that he could leave the place for a couple of days and that the cattle wouldn't all be dead by the time he got back, maybe he could take your mother south to the hot springs in Montana for a little holiday. But I guess that's more than a person should be able to ask for."

My mother witnessed daily that my father and I did not make good partners, and she ended up stuck in the middle of all our battles, and so she urged me to go to university, but that meant I would have to finish high school, having failed grade twelve English because I'd been caught plagiarizing my final paper on *Hamlet*. The teacher, Mr. Whiteman, had already graded my paper on *The Cruel Sea* at twenty-five per cent—I'd handed it in a few hours late after not showing up for class the morning it was due because I'd been up until four a.m. helping my father attempt to pull a calf from a heifer. We succeeded, but the heifer and calf both died. Mr. Whiteman saw himself as the gatekeeper between hayseeds and higher education, and did not see the attempt to pull a calf as an adequate excuse for not handing in a paper on time, and so docked me fifty per cent for being a day late. He followed this up by seizing on some uncredited ideas in my *Hamlet* paper, calling me in to confront me with the library book I had borrowed them from and the evidence of my having checked out the book, and pointing out that there was no citation acknowledging the source. The whole incident was all the more upsetting because I had not realized that I was doing anything wrong: the ideas I paraphrased from the book were good ones, I thought, and I truly believed the point of my studies was discovering good ideas. I had no concept of how to continue on in an academic career without borrowing others' ideas, and so feared I would only repeat the process with the same embarrassing result, thus plagiarizing my own sorry past.

Besides, I knew that university would mean I'd have to pass through years of accepting money from a man who would only give with great grievance, so when I set off to the city, I had a vague plan for a life that had no dependence on my father or any other Mr. Whiteman. I'd heard that the stock market business was an easy way to make money. A career in trading stocks and bonds would subsidize me until I sold my first book. I hoped that my grandfather, a successful Canadian artist, would mentor me along my chosen path.

—

It has been fascinating and humiliating to read my journals from those first days in Vancouver. My younger self marvelling at the balmy January weather compared with Saskatchewan's polar bite. From the perspective of Saskatchewan, it was impossible for me to see Vancouver as the edge of anything.

What do I make of that unspoiled innocent youth wandering in the morning rain through the cavernous streets of downtown Vancouver handing out resumes to brokerage firms? He still believed he was going to be a famous artist like his grandfather, but he needed a job to pay the rent and get his start in the big city. The mountains across the harbour made him feel special just being in their distant presence, so far from the farm and so exotic in their beauty he felt he might be on television or in a movie. On clear mornings, to the southeast, there was Mount Baker, perfectly snow-capped, apparently volcanic.

A Barbie-like receptionist advised me that the back door into the brokerage business was to get hired as a courier and work my way up. She assured me there was an opening and she'd slip my resume into the right hands. Her lips were the colour of a candy apple. She sat alone near the elevators in the ethereal glow of a mirrored lobby like a mannequin in a department store window. I wanted to touch her to test if she was real. Instead, I thanked her and backed slowly away. By the time I got to my apartment there was a message on my machine asking me to come in for an interview the next day with office manager Leonard Billingsley.

Cage manager. The area where they handled dollars and securities in a brokerage house was called the cage. Couriers worked out of the cage.

Leonard Billingsley, pale chain-smoking cage manager of Universal Securities, had a glass-walled office in the corner of the cage, from where he surveyed his domain without leaving his chair. Things didn't start well at the interview. Five minutes and half a dozen questions in, Mr. Billingsley was explaining that he was looking for someone with experience. I pointed out that the artist who'd painted the print hanging on the glass wall over his stock terminal was Philip Bentley. I actually interrupted him by stabbing a finger at the print and saying, "That's a Philip Bentley."

Leonard Billingsley did not look the least bit impressed. In fact, he looked more than a little annoyed at being interrupted. He glanced up at the print.

"Yes. Actually, a reproduction. Philip Bentleys are out of my price range."

I nodded and smiled.

"He's my grandfather."

A few minutes later Mr. Billingsley—"Call me Leonard"—was telling me that the pay was a thousand dollars a month and I could start on Monday.

—

My supervisor, the head messenger at Universal Securities, was Sid. He was a year younger than me, still is, with GQ model looks (still has those too): thick brows over Rudolph Valentino eyes and bangs that tendrilled in a naturally contrived way over his forehead. His real name was Madison Fairmount Hedges III. His father, who Sid called MFH2, was a close friend of MacMillan, the senior partner of Universal Securities. His mother, who had been a model, had died of breast cancer when he was a teenager.

The day I met Sid, my first day on the job, he led me through the fog and exhaust down Dunsmuir Street, demonstrating how to plot out a route according to the different stops I'd normally have to make, and introducing me to the

clerks at the various brokerage firms. There was no point
introducing me to the tellers at the banks, he said, as there
were so many of them and they weren't usually very friendly.

"Banking makes 'em bitter. Must be having all that money
pass through their fingers while the bank pays such a measly
salary. But if you see one you like, let me know, cause I probably know her. Bitterness is nothing a little lovin' won't cure.
At least for an evening or two. I wouldn't bet on a long-term
recovery. That's my experience anyway."

Sid's shoes were beautiful. He caught me eyeing them and
ordered me to feel. "Italian," he said. I knelt and touched the
soft brown leather.

As we were passing through the mirrored lobby, I said
hello to the receptionist.

"You got the hots for Tanya?" Sid asked. "Forget it. She's
fucking one of the brokers."

I told him how she had told me about the job and passed
along my resume.

"Don't read into that. Just keep reminding yourself that
none of this is real. It's all illusion: pretty on the surface but
a cesspool underneath. Don't trust anyone. Don't trust me.
And especially don't trust women. They're too weak to save
you from the sharks, even if they see one coming before you
do. The business is sexist like you wouldn't believe, my artsy
girlfriends keep pointing out to me. The sexual revolution's
barely dented it, which isn't your problem since you're a
man. Ride it as far as it will take you, but have no faith that it
will be there to carry you tomorrow. Listen, but don't ask too
many questions. Curiosity choked the chinchilla. You know
what I mean?"

I nodded. I didn't.

Despite his last advice, or maybe to test me, he asked, "Any questions, Bentley?" as we approached the cage door. I looked around.

"Why all the mirrors?"

There were mirrors everywhere at Universal Securities: in the elevators, lobby, hallways, and boardrooms.

"They give the illusion of space. Make things look bigger than they are. And a lot of people in this business like to look at themselves. Don't you like to look at yourself?"

"Not all the time," I said.

I mentioned that there were mirrors over the urinals that enabled you to watch yourself while you peed.

"Look at your dick if you'd prefer," he winked. "You're not that hard on the eyes." As he punched in the code to get into the cage, he asked, "Is that your graduation suit?"

I denied it, but did not explain that I had failed to graduate.

—

Strange, Mary Abraham, seeing Sid again for the first time in the awkward sentences of that old journal. Always charming. I'd forgotten touching his shoes. Leather like butter. Funny how the lost moment returns when you read the words. It's all folded into the brain, no protection but the skull, stored away like files in a machine. Kneeling down to him on day one.

November 5, 2012

I miss the subway at rush hour.

As I woke this morning, for a moment I was overcome by the familiar contemplation of pulling myself out of bed, staggering to the shower, and bolting down some breakfast so that I could rush to catch the bus to the train. Only then did I wake up enough to realize there was no reason to get out of bed.

We have a black Lexus and I could easily have had Argyle rent a parking space so that I could inch into work each morning with Coltrane on the stereo, but for the sake of the earth I chose to take the bus and the subway. The point of existence, I decided, was to vanish with as little trace as possible. Stay out of the frame. Sid liked to make fun of even this tiny goal, my aspiration for an ethical life, insisting that within a few years artificial intelligence would solve the problem of climate change and everything on the planet would be powered by the sun. But the courage of my convictions led me to troop onto a bus each morning and transfer onto the Bloor-Danforth subway line, where I could generally wedge myself through the sliding doors and find a space to stand, staring out the window at the dark walls of the tunnel. At least once a month there would be some delay—mechanical, medical, suicidal—and afterwards the platform would be so crowded I would have to watch four or five or six trains pull up and stop, too full to accommodate any more than one or two extra passengers.

That last Friday morning, ten days ago now, October 26, I had a nine o'clock meeting with Sid, and so considered taking a cab, but knew from past experience I'd have as much trouble claiming one and that even when I did it would crawl in traffic so thick I'd probably get there later than if I'd continued on the subway. Not to mention the ridiculous price that taxis charge. Uber is worse than the regular cabs on mornings like that.

Across the westbound tracks, on one of the stanchions supporting the tunnel, Beth stared back at me from a larger-than-life poster, her right hand balled into a fist before her:

Seize the Future
ARGYLE

Strange to see her there each morning watching me watching her, and watching the other men watching her. They'd photoshopped away the tiny crow's feet that had begun to web from the corners of her eyes. That last morning I ignored the beseeching blonde (our good doctor believes we should be separated by now), glanced at my watch for the fifteenth time, and edged my way to a spot by the yellow line, anticipating from experience where the doors would be when the train came to a stop. I brushed against a young man

with a neatly trimmed beard and a tattoo of Marcus Aurelius
on his neck, and he scowled at me before looking back at his
phone.

When the train thundered into the station and squealed
to a halt, the doors slid open directly in front of me, but
there wasn't an inch of space on the car and no one got off.
A flattened man in a grey suit, exposed when the doors slid
back, eyed me nervously, hoping I wouldn't try to shove my
way inside. After a few seconds the chime sounded, the doors
slid closed, and the train pulled away. Beth was revealed once
more, smiling suggestively from across high voltage rails.

I managed to squeeze onto the next train and stood for
ten minutes trapped against the hostile tattooed man from
the platform, meditating on Marcus, smelling his Old Spice
and trying to convince myself that I did not need to sneeze.
Another man breathed cigarettes and garlic against the back
of my neck. At Yonge station I got off and trudged up the
stairs in a great mass of marching humanity that always
made me think of cattle being forced through a chute. My
father was the man behind me, twisting my tail, forcing me
along, muttering "Act like a man!" as though it couldn't possibly be anything more than an act. When I reached the top of
the stairs, I jammed my way onto the southbound train and
rode two stops to College, where I disembarked and took my
place in line on the escalator. Once at street level, I had to
walk five more minutes, mostly heading east, in the direction
of my home, which always made me feel like I was going
backwards. That morning I sprinted those final blocks, dodg-
ing pedestrians, glancing at my watch every thirty seconds,
hoping it might stop telling me that I was already late.

Time, uncooperative, kept moving relentlessly clockwise.

The offices of Argyle are on the sixth and top floor of the Mechanical Engineering Building, a nineteenth century brick warehouse converted by the university in the late eighties. Sid had calculated that renting space from the university would lend credibility to our endeavours. He persistently implied that there was some actual relationship between Argyle and the academics in the building studying the field of nanotechnology, and the implication had begun to take on the breath of truth, just as the mask begins to become the face.

I dashed through the lobby to find the elevator was, as usual, out of service, leaving no option but to climb five flights of stairs. Fifteen minutes late. Clutching at the pain in my side, I swiped my keycard to open the stairwell door at the sixth floor, and immediately met Chief Operations Officer Harold Swelling's eyes. Harold is the current overseer representing the interests of Argyle's multinational mothership.

"Sorry I'm late. Subway—you know."

"Good morning, Mr. Bentley. Mr. Hedges isn't in yet," Harold Swelling said.

Mr. Hedges is what Harold Swelling calls Sid.

"Oh?" I said. "Good morning."

I felt Harold Swelling's eyes follow me to my office.

—

Sid never appeared that morning. After lunch I returned to find the elevator still out of service and so plodded up the stairs, pausing in the stairwell at the third floor to look out the window at a squirrel perched on the edge of one of the dumpsters, chomping away at some rotting treasure, something both frantic and deliberate in the way it went about the task of eating and storing away some fat for winter. I had just eaten at a fast-food Thai restaurant on Yonge Street. I usually ate at my desk (a sandwich, an apple, some milk and a couple of cookies), but I'd forgotten to bring my lunch that morning. It was sitting at home in the fridge. It was Friday. By the time Friday rolled around each relentless week, I had difficulty remembering my own name.

I continued my way up to the sixth floor, swiped the keycard, and walked in to see Sid chatting with Marjorie, the receptionist.

"I pick him up and take him to soccer after work," Marjorie was saying, "and then I barely have time to pick Sheila up from basketball at school." It did not take much encouragement to get Marjorie talking about her children. Both she and Sid turned as if to acknowledge my presence, but neither spoke.

"How did the meeting with Mary Abraham go?" I asked.

"Morning, Bentley," Sid nodded. "We'll talk about it in our meeting with Harold."

"I believe it's past noon. I just ate my lunch. You want to talk right now?"

Sid shook his head, and those naturally contrived tendrils of his bangs shook in rhythm: his hair has not changed an iota since he was twenty-two.

"No rush. Get settled. Check the numbers. I believe we're scheduled for …" he looked at his watch, "two o'clock?"

"Two o'clock? We were scheduled for nine." Marjorie self-consciously moved papers from one pile to another, pretending to not be listening. "I was here. I've already checked the numbers. I come to work in the morning."

Sid smiled and walked away. Marjorie glanced up to see that I was still there before returning her focus to the shuffling of papers.

I walked down the hall to my office and had only just settled behind my desk when Sid entered, closing the door softly behind him.

"Mary Abraham called Arabella and, as a result of their very disturbing conversation, Arabella ended up in the hospital," he said.

Arabella, childhood friend of Sheena's, was named after her mother, Arabella Wiseman, the founder of Argyle, who has been stored in The Beautiful Place for more than twenty-five years, awaiting resurrection. Arabella the younger, twenty-four years old, suffers from anorexia nervosa and is often in hospital, and so I was skeptical about Sid's inference of a causal connection between your phone call, Mary Abraham, and Arabella's hospitalization. As far as I'm concerned, Sid's life-long neglect of his daughter is the root of her maladies. She never knew her mother in any way, as she was not born until after her mother had been frozen: an Argyle child, she was conceived in a petri dish from Sid's seed and her mother's preserved egg.

"That's terrible! Why would she call Arabella? Did you talk to her?"

"She did not even respond to my invitation. She obviously didn't want to talk to me. For some strange reason she wanted to talk to my daughter and so she tracked down her phone number. And you know what she asked her? She asked her if she knew where her mother's body was *entombed*. Apparently, that's the word she used. Entombed. She said she wanted to find Mr. Abraham and she wondered if my daughter could give her directions. She asked if her mother had ever risen and come to her, asking to be buried. Why didn't you tell me she was nuts?"

I picked up my phone to check my messages.

"I'll talk to her."

"Like I already asked you to talk to her? I would have hoped I could count on you. You said she had the hots for that pretty face of yours. But it's too late for that now."

I never said that, Mary Abraham. I said that I thought we had a connection.

"I'm sorry? Is Arabella okay? What do you mean it's too late?"

Sid was looking out the window, over my shoulder, at my view of the CN Tower thrusting into cumulous cloud.

"Arabella will recover. I mean the time has passed for any of your pitiful damage control."

The first message was from you, asking me to return your call, your voice calm, professional, in its elegant, part British, part South Asian way. Scrawling down your number, I told Sid you'd called and that I would call you.

"Don't you dare! Leave it alone! Too late. We've known one another a long time, Bentley. So much time has passed."

By the time I set down the phone and my pen and swivelled my chair toward him, Sid was already gone.

—

Harold Swelling is only thirty-five, and had been forced to move from Silicon Valley to Toronto to shepherd the Argyle ship. This makes him bitter. Or perhaps he is just naturally bitter. When I entered his office, my notebook and graphs tucked under my left arm and a cup of tea in my right hand, Harold was at his computer studying some data with an intensity suggesting he'd caught an image of God in the arrangement of the numerals across the screen. Sid was nowhere to be seen.

"Are we still on for two?"

Harold glanced up and then returned his eyes to the screen.

"Yes. Close the door. Sit down."

"What about Sid?"

"Mr. Hedges is busy. He's no longer in the office."

"Oh? We should reschedule."

"Mr. Hedges said to go ahead without him."

I shrugged. "I don't see how that's going to be very productive."

"Sit down, Mr. Bentley."

I closed the door and sat, placing the tea on the edge of Harold Swelling's desk. Swelling glanced up for the second time, looked at the steaming cup of tea, picked up a beige coaster from beside his mouse pad and placed it next to my cup. I placed the cup on the coaster. Swelling had already turned his attention back to the data. For more than two minutes neither of us spoke. Licking his lips, Swelling stared at the screen. I fidgeted in the chair and sipped my tea, watching his tongue flick between his thin lips and disappear.

"Mr. Hedges tells me we have a serious situation with one of your clients."

"Not my client. Sid's client. The daughter of Sid's client. I don't even know that it's all that serious. The client is already in The Beautiful Place. I'm going to talk to her. I've left a message ..."

"Don't! You must not speak to her." Slowly, Harold's Swelling's lizard eyes left his screen and found their way to my eyes. "Mr. Hedges certainly feels it's serious. Lawyers have been called."

I nodded. "I don't think it will come to that. She has no case. I'll talk to her and explain the situation to her again."

"Don't!"

Harold Swelling swung his chair to face me, clasping his pallid hands together under his chin as if he were praying.

"You've been with Argyle a long, long time."

"I have," I confirmed. I considered telling him that it had been almost twenty-five years, but I guessed that he already knew and, anyway, was not interested in the details of my servitude. He was staring grimly at my cup of tea. I wished I hadn't brought the tea. "Shall we look at the numbers?" I said, to break the silence. "I think to get the proper perspective you need to look at them in the longer term. The human reanimation division is having a bad year, but six of the past ten years have shown growth ..."

"I'm sure you've seen many *changes* over those years."

"Yes."

"You know that I've long been concerned about the human reanimation division's role in the organization, and after careful analysis and much discussion, and taking into consideration the impact of the present situation with your client, Mr. Hedges has agreed that it is time for the organization to move in a new direction."

"A new direction?"

Harold Swelling nodded. "He asked me to communicate this to you. We're going to have to let you go."

I sat back in the chair. My ears rang like an alarm had gone off. I couldn't speak and so I waited for Harold Swelling to say more, but he simply stared at my tea.

"Let me go," I said.

November 7, 2012

This morning my ritual walk was diverted by a stop at a hardware store on Queen Street where I asked about nine-millimetre ammunition and was told I needed a license to purchase.

"Oh, I see. I don't have a license. It's my grandfather's gun."

"He'll have to come with his license and get it himself," the proprietor said, studying me intently.

"He's not able to do that. He has trouble getting around." I pictured him frozen in a pod in The Beautiful Place; his whole body there, awaiting resurrection, somewhere near your father's head. "It was his service pistol. From the Second World War. Browning Hi-Power."

The man nodded. "Nice gun. WW Two vet! He must be getting up there."

"Way up there. Okay," I said, turning to leave, "Thanks very much."

"How much does he need?"

"Pardon?"

"How much ammo does he need."

"Just one box of shells."

He looked toward the door.

"Can you show me some ID?"

I took out my driver's license and he compared the photo to my face before leading me to the back of the store where he unlocked a cabinet and produced a box of ammunition. I thanked him and paid at the counter. He put the heavy box in a paper bag that fit easily in my coat pocket.

From there I was off on a birthday quest for Tony. My idea was to get in Beth's good books by taking this chore off her hands. She refused the offer, but I decided to do it anyway. Often she insists I should not do something and then complains when I don't.

I spotted an album in the window of the vinyl store on Queen Street, the young woman peering out from the photo with a lost little girl tilt to her head. Feral eyes. Hair groomed so carefully you could count the brushstrokes. I recognized the name. A punk-folk harp player Sheena introduced me to, and just perfect for Tony. The singer had a voice like her face, the little girl turned loose on a hostile world, and her lyrics were about killing dinner with karate and other notions in that vein, if that could be considered a vein. Capillary at best. Tony might even be impressed that I know music balanced so cleanly on the razor's edge. Though Tony would never admit it. Tony is the kind of guy who lives primarily to outdo everyone else with his coolness, despite his male white straightness. He wishes he were indigenous; he wishes he were gay.

A fluffy blond dog lay in the doorway of the vinyl store. Dogs tend to like me and this one didn't look the least bit threatening, but I couldn't help feeling the elemental nature of a dog blocking a doorway, and so stepped gingerly over to get inside. The dog stretched lazily and wagged its tail but did not lift its head. As I searched the racks for the record, I tripped on something and looked down to see a large, slightly bloody, beef bone, a dark space where the marrow used to be. I stepped over the bone and continued my search. Unable to find another copy of the harp music, I approached the storeowner for help. Three young people with Down syndrome were at the counter taking instructions on walking his dog, so I couldn't get his attention. Finally, I reached in and took the album right out of the window display.

As I waited to pay, I began to worry that maybe Tony didn't have a turntable. Maybe he streamed his music directly from the Internet like any normal person. But why would a store that sells vinyl still exist if people like Tony, people who need to be cool, weren't buying records? It seemed like a very risky business. What was this fellow thinking, investing good money in bricks-and-mortar music retail, sending his beloved dog off with three young people each with an extra chromosome? But something about the abundant faith that inspired these graceful acts made me feel reassured that I was doing the right thing buying this harp music for Tony.

Once the three kids had been led off by the excited dog, the proprietor rang up my purchase, very impressed by my recognition and appreciation of such an avant-garde performer. "Oh, she's great, isn't she?" he said. "Nothing like her."

"I love her stuff," I ventured a bit self-consciously.

The storeowner peered at me over his glasses. I could see a kind of admiration in his eyes, only a little overwhelmed by doubt or surprise. He didn't say it, but I got the definite feeling he might have said that I didn't look the type to know this young woman's music. It made me feel younger. Tony would be impressed. Maybe even Beth would be impressed. I thanked the proprietor, wished him a good day, and walked out of the store feeling a deep connection to all the world's faithful.

I passed the little man who sells pencils in front of the grocery store, singing his "Hey, Hollywood" song. No change in my pocket, only that heavy box of ammunition, I pulled out my wallet but had nothing but twenties. He looked up at me, his kind eyes smiling out of a jaundiced face that seemed about to slide off his skull.

"Hey there, Robert Redford. You wanna buy a pencil?"

He always calls me Robert Redford. Calls Beth Marilyn Monroe. He probably calls all men Robert Redford and all women Marilyn Monroe. I handed him the twenty and took the pencil. We thanked one another.

As I wandered along the north side of Queen Street, enjoying the pale November sunshine, feeling the satisfaction of my altruism, thinking about how I'd go quietly off into the woods north of the city, load the fresh ammunition into my grandfather's gun and help Sheena live her dream in Manhattan, I remembered, with a tightening in my chest, that I'd bought an album by the same harp singer a couple of years before as a present for Tony.

A woman bundled in a knee-length burgundy winter parka, hood up so that I could not clearly see her face (a bit extreme, I thought, for such a lovely day), was watching me from the corner that I was approaching. She was smiling a grim smile and as I made out her features I saw there was something familiar about her face.

It was you, Mary Abraham.

"Hello," I said as I reached you. I stood shuffling nervously and you responded, "Hello, Mr. Bentley."

"Beautiful day."

"Is it? A little cool. Shopping?" You motioned toward the bag in my hand.

"Yes. Birthday present." To fill the void of my confusion in seeing you standing there on Queen East, a woman who has walked with Christ, I pulled the album from the bag to show you, vaguely hoping, since I could not tell you I had paid twenty dollars for the pencil in my breast pocket or that I was preparing to blow my brains out to give my daughter her dream, that I might impress you with my choice of music, the way I had the store owner, and thus be granted some absolution for all of the sins I had committed and had yet to commit. "Have you heard of her?"

You shook your head.

"Talented?"

"Yeah. She plays the harp. Not a blues harp. A real harp. Like the angels? My daughter introduced me to her music. The only problem is that as soon as I walked out of the store I remembered that I'd actually bought the fellow the same album—it's a birthday present—bought him the same album a couple of year ago. The exact same present."

You looked perplexed.

"Angels? He must have liked it very much?"

"I don't remember." I chuckled. "This has happened before. I buy somebody a gift, and then I remember I've bought them the same gift before. But I really haven't. I don't think I have. I just get anxious about whether I've bought the right gift or not and so I think I remember buying it. A kind of déjà vu."

"Is it? Interesting. Perhaps a form of—how do they say—buyer's remorse?"

You had a rather ironic look in your eyes that made me feel uneasy.

"Maybe. I suppose that might be. Do you live around here?"

"No. I've been here only once before. I was remembering. With Joseph. We drove out one Sunday and walked on the boardwalk. Actually, it was my idea, not his. He was not one to walk and he was uncomfortable that everyone was so … white. Despite his rebellions, he was uncomfortable being in the minority. He did not like to stray from Mississauga. Even the airport is here, he used to say. I had heard of this part of the city and thought it would be romantic. The lake and the boardwalk."

At last you paused and waited for me to respond.

"Romantic?" I stammered.

You nodded. I was realizing that daughters do not want to be romantic with their fathers and I was remembering with terror and embarrassment what Joseph Abraham said to me the last time I saw him, in my dream. *Look after my wife.* "Well, that's too bad. I'm sorry about that. You come here to remember him and you run into me."

"Oh, that was not my intention today. I came here to see you, Mr. Bentley."

You didn't smile when you said this. To avoid the intensity of your eyes, I glanced away, looking for somewhere to hide, thinking of Beth's accusations, making sure that she wasn't watching from nearby. I could feel her eyes.

"Pardon?" I said, staring at the yellow leaves trampled on the sidewalk.

"I thought we had agreed to meet? Why did Mr. Hedges call me?"

"I thought it would ... be better."

"Did you? It isn't." I nodded, but could think of no adequate response. You continued, "Shall we have coffee now?"

"No!" I blurted. "I'm sorry, I can't."

"Why is that?"

I looked at my watch.

"I have to be somewhere."

"Really? Where?" All I could do was stare blankly and so you added, "My apologies. Not my business. But I really must talk to you about Joseph."

Your burgundy hood framed your caramel skin, contrasting your brown eyes, speckled with gold, making me look at the sidewalk. Perhaps Beth was right. Maybe you were in heat. Perhaps you were exuding pheromones and I could subconsciously sense your swollen clitoris. I couldn't help imagining you beneath the parka, my lips on your breasts, moving down your belly to your thighs.

"Joseph?"

"Yes. My husband."

Why had I thought you were his daughter?

"Your husband?"

"Yes. Joseph Abraham. Your client."

I shrugged.

"Not my client. Sid ..."

"And your grandfather. I must talk to you about your grandfather. He came to me last night."

"My grandfather? I see." Abruptly, I started to walk and you fell into step beside me, matching my strides.

"I'm not crazy, Mr. Bentley. A few weeks ago, I may not have believed it myself if someone had come to me and told me the same thing. But it happened. Your grandfather came, as real as you walking beside me now, and he spoke to me. I was sitting … in meditation, staring at a candle, and the flame went out. It wasn't blown out—not a breath of a breeze—it was as though there was all at once no oxygen in the room and the flame shrunk and died to a thin wisp of smoke. When I looked up this old man was standing there looking down at me. Not a shimmering ghost. It was him standing there, your grandfather, as solid as any person I've ever met. I wanted to stand and greet him, but I could not. I could not move. I was paralyzed, sitting there on my cushion. And then he started to speak. He introduced himself, Philip Bentley, and said that he'd made a terrible mistake. He told me he wanted to be buried. To be taken back into Mother Earth is what he said. He told me that I should come and tell you. He was very clear that I should talk to you."

I stopped and faced you.

"This old man that broke into your meditation room told you he was my grandfather?"

"He did. Philip Bentley, he said. And when I looked at photos on the Internet I saw that, indeed, it was him."

"I'm really sorry about your loss, but you should be talking to … someone else. I know that bereavement can be devastating. But I can't help you."

You shook your head the same way you'd done that day we'd met in my office, lifting your hand to brush back a strand of your hair that had escaped, pushing it back under your hood.

"Yes, you can. I think you know where it is: The Beautiful Place."

I'd explained to you during that first meeting that the name of Argyle's state-of-the-art facility had been borrowed from the Ancient Egyptians: the Pharaohs' embalming centre was called The Beautiful Place. It was a name chosen by Argyle's founder and benefactress Arabella Wiseman, who is now preserved there. Arabella's first husband had been Egyptian. The architect she hired to design The Beautiful Place was inspired by the pyramids. Arabella's first husband was an arms dealer whose body had been cremated when his limousine was hit by a rocket he had profited from the sale of. Her second husband was Sid.

"I've already told you, Ms. Abraham, that I have no idea where it is. The site of The Beautiful Place was selected with every kind of security issue imaginable in mind, from rising ocean levels, to earthquakes, to civil war, to nuclear attack. Your father may need to be there for five hundred years until all the necessary technologies to awaken him have been perfected, and until then the fewer people who know where he is, the better. And anyway, your father signed a contract which made his wishes very clear."

"My father?"

"Your husband," I corrected myself, the mistake stalling my rhetorical momentum. How could I have thought you were his daughter? You are much younger than him, probably thirty-five, forty at most, but it was stupid of me to have assumed, not to have checked and understood your relationship. But he was Sid's client. Why didn't Sid know? Why hadn't he told me?

"You're quite an inadequate liar, Mr. Bentley. I can see in your eyes that what you say is not true. You know where this facility is. You know where *he* is."

Dead leaves skittered across the sidewalk in a slight breeze. Not wanting to meet your eyes again, the image of your naked body appearing again out of *spiritus mundi*, I concentrated on speaking to the leaves. Emotionally unfaithful, I could hear Beth saying.

"I'm very sorry about the feelings you're having, but I can't really discuss it with you any further. You should talk to Mr. Hedges."

"I don't want to speak with Mr. Hedges. I want to speak with you, Mr. Bentley. Your grandfather wanted me to speak with you."

"I have to go." I started walking again and you started walking again.

"Please! It is your grandfather's wish! Why won't you have coffee with me?"

"Because I promised that I wouldn't," I said, marching beside you, as if in formation, my shoulder parallel to your much lower shoulder.

"You promised Mr. Hedges?"

"I promised my wife. I was keeping that promise, but Mr. Hedges fired me for not having coffee with you. I do not work for Argyle any longer. So, you see, this no longer has anything to do with me."

That left you silent, both of us still marching, feet clipping pavement.

"I don't understand."

I did not respond, and at last you slowed and let me go.

When I glanced back a moment later you were standing, watching me, under a naked ash planted on the boulevard.

—

I arrived, a little breathless, at my Victorian home and climbed the front steps, where I stood on the veranda for a moment, gazing at the blue of Lake Ontario just a hundred yards away. A streetcar bell clanged, the traffic hummed, and there were distant sirens rushing to a fire or accident or hurrying some injured or dying person to a hospital downtown.

I love this house. Casa Equity. It's worth enough to keep Beth and Julia comfortable for the rest of their lives. If she sold it. Which she would not do. "Where would I move if I sold it?" she'd ask me when she found my corpse, and I would not answer.

I checked the mailbox: flyers and bills.

Once inside, I placed the album on the kitchen table and fetched the DVD of *Who's Afraid of Virginia Woolf* from the shelf in the basement and placed it on the book.

In the dining room, I paused to look at my grandfather's painting hanging above the credenza: blobs of grey and black pigment dripping down a white canvas. The painting, and modern art in general, has always puzzled me, making me feel a bit stupid and inadequate. Beth calls it an unrecognized masterpiece and tells me that standing in front of it makes her feel calm and alive. "Recalibrated," she says, "the way you feel after your walks on the boardwalk." I stood for a moment, trying to recalibrate myself, but felt nothing at all.

Well, not nothing. Stupid and inadequate.

A few minutes later, I was sitting on the toilet upstairs, the bathroom door open, when I heard the key in the front door: Beth arriving home with Julia. She called to ask if I was home. I answered that I was. Julia must have seen the DVD and the record on the table. I heard her ask her mother, "Who's Virginia Woolf?"

"A writer," Beth said. "From the 1920s."

Could a writer's life somehow be encompassed by a single decade, Mary Abraham? Raising myself from the toilet and flushing, I wondered if maybe we couldn't all be summed up in one significant decade. Everything else was just repetition, a crouching and wiping and flushing. My own significant decade, the eighties, when I'd rebelled against my father and left the farm, was already long over and I was about to end my impotent time on earth. But let's face the truth: I have no decade. Most of us don't have even one important year; one important day; one important hour. Most are simply mankind's effluvia drifting through time like dust motes in narrow shafts of sunlight. All that matters, Sid likes to say, is the genes that drive us to copulate and survive and preserve ourselves in our offspring. Genes are the tiny machines that power the human race.

I would never share this with Beth. She wouldn't appreciate the conceit. She'd think I was making fun of her. Beth fears her significant decade was the nineties, which produced her popular but superficial television series, *The Trials of Trudy*, very much part of the last millennium.

"But why would they be afraid of her?" Julia asked. I was about to turn on the tap to wash my hands, but I paused to hear Beth's response.

"It's the name of a play. I acted in it years ago. Your father has fetched it up from the basement. I have no idea why. We could stream it if we actually wanted to watch it. But it's not appropriate for someone your age."

I washed my hands and trotted down the stairs. As I walked into the kitchen Beth was trying to explain the play's inappropriateness: "It's about a history professor and his wife and they have this joke they both find hilarious where they turn an old song 'Who's Afraid of the Big Bad Wolf,' into 'Who's Afraid of Virginia Woolf.'"

In an attempt to make a joyful and comic entrance that would illustrate what Beth was saying, I sang a bit of the song and did a little jig before banging my head on one of the pots hanging over the marble-topped island in the centre of the floor. I stood rubbing the invisible wound, the pots swaying slowly. Beth ignored me and Julia studied me and the swaying pots without cracking a smile. My daughter is a very pretty girl. You can see her mother in her face, but those ideal features are marred slightly by the imprint of my coarser composition.

"Why would they think that's funny?" Julia asked.

"I don't know, ask your father," Beth said. She looked tired, dark hollows under her eyes. She'd complained this morning that she was not sleeping well. "What are you doing home? Shouldn't you be out pounding the pavement?"

She stuck a small box of chocolate milk into Julia's hand and Julia grasped it without looking, still watching a pot sway, waiting for it to fall.

"I was out," I said. "Bought a birthday present for Tony. Just got back. The pavement seemed suitably pounded."

Beth looked me in the eye.

"You bought him a used DVD?"

"I didn't buy the DVD. I bought the record album. Real vinyl. I thought he might like the DVD too, if you think that makes sense? He'll remember you in it."

"I'm sure he'll be thrilled. No one watches DVDs anymore. What century do you live in?"

"Okay. Just an idea. We don't have to give him the DVD."

"Why *did* they think it was so funny?" Julia eyed me coolly, waiting, but before I could answer, her mother interrupted.

"My, you are a messy man!" She was crouched on her knees beside the gas stove. It was a stove she had demanded and it had cost us more than two normal stoves. "I stacked these containers properly in this cupboard yesterday, and now I have to do it all over again. If you're going to lounge around the house all day, then perhaps you could try to leave things in a reasonably ordered state?"

I lifted the DVD and read the cover.

"It's a very interesting play. I saw you mother in it before you were born. It's hard to explain why they thought their song was so funny. Maybe because Virginia Woolf never blew a house down? Not that I know of, anyway."

I was thinking about how I'd dug through that cupboard to find the proper sizes of plastic containers to freeze the leftover pasta sauce after I'd made our dinner last night and how I'd used steel wool to scrub away the spot on the ceiling above the stove that Beth had complained about, and she hadn't even noticed. Or if she had noticed, she hadn't said a word to signify her appreciation of my effort.

"Virginia Woolf drowned herself by putting stones in her pockets and walking into a river," Beth said as she firmly wacked a plastic container into place.

Julia considered this carefully.

"Drowned herself? Why?"

"I don't know, dear." Beth paused to glance at the gas stove. "I guess she must have been unhappy."

Julia slurped chocolate milk, sternly contemplating Virginia Woolf's unhappiness.

"Or maybe not," I said. "Sometimes people kill themselves for … better reasons."

"This conversation happened before," Julia said.

I coughed and looked at Beth, whose complete attention seemed to be focussed on the stacking of plastic containers.

"Why do you say that?" I managed to ask Julia, though my throat felt suddenly constricted by some uncanny fear. She raised her eyebrows. I love her perfect eyebrows, a miniature replication of her mother's.

"I remember having this conversation before. I remember Mom talking about Virginia Woolf before. Just exactly this way."

I laughed and took a nervous step toward Julia, stood touching the space between her shoulder blades through her King Tut t-shirt, and was overcome by a sudden image of my father running a calloused right hand, his good hand, with all four fingers and a thumb, through my hair to muss it up. I must have been very young. I can't remember my father touching me as I grew older, except in recent years when we shook hands in greeting. I'll never again feel that self-conscious squeeze. A heart attack took him one day last spring when he went out to check the cows. My mother watched from the truck as he walked toward a cow in labour, and he slowly knelt and lay down in a patch of tall grass. By the time Mom got to him he was gone, marble eyes staring up into the sky. I could feel Julia feeling the weight of his hand through my hand, and I hoped it felt like love.

"Mom talked to you about Virginia Woolf before?"

Beth, still not finished rearranging our bottomless collection of plastic containers, refused to confirm or deny.

"Yes. You and Mom and me. This conversation. Exactly this. These words I'm saying right now. The ones coming out of my mouth. I remember for sure all of this happening exactly this way once before."

Beth finally stopped what she was doing to turn and stare at Julia. She tilted her eyes up to mine, and I looked back at her, and before she could turn away we had both realized that our daughter was absolutely correct and that everything we'd convinced ourselves that we were now experiencing was only a flawless forgery of an earlier moment.

"Sometimes it feels like something's happened before, but it really hasn't," Beth said.

Julia shook her head and thumped the empty drinking box on the counter.

"This happened before. Exactly this moment."

November 8, 2012

My daughter is Nietzsche's demon (or god), warning me that I am doomed to repeat this same meaningless life over and over again. What's the point in killing myself, Mary Abraham, if I only come back to exactly the same mess? At least the Buddhists give us a chance for something better. Enlightenment in exchange for our sacrifice. They tell a story of a prince who gives himself to a starving tigress so that she can feed her cubs. The tigress consumes his body and the prince is given the gift of rest: eternal death instead of eternal life.

Can it be a sin to want my tigress wife to consume me, Mary Abraham?

Went for my walk this morning. Looked out at the lake. Imagined filling my pockets with stones and walking into its cool embrace. Imagined the chill beginning to enter my bones, the numbness enveloping and pulling me under.

I ended up refusing to attend Tony's birthday party, though Beth tried her best to convince me to go. I did drive Beth and Julia across the city to Tony's front door, sending along my best wishes and the wrapped gift of punk-folk harp player music. We didn't discuss what excuse she'd give for me, but I assume she'll use my firing, my terrible failure, and everyone will understand that I am in no mood for celebration. We pretended that was the reason, but I know Beth understands me to be making another puzzling statement that will only further estrange us. She's begged my presence and I have turned away.

After dropping them off, I drove straight home, whizzing along the Gardiner Expressway, passing sports cars and cabs, so that I was home twenty minutes later. I went straight up to the bedroom, took this journal and my grandfather's pistol from under the bottom drawer in the dresser, and loaded the gun with the shells I'd bought yesterday. Practiced pointing it at my image in the mirror and into my mouth. Phoned Sid and listened to his voice on the machine. Replaced the gun under the dresser still loaded. Thought of Julia finding it. Pulled out the drawer again, emptied out the bullets, and replaced it again. Found another hiding place for the bullets.

You say my grandfather came to you, Mary Abraham. Does that mean he will come soon to me to retrieve his painting and his gun? Why did he come to you and not to me directly? Had he tried, but was I too material, too full of blood and guts, too distant from the spiritual realm, while you live on the threshold, there to answer and welcome him across and into your room?

Like your husband, all he wants is to be buried. Is that all anyone wants from you? No. I want more.

I lit the wood stove in the basement and burned my stories, my poems, the pitifully bad novel I'd begun and never finished, and those journals full of purple prose. The past, gone. Embarrassment gone. Ghosts gone, taking with them all their silly demands. To be buried instead of frozen. I realized I would prefer cremation as I watched the orange flames through the smoky glass door. I will live in the present moment.

There was a Raptors game on television. Sports are always a good substitute for intimacy and a somewhat effective distraction from anxiety and pain.

Beth said she and Julia would be home for dinner, so I roasted a chicken and potatoes and planned to stir-fry broccoli with garlic. Rice for Julia, who does not like potatoes. They were late, so I turned off the oven so as not to overdo the chicken. I hadn't done the broccoli yet, but had it cut to size with two cloves of chopped garlic on oil, waiting in a heavy pot. I sniffed the garlic on my fingertips and thought I could detect a hint of sulphur. I washed my hands again.

Just when I began to think they'd decided to have their dinner with Tony and his gang without informing me, a cab stopped in the spot Beth's cabs always pull up across the street. I unbolted the door and turned on the gas under the broccoli.

As I set the food before them, I made terse comments about how I was sorry if anything was overdone or wilted but I'd been planning the meal for an hour earlier. I felt a little ashamed of myself for being petty. Once upon a time it would not have concerned me, but I have learned not to yield any possible advantage. There were always verbal grenades from Beth for me to dodge these days. My shrapnel didn't injure her in the least. She talked wistfully with Julia about what a lovely time they'd had and how it was too bad I hadn't been there to meet Tony's new girlfriend, a successful young talent agent who was just great with kids. Julia loved her and volunteered that she was the most beautiful woman on earth—aside from her mother, she quickly added. It was clear they had not missed my company.

"Did Tony like the vinyl?"

"Oh? Yes. He said to thank you. He put it right on and we listened to both sides. Very cool. He said he has some of her others, but not that particular one. Tony was so sorry you couldn't come. He understands. He feels terrible about what happened. He said if you need someone to talk to …"

She mentioned that he was having problems with his back; his pain gave me some small feeling of satisfaction.

November 20, 2012

Almost two weeks have passed, Mary Abraham, and I am still here, breathing the precious air, eating fruits and vegetables delivered from all corners of the globe and sucking the marrow of various wonderfully tasty creatures, while promising Beth that I'm looking hard for a job. Beth is skeptical, her cynicism well-founded. Julia likes that I walk her to school every day and meet her outside to retrace our path when the home bell rings.

I was reading, watching the clock, waiting for school to end, when the phone rang this afternoon and it was my ex-wife, Denise. I had not heard her voice in many months.

"I thought I'd better let you know that your daughter overdosed this morning."

"Denise? Pardon? Sheena?"

"Yes, it's me. Sheena overdosed on her meds. We're at the hospital."

"Is she okay?"

"She's very much alive. We were fighting and she said she was going to stay with a friend, which she does a lot lately, and so I checked and she hadn't packed her meds and so I took them down to her. She was standing at the front door with her backpack, about to leave, so I handed them to her. I'd opened the bottle, because she obviously hadn't taken one today and she needed one. She took the bottle from me, looked me in the eye, and in one motion she downed the whole thing."

"Was it full?"

"Maybe ten pills. I got her to throw up. I gave her a raw egg to drink and that did the trick. But I called her doctor's office and they told me I should take her to emergency and now they won't let her go until a psychiatrist talks to her. Suicidal ideation."

"That's ridiculous. You were fighting. She's likes to be dramatic. She's okay?"

"I guess you could say that, if you think downing every pill in a bottle is okay."

"You were fighting. What were you fighting about?"

"Money. What else? Apparently you don't have any. Lost your job, she tells me. With friends like Sid, who needs enemies, hey? So now it's all got to come from me."

"That's not what I said. I'll do what I can."

"And what can you do, Bentley?"

"I'm not sure. I've been thinking. Making some plans."

"What plans?"

"I'm looking into selling my grandfather's painting."

"And what do you think that's worth?"

"I don't know."

"It's not going to be nearly enough. She needs this, you know. She needs hope. She needs her dreams. I'm afraid she does a lot of suicidal ideating. Suicide is a bit of a fetish for her and her friends."

She left that hanging there, somewhere between Vancouver and Toronto, billowing in contrails over Saskatchewan.

"You were fighting," I said.

"We were. We do a lot of fighting. I think you should consider that if she doesn't get the money from you and me, she'll think of other ways. I've seen evidence of that already."

"What do you mean? Get a job?"

"Selling her body. Maybe an escort service."

An image came into my head that I forced away. I did not want to believe Denise and so I did not. I do not believe her. Mother and daughter drama. They are close, but they hate one another as much as they love one another, which causes Denise to make these kinds of furious accusations. Maybe she even believes it. She always did expect the worst.

"She wouldn't. She doesn't even ... *like* men."

"Selling your body is a pretty sure way to make you dislike them."

"You've seen evidence of this?"

"I have. Unexplained deposits. I check her bank transactions."

"How do you know that's where they come from?"

"I suspect. I ask and she gives me bullshit for answers."

"So you don't know this for sure?"

"You can tell yourself it isn't true if it makes you feel better. That's what Bentley does best. If he's not lying to you, he's lying to himself."

"Just like old times."

"My deepest apologies. I only called to tell you what a great father you are. Sheena needs her father. If you're not working, you must have some time on your hands. It might be a good idea if she were to come and stay with you."

"I'll talk to Beth. We have room. I don't see why not. If she wants to come."

"I'm not sure she wants to come, but *we* need a break, and I don't think it's a good idea for her to stay with her friends. I think that's where she got the entrepreneurial streak."

"I'll talk to Beth."

"You do that and let me know. Nice chatting."

She hung up.

—

Selling her body. Might it be true, Mary Abraham? Or is it only the depths of Denise's imagination that she's inflicting on mine.

If it is true, was Denise implying that it is my fault. Do you have children, Mary Abraham? How do we protect them from the world and from themselves? We can't help but feel responsible for their actions and misfortunes. What exactly does a daughter want from her father? Love and respect? I've tried to give her both, but from such a distance, across the continent, that she must have felt abandoned when I left. Must feel I am practically a stranger. Despite the distance, I can feel her wanting something from me.

Pride. She wants my proud love.

Before I burned them, I had read through my old journals, the pages slightly yellow, for an account of Sheena's birth. Like Julia, we almost lost her before she was born. It was different, of course. No duplicate is ever really exactly the same as the original.

I wanted to read it in my own hand as I was living through it that first time, but there was nothing. Sid must have already convinced me that my account would never equal a machine's. It had been recorded in words and numbers by various doctors, nurses, technicians and medical devices and stored in the archives of St. Paul's hospital in downtown Vancouver, but I imagine they've incinerated the data by now, just as St. Mike's in Toronto later incinerated my lost daughter, Louise.

Denise is a decade older than me. Because of her age, they recommended amniocentesis. I was watching the ultrasound monitor as the technician pushed the needle into her womb to draw out the amniotic fluid and I saw Sheena reach up to touch the needle like Adam reaching out for God's fingertip. The technician saw it too and drew the needle out fast. Too fast.

This is what I believe happened. The technician never confessed.

They sent us home, telling Denise to stay in bed for a day. She got up to go to the bathroom and on the way her water broke.

We rushed back to the hospital. After examination, a doctor told us to go home and wait. Denise would abort, the doctor said. We would lose Sheena.

Instead, over the next weeks the fluid reaccumulated. A small miracle, another doctor said. The baby looked fine. One of the technicians pointed out, while watching her on the ultrasound monitor, that she appeared to be sucking her toes.

Denise gave birth in a maternity room at St. Paul's Hospital in Vancouver. Like Beth, they gave her an oxytocin drip to speed things up—she was three days past due—but with Denise the oxytocin worked. Her water broke for the second time, and we clocked the labour pains until it was time to go back to the hospital. The labour proceeded quickly and by that evening Denise was in great pain and in the process of pushing Sheena into the world. Denise's doctor was away on vacation, and the on-duty physician, whom we had never met before, asked if we minded if a class of medical students came in to watch the birth. Denise said it was fine with her. The entire class trooped in and stood watching Denise, legs spread, moans escalating into howls, while I massaged her back.

When Sheena emerged, it appeared to me that there was something wrong with her legs, but the nurses swooped her up and wrapped her in a towel and I thought I must be mistaken. There was an awkward silence in the room, except for Denise's blissful gasps of relief, before the doctor started motioning the medical students out of the room and a nurse pulled me aside.

"Did you notice the baby's legs? You'd better tell your wife about her legs." She unwrapped Sheena to show me what she meant. Her knees were bent the opposite direction to normal, at forty-five degrees, so that her feet pointed into her face. To comfort herself, she was sucking her toes.

Deformed. The word went through my head, repeating. *Deformed.*

I told Denise, at the same time asking the doctor how this could be. He said he didn't know, but that it was likely related to the loss of amniotic fluid at three months in the womb. He hustled off, presumably to examine our child more closely, leaving us with the nurses. We asked more questions, but they told us they didn't know anything more than what the doctor had said. They took Sheena for further examination and left us alone to mourn our child's and our own futures.

When the doctor returned, all he would tell us was that we'd have to see an orthopaedic specialist. He couldn't say anything more. He'd get us in for an appointment as soon as possible: the following Monday morning.

Our baby was not shaped like all the other perfect babies. *Deformed*. We believed she would never walk. We sat up that night talking. At two in the morning they let us descend to the paediatric critical care unit where they were keeping Sheena. Denise held her. An older nurse in charge of the ward showed her how to breastfeed, trying to get the baby properly latched on. She assured and reassured us that we should not worry about her legs. This would not be a problem. The orthopaedic specialist would fix Sheena up as good as new.

On Monday the orthopaedic specialist, an older man with a large white Santa Claus mustache, confirmed what the old nurse had said. "It's just a packaging problem. Nothing else wrong with her at all. It'll take some time, but we'll have her legs in good order in a few months." We were, of course, ecstatic. Our baby was getting her legs back. She might look deformed, but in a few months, with the help of medical science, she would be returned to her perfect self.

When the fluid escaped and the tiny fetus fell to the bottom of Denise's womb, Sheena's knees were trapped under her weight and hyperextended, bending back the wrong direction. As the fluid reaccumulated, she continued to develop that way.

Over the next six months we took Sheena to the hospital once a week to have casts taken off her legs, then reapplied. In this way they gradually stretched her ligaments and forced her legs back to their normal position. Due to this procedure, Sheena began her life in constant pain. At nights she cried for hours while I marched around the bedroom, trying to rock her back to sleep. But gradually she no longer looked deformed. Now her legs might be mistaken for perfect, though her knees would never be quite right. She'd never run a five-minute mile.

All of this contributed to her becoming an artist. She had my grandfather in her; pain bred in her bones. From the beginning she suffered and her body was marked as different. It took her longer than normal to walk, but by nineteen months she was on her feet and by two she was running around the house stark naked except for her mother's Christian Louboutin high heels.

Sheena's always had expensive tastes.

November 28, 2012

When I broached the subject of Sheena coming to stay, Beth was surprisingly supportive. She was obviously not thrilled, but she tried very hard to sound accepting of the fact that it was natural enough for my daughter to spend time with us.

"It will be nice to have her with us for Christmas," she said. "Just like the good old days. Julia will be delighted. Maybe the two of you can look for work together. If she's planning on going to school in New York, she'll need to save some money."

"Maybe we will," I said. "Maybe we will."

When Sheena was younger, she and Beth got along famously. She'd spend entire summers with us, and every second Christmas, and every March break. In summers we'd rent a cottage on Georgian Bay and spoil her with anything she wanted. Beth was always buying her presents, which Sheena appreciated greatly and Denise not at all. That was the shape of things at the time: the two women competing for the love of the single daughter, and Beth winning easily. To be fair, I was a part of the competition, and happy enough to be on the winning team. I even derived a certain pleasure listening to Denise's phone complaints about all the ways we undermined her in her daughter's eyes. At the same time, Denise enjoyed the breaks enough that she was not about to stop sending her.

After Julia was born, the competition gradually shifted into a bloody tussle between Sheena and Beth. This was not nearly so pleasant for me. No matter what I did, both of them were convinced they were losing the battle for my love, and battled all the more fiercely. Beth's enmity could generally be traced back to the idea that Sheena's expensive tastes, which had been modelled from and nurtured by Beth in those early years, were now a threat to Julia's future. (Our staggering line of credit is actually Julia's greatest threat, and that is mostly Beth's doing). Sheena had quickly detected Beth's evolving attitude and constantly accused me of siding with Beth. For the sake of sanity—I'd already screwed up one marriage and did not want to fail again—I generally did try to appease Beth. This tortured battle accelerated as Sheena became a teenager.

In recent years both had realized I was not worth the fight. Sheena's visits became less and less frequent, leading Denise to regularly accuse me of being the neglectful father at the root of his daughter's self-destructive actions.

Perhaps she is right, Mary Abraham.

—

This morning the doorbell rang and Beth got there first.

"There's someone here to see your grandfather's painting," she called. I was already coming down the stairs and saw a small man standing in my doorway wrapped in a red scarf and a ridiculous faux fur hat.

"You said we'd arrange a time," I said to him, perhaps a little sharply.

"Didn't we? It's in my calendar." He flashed his phone at me. "I believe I talked to your wife. Is right now a problem?" He looked from Beth to me and back to Beth. I'd asked him to call me on my cell phone.

"Now is perfect," Beth said. "The painting is right over here." She motioned him to enter, and he pulled off his boots, glancing nervously at me.

Beth led him across the living room, and we all stood gazing into the Philip Bentley for thirty seconds, recalibrating ourselves.

"Interesting," he finally pronounced.

"Isn't it!" Beth exclaimed.

"Not what I was expecting. The problem is it's not part of the Bentley vernacular. The prairie town thing. Horses. Formalist. I'd heard he did these before he died but I've never seen one before. You're his grandson?"

"As opposed to after he died?" I asked. He did not respond. "I am. He left it to me and some others like it that I sold years ago."

He studied it again and shook his head.

"I doubt you could even get ten for it."

"Ten what?" Beth asked.

"Thousand? Maybe five. I'm pretty sure we could get five."

"No, thank you," Beth said. "It's not for sale."

The fellow nodded, pulling at his red scarf to give himself some air, and looked from Beth to me.

"It's not for sale for five," I said. "Five or even ten is not nearly enough. The other abstracts I sold twenty years ago went for twenty-five. Each."

"Well, I'm sorry, but even classic Bentleys aren't holding their value, and this is not what people think of when they think of a Bentley."

"People often don't know what to think when they think of a Bentley," Beth said.

"Sorry," the man said, already heading for the door. "I should be going."

Once he was gone Beth blocked my retreat.

"What right do you have …!"

"It's my painting!"

"Yours? Is this not a marriage? I thought this was a marriage. It is *our* painting. I realize you don't like the painting, but you know that I do. How dare you try to sell it without even discussing it with me."

"My grandfather gave it to *me*, before I ever met you. You never knew my grandfather. Sheena needs the money. Her talent—and I believe she has talent—and I believe her talent comes from him … I thought it was appropriate for his painting to finance her dream."

"Appropriate? It would be appropriate for you and Sheena to realize that you are not wealthy, and you have no way of financing her selfish and ridiculously expensive fantasies. This is the arts we're talking about. Unlike you, I have some personal experience with the difficulties of a career in the arts. Did I ever get the chance to go and screw around in New

York City? No! But now I'm expected to support Sheena's illusions, since I'm the only one making any money in this house? What about Julia's dreams? What about my dreams? If you want to be Sheena's sugar daddy, then it would be appropriate for you to get busy and get a job. You're not quite dead yet."

Another image out of *spiritus mundi* flashed through my mind: my grandfather's gun pointing into my mouth.

Philip Bentley came to your room while you were meditating, Mary Abraham. The candle went out, the wisp of smoke curled into the air, and he was there. Now that I think of it, that's not so different to how he first appeared to me.

April 1986, Vancouver

I was sitting in my favourite coffee place skimming *The Georgia Straight,* when I glanced up through the window and saw, across Denman, an old man coming around the corner from Comox Street, eyes trained on the sidewalk at his feet. I'd seen photographs of Philip Bentley, but it wasn't his face I recognized. It was something in his walk, an awkward sidle that for a second made me think maybe Dad had come to fetch me home. But then I saw something else: a tremor and a stumble that made me think this person who was obviously not my father was about to fall. The man was much older than Dad, and there was something in his profile that reminded me of a photo of myself that Grandma had framed and placed on her piano.

And then I noticed he was wearing a pair of navy blue bedroom slippers.

He staggered to the sandwich shop directly across the street, where he managed with some difficulty to push open the door and stumble inside. It was five minutes before I finished my coffee and mustered the courage to stand and leave the coffee shop. Jaywalking across Denman, I spotted through the window the man I suspected to be my grandfather sitting at a table with a cup of coffee before him. His skin was the colour of the fog obscuring the mountains to the north and his hand resting beside the cup on the table shook noticeably. He looked up and, through the space between some letters etched in frosted white on the glass (*Fully Licensed*), met my eyes. I thought I saw a look of recognition cross his face. There was a large ugly bruise over his right eye and his head trembled.

The door to the sandwich shop *was* heavy. It was new to me, feeling the weight of a door and thinking what such a weight would mean to an old man. Once inside, I saw that the old man's eyes had not followed me; he was still looking blankly out the window, and I realized he hadn't recognized *me*; he'd been watching anyone who happened to pass. I approached the table and stood waiting for him to notice me. This took a long time, but finally his eyes glanced my way, and I could see him waiting for me to explain myself.

"Philip Bentley?"

He sat up a little straighter and scanned my face and the rest of my body before nodding his quivering head. "It's about time you got here," he said.

I considered this, the scolding tone reminding me again of my father, and was unsure how to respond. It was him, the grandfather I'd never met, and it seemed he'd been expecting me.

"Are you okay?" I asked, feeling a little dizzy myself.

He looked bewildered, raising a shaking hand to the yellow bruise above his eye.

"Yes. I was trying to get out of the bath and came down on my forehead. Crawled for the phone but couldn't make it. Blacked out right there on the floor, I must have. Didn't wake up 'til this morning. Is it morning?"

It was four in the afternoon. "We should get you to the hospital."

The old man sighed, a childish expression of self-absorption passing over his face: he looked as if he might burst into tears. "Maybe you're right."

I went to the counter and asked them to call a cab.

"Do you want another cup of coffee, I could get you one to go?" I asked when I returned to the table, but my grandfather shook his head, motioning with his unsteady hand for me to sit. When I did, the old man leaned closer and began speaking in a self-pitying tone.

"The woman in the apartment over me is always banging on her floor for me to shut up. Not that I have anyone to talk to. I'm losing my voice. Any noise I make, she disapproves. If I play my music loud enough that I can hear it she's banging away up there. I suppose my ears are going and I have it too loud. Do I seem deaf to you?" I shook my head. "My hands shake from the Parkinson's, and so sometimes without noticing I'll be banging my hand on the table, and the next thing I know she'll start banging on the ceiling in exactly the same rhythm." To demonstrate, he allowed his hand to tap the table. "My shrink thinks I'm imagining it."

He leaned closer.

"I used to find young men attractive. Once. Too attractive, I mean. Not any more. Now they don't have any meaning for me. Too old. Might as well be dead." I squirmed in my chair. "You can't control it. All those priests and politicians who want young boys and give in even though they know it will ruin them. The feeling finally gets the better of them and they fall."

The cab pulled up outside the window and I jumped to my feet. "It's here!"

Wearily, my grandfather turned to look where I pointed. "Our coach awaits," he said, struggling to stand, hands flat on the table, pushing down for support. I stood back, waiting, until I realized I should offer to help and took his arm. There was an unpleasant smell that I couldn't entirely place: urine and something else.

In the cab, he was mostly quiet, but at one point he said, "I'm afraid of hospitals. You never know. You go in, you might never come out. Once I'm inside I'm generally okay, though. It's kind of nice to have someone looking after you."

The waiting room at Emergency was crowded. We sat and watched the circle of injured humanity: parents with bored or weeping children, a man in work clothes holding his arm and gritting his teeth, an elderly woman with a man who must have been her son.

"When it happened," Philip Bentley suddenly said, "I thought about what it would have been like to have gone off the balcony. Instead of out of the tub and onto the bathroom floor, over the rail of the balcony and down twelve floors. Tumbling head over heels. There's a parking lot down there. Make a terrible mess, the insides coming out of you, and somebody would have to clean it up. I never even use the thing. The balcony. There's always people out watching. There's a man who dances with himself in the next building over."

The woman across from us, her daughter's nose in a book, glanced in our direction and away. Nothing to see. Just a young man and his grandfather waiting to see a doctor. An anchorman's mouth moved on the muted television mounted high in the corner.

"It shouldn't be too much longer," I said.

Three hours later we sat behind a curtain listening to the doctor in the next cubicle telling a woman there was nothing wrong with her son.

"But he's been crying all day. He won't stop crying. I don't know what to do with him. I can't stand to hear him cry another moment."

"Sell him to the circus," Philip Bentley murmured.

They took him away for X-rays. I called Denise to tell her I would not be able to meet her at the bar as we'd planned, but she wasn't home and so I left a vague message of apology. An old woman watched me talking into the payphone, her right eye open in a way that reminded me of Denise in her hunting pose: aiming down the barrel of a gun. I got hungry and went to buy a bag of potato chips. Worried I'd missed him, I rushed back to the waiting room. An hour or more later, the old man came stumbling in and told me they'd found nothing serious.

"Apparently I'm unbreakable. They're giving a money back guarantee. If you want your money back. You don't look like you have much money."

We emerged to a darkened land, the pedestrians on Burrard giving no hint they believed in a world of sick or dying souls. The cab whisked us up Nelson Street toward his apartment by the park. I swivelled my head as we passed my building.

"Did you see that doctor?" my grandfather asked.

"Which?"

"I guess you didn't see him. Curly black hair? Knew his way around a problem. Told me when to cough. If I'd had the opportunity I might have been a doctor myself. Not a chance, coming where I come from. Bastard child of a prairie town. That's what the other kids called me after Sunday school: bastard. They might have forgotten, but their parents reminded them."

"I'm from there too," I said.

Some expression of warning settled into the old man's eyes. "You're a bastard?"

"No. I don't think so. I'm from not that far from Horizon. Near Broken Head."

He looked at me steadily, his shaking suddenly gone. "My condolences to you. I'm not from Horizon. Lived there once a very long time ago. Only for a year or so. Didn't like it much. How in the hell did you get here?"

"My father is your son. You named him after you. Philip. I'm your grandson."

I might as well have punched him in the stomach. His yellowed eyes widened, as if he were trying to see what he'd been missing. When he saw for certain I was speaking the truth he lowered his head to gaze at his dusty bedroom slippers. "I knew I'd seen you somewhere before." I didn't correct him. He didn't say another word until the cab stopped in front of his building. He paid the fare. I got out and ran around to open the door.

Inside his building, in front of the elevator, he finally looked me in the eye and said, "How did you find me?"

"You found me. You walked by and I recognized you. You look a little like my dad."

He nodded, but didn't want to pursue it any further. "Are you coming up?"

It was a large airy apartment overlooking the park. The furniture was fifties modern, more expensive than Ikea, and the patio doors to the balcony might have let in some light if it were not already dark. Some large abstract paintings covered significant portions of the walls. There was blood drying on the bathroom floor and I wiped it up with paper towel and some abrasive cleanser I found under the bathroom sink.

When I emerged from the bathroom with the can of cleaning powder, my grandfather was sitting on the couch, watching me.

"You remember Old Dutch Cleanser? I guess that's before your time. There were all these women in bonnets chasing dirt around the cans. They had blue dresses and bonnets like white hoods and their faces were turned away from you like they couldn't look you in the eye. They carried sticks: 'I am coming to clean up the town'. That was their motto. Could be that's what they need here in Vancouver: a gang of hooded women to clean up the town. All the queers and addicts and the like."

He smiled ironically and pretended to swipe an imaginary stick. My mind had somehow formed an image of the label of Old Dutch Cleanser. Maybe Mom had once used it, or I'd seen an old can of the stuff tucked somewhere out in Dad's shop.

"It looks beautiful on the surface but it's dirty underneath. Right? Dirty dirty dirty. Vancouver." This sounded like something Sid might have said and he said it with a similar delight. To fill the awkward silence, I studied the abstract paintings, bleak hulking things, mostly black and metallic shapes hanging ominously against grey backgrounds, paint dripping down. "My latest self-indulgence," he said when he saw me concentrating so deeply. It made me feel uneasy, being watched as I studied them, the old man perhaps waiting for some word of appraisal, but I had no idea what to say. I could hear my father saying that they looked like something he could have done himself in an afternoon if he had the canvas, a wide brush, and lots of black paint. I had no idea what I was supposed to be looking for, in order to properly appreciate them, but the metallic hues appealed to me; they gave them a precious metal burnish.

When I said goodbye, I offered to come and check on him the next day and he smiled.

"If you wish. Don't knock yourself out. I get along just fine on my own. It's been a long time since I had family to check on me. But I do thank you for coming to my rescue today."

I promised I'd return.

"All right. Well, if you do decide to visit again, could you bring me some bananas?"

I nodded and he closed the door between us.

—

Those paintings entered my mind that day in, perhaps, exactly the way that Beth feared the image of the mummified fetus of my daughter might enter me and infect our marriage. My grandfather left each and every one to me, Mary Abraham. I sold all but one to Sid's father, who appreciated them even less than me, but who hoped they would appreciate in value. He died disappointed.

If he'd looked more carefully at the paintings, he would have seen their warning. They are portraits of failure: my grandfather was painting the parts of us that we'd rather not recognize.

—

The next morning, I pressed the button beside my grandfather's name and told him I'd come bearing bananas. There was a long pause filled only with static.

"Hello?" The lock buzzed to let me inside. I rode the elevator up, knocked on the door and, after another long pause, it opened a crack.

"That's okay," his gravelly voice came through the opening. The chain, I could see, was connected. "I'll be fine. You don't need to worry about me."

"You feeling all right?"

"Just fine. Much better. Thanks." A yellow eye peered out.

"I brought you bananas." I lifted them, as if in a toast, to demonstrate. "And a rubber mat for your bath tub. So you don't slip again." There was no response except the hum of some ceiling fan or air conditioner, but finally I heard the chain being removed and a shaking hand reached out through the opening and took the bananas. A moment later, the pale hand reappeared and snatched the rubber mat.

"Thank you." The door closed and the bolt slid into place.

"You're welcome."

I studied the door —it looked like a new door, but a chip of paint had flaked off, leaving a mark roughly the shape of Italy—before I turned and walked to the elevator.

November 30, 2012

My first wife, Denise Davis, had a pixie cut when I met her in 1986, her brown hair dyed jet black to contrast with her ivory skin. She was only a little more than five feet tall, but made up for her lack of height by standing aggressively close to people and staring directly into their eyes, daring them not to look away. The first time she spoke to me was at an office wine and cheese. She sat down between me and a broker, Miles Jones. Having her so close made me nervous. Sid had told me she was MacMillan's (the top dog's) mistress.

Jones was touting a company that claimed to have developed an effective treatment for AIDS. The pharmaceutical authorities hadn't cleared it, and in the meantime they were marketing it as herbal tea. But the stock, Fountain of Youth Explorations (a medical company mostly involved in the field of cosmetic medicine), was doing well on speculation. They were releasing a new issue and Denise wanted in, but Jones wouldn't bite. Instead, he was pitching her for a meeting with the widow of a recently deceased Middle Eastern arms dealer.

"I heard you and MacMillan had dinner with Arabella Wiseman last night. Is that true?" Jones wrapped an arm around her and squeezed her shoulder. "Come on, Denise. I can smell her perfume on you. Where's she staying? Point me in her direction."

She arched her pencil-thin eyebrows in a way that would become all too familiar to me.

"She's in a motel on the Kingsway. The Dew Drop Inn."

Jones snorted an annoyed chuckle. "I'll track her down, you'll see. I'll touch her up for a feel inside her purse."

"And what would you want with her, Miles? You buying rocket launchers for your weekend hunting excursions? I hate to think what one of those things would do to a deer. You heard what one did to her husband? Hoisted on his own petard."

"Yes, wasn't that a terrible thing to happen to a beautiful Rolls Royce. But Arabella's interests are more spiritual than that camel jockey husband of hers. More life affirming, like Fountain of Youth. I'll tell you what: if you can get me a meeting with her, I'll give you a piece of the new issue."

"She has millions. She's not interested in penny tea stock."

Jones pulled himself up to his full sitting height.

"There's no reason she shouldn't back Fountain. I mean, we've got unlimited market potential. Some people haven't got that through their heads. They think AIDS has stalled with the homos, but it's movin' on the straights, and when that fact sinks in the governments will start to pay attention. This is a plague we're dealing with. This is all of our lives at stake—how do you know the man you fucked last night didn't fuck somebody else with it the day before? When there's that much at stake, there's definitely money to be made."

"Except there's no proof your tea has any positive medicinal qualities …"

"There is proof! There's a few ornery scientists disputing facts, but there are fags still walking around because they drink our tea. The proof is in the pudding!"

Denise's eyes had glazed over, and she leaned away from Jones, who didn't notice, kept on spouting homophobia—he was already pretty drunk, though it was only two in the afternoon. I glanced away for a moment and when I looked back in the mirror across the room, I saw that she was staring directly at my image. I watched her head turn to me and I turned from the image to face her brown eyes and those arching dark eyebrows.

"Are you gay?" she asked.

"NO!" I said. When she smiled at the violent reaction, I said, "Oh, sorry, I …" and then realized I couldn't explain.

"It's okay, it's okay. Some of my best friends are homosexuals."

"I'm not!"

She looked me up and down with her ironic smile that widened the right side of her mouth a little more than the left, revealing very white teeth.

"Oh, I'm sorry. I thought maybe you and Madison's boy…. Although, you don't dress well enough." She winked. "I'm not going to take your word. You'll have to prove it."

"Denise!" MacMillan called her from across the room, waving an arm like a third base coach directing a runner home. "Come here and tell Harrison what an asshole he is."

With a quick pat on the knee, she left me very much alone.

—

Not an ideal relationship. I was twenty-three and almost broke and she had money. She was a decade older and we had little in common. She was attractive, her pale complexion next to her artificial vampire-black hair, but her skin had begun to soften and she would soon see her beauty fading in the reflection in my eyes, sending her in search of young Brazilian sailors and old visual artists who still looked at her in ways that allowed her a glimpse of her lost allure, or who she thought would make me jealous enough to fight for her.

She gave me Sheena.

If I'd gone for coffee with you, Mary Abraham, would you have reminded me how lucky I am to be alive? The world a heaven all around me. Birds and trees and wind moving across the water, light shimmering on each tiny wave. This morning I told myself to be grateful and jumped out of bed and was ready by eight to walk Julia to school. A killing frost in the air. We had to bundle up. Julia skipping beside me, I told her that it was strange how I used to hate the endless grind of pulling myself out of bed in the morning, but now I found myself missing dragging myself in to work.

"What did you do there all day?"

"Looked at numbers. Answered emails. Had meetings. It was all pretty boring."

"Yes," she agreed. "I'm never going to do anything boring. Even for money. I'm going to be an Egyptologist. When are we going to Egypt?"

"Sometime."

The time has passed.

When I got home again, Beth was out, so I used her office

phone to try calling Sheena and got no answer. Left a message asking her to call me back, then phoned my mother. I'd used the landline in Beth's office because Mom couldn't hear me properly when I called on my smart phone. I was feeling guilty because I had neglected to call her since before I was fired.

She answered with her familiar confused hello. The way she spoke the simple greeting made her sound vulnerable to the entire universe and I felt another flood of guilt for not being there to protect her.

"How are you doing, Mom?"

"Not too badly, I guess. Who's calling?"

"It's me, Mom."

"You?"

In the background I heard the clock chime. I'd grown up with that clock—that chime on the half hour to punctuate the other tone that counted off the hours. As a child I'd thought the hours would never end, but my life on the farm was so long gone, so distant, it was almost as if that part of me existed outside of time. The clock had been a wedding gift and had ticked off every second of my parents' marriage. Over the years Mom often reminisced about who'd given them the clock, but I can never remember.

"Who was it who gave you that clock?"

There was a confused silence.

"Oh? Did you want to speak with your father? He's out in the shop."

"No. That's okay, Mom. Who was it gave you the clock? I remember you telling me when I was a kid."

"Clock? What clock?"

"Your clock. The wedding present? In your kitchen? The one I just heard chiming?" Another longer silence was filled only by the ticking of the clock here in Beth's office.

"I don't remember," she finally said.

"How is Joan, Mom?"

Joan was a neighbour from the next farm, only a couple of miles away; a friend who came over for tea almost every afternoon. Or so I liked to imagine.

"Joan? Joan's gone."

"What do you mean? Are they in Arizona?"

Many of the neighbours winter in mobile homes they rent in Arizona, but, as far as I knew, not Joan and her husband.

"Arizona?" Mom asked and was silent again. I didn't interrupt this silence, as I could sense she was following some path in her mind toward that southern state. I wished I was on my smart phone, sitting on the front stoop, looking down the street toward the lake, instead of tied to the wall, looking at the green glass shade of Beth's bankers lamp.

"Arizona? I don't think so," she finally said. "Joan passed away. I went to the funeral. Mildred and Ken took me. It was very nice. Not too long. They had some lovely desserts. Nanaimo bars and date squares and the whole nine yards."

"Oh!" I spun a one-eighty in Beth's office chair and peered out the window at our neighbour at her desk, staring into her computer. "Is Mildred looking in on you, Mom?"

"Yes. I see Mildred. I can't recall who gave us the clock. I'm not sure why we have to memorize all these facts about the past. There's no one to replace us anyway."

I carefully considered the profundity of this sentence, listening for other sounds in the background, other hints of my childhood, watching the woman next door staring at something on her computer that seemed to trouble her greatly. "Yes," I finally said. "I think I know what you mean. Are you spending Christmas with Mildred and Ken?"

"Oh? That would be nice. I thought they were going to Medicine Hat to spend it with Delores."

"Are they?" I asked, but she didn't answer, and we both sat for many seconds listening to the line buzz. "Maybe you should come here for Christmas, Mom. Would you like that? Spend it with Beth and Julia and me? Sheena's coming too. I'll get you a ticket and talk to Mildred and Ken about getting you to the flight."

"Flight?"

"Yes. We're in Toronto. You'd need to fly."

"Oh, I don't know about that. I'm not much of a flyer. Airports make me dizzy. I don't much like escalators."

"Are you sure? We'll get someone to help you through the airports. We'd like to have you. Beth and Julia and I. And Sheena."

"For Christmas? In Toronto?"

"That's right. Would you like that?"

"That sounds very nice. Your father will be in soon, and he'll be hungry. It's getting toward dinnertime. I'd better get some food together."

She hung up. I set the phone down and the woman next door looked up and saw me, then pretended she hadn't.

Dinnertime meant lunchtime, but it was only eight o'clock in the morning in Saskatchewan.

December 1, 2012

I found Mildred's number and called her and she filled me in on Joan's death, a sudden heart attack, reassuring me that Mom seemed fine, though she did often think that Dad was still alive and working out in the shop. She was constantly expecting him to come in for tea.

"I think she would prefer it so," she said. "She seems to be eating well. I go over and play Scrabble with her every few days and her mind is pretty sharp. She usually beats me. Are you coming to see her?"

It was true that they were going to Medicine Hat for Christmas. She offered to take Mom with her. I asked if she and Ken would be able to get her to the airport in Medicine Hat if I booked a flight for her, and she said they'd be happy to do that. She hoped the weather wouldn't be a problem. Mildred has email and said she'd print Mom's ticket. I thanked her and told her I'd let her know once it was all arranged.

I put Julia to bed and was in bed myself, watching the news, when Beth got home from her story meeting. They were on a hard deadline because the holidays were coming up. According to the television nothing new had happened in all the world. Beth brushed her teeth, pulled on her warm flannel nightie and collapsed onto her side of the mattress.

Beth's face softened when I told her my mother was not well and when I told her that Joan had died her lips rounded into an expression that reminded me of when we had first met.

"Oh, honey! You'd better go. Go!"

She touched my arm and left her hand there.

"I was thinking of inviting her for Christmas."

She withdrew her hand. There was a long silence, her brow furrowing into a more recent physiognomy.

"Why not? That would be nice. I'm really busy, though, so it would be on your shoulders to look after her. I'm sure Mom and Dad would be happy to have her."

We always go to Beth's parents' for Christmas.

"Okay. I'll book the flight tomorrow."

"All right. For just before Christmas?"

"Fares are lower a little earlier. Maybe the 19th"

"Okay. The 19th. It'll be on your shoulders."

"Of course. I'll book it tomorrow."

"Tomorrow."

Beth sighed and shifted on the bed.

"And Sheena's coming too. Don't forget you'll need to entertain Julia full-time, once the holidays start."

"I'm sure Julia will be happy to have Grandma here."

Beth was silent. I lay there bracing myself for an explosion I could smell like a fuse burning. A few minutes later she muttered, "Good night."

An hour later, I could not sleep and so got up to write down this day and a memory of Vancouver that my burned journal had recalled.

April 1986, Vancouver
While Denise slept, I slipped from the bed and out the door, bought a bunch of bananas from a Korean grocer and walked, meeting runners in spandex, tweedy dog walkers enjoying the morning, and German tourists seeking suitable sausage on Denman Street. As I approached my grandfather's building, a cacophony of birdsong rose from Stanley Park, the birds stubbornly attempting to drown out the hum of the city. It reminded me of waking on the farm where, on a spring or summer morning, the birds could seem deafening in the silence. My jaw ached from grinding my teeth while I slept. The constant drone of the city made me grind my teeth and walking on cement all day made my knees ache. Still, I felt happy. It was a happy time, Mary Abraham. Or that's how I remember it.

I buzzed and identified myself. There was silence before my grandfather responded, "What do you want?"

"I brought bananas." I held them up to the intercom but the bananas did not speak. Finally, the lock buzzed and I pulled open the door.

When I got out of the elevator I saw my grandfather's door was open a crack. My knock pushed it wide enough that I could see him staring at the ceiling.

"Hello?"

He brought his eyes down to meet mine, but his mind was still above him. He pointed over his head. "She's at it again. You hear?"

I heard nothing and so coughed to hide my discomfort. Despite the sunny morning, the apartment was gloomy, the curtains all drawn.

"I brought bananas."

My grandfather shushed me, a hand held high, and I was reminded of suppertime on the farm, my father halting all discussion because he was trying to hear something on the six o'clock radio news. The hand, raised like Moses parting the Red Sea, trembled as though some higher force were channelling through the old man's body, until finally he lowered it self-consciously.

"You don't hear her, do you?"

I shrugged. "I guess she stopped."

Philip Bentley sighed.

"She's a tricky one, she is. Wants me out of here. Says I belong in a home. As if it's any of her business where I belong."

I nodded. "I brought bananas."

The old man finally focussed on the offering and, with quivering hands, accepted.

"Thank you. I need potassium, my doctor tells me. We all need the potassium, apparently. Don't know how we managed to survive when I was a kid. There was nothing so exotic as bananas until I got to the city and then the only kind I could afford were the ones as black as the devil's nutting bag. Got used to eating them like that and I still like them that way. Kind of melt in your mouth rotten. Like me. But I'm not patient enough to leave them that long. How much were they? I believe I forgot to pay you for the last ones. And the bath mat. Thank you for the bath mat. It's a real improvement. It's raised the value of the entire property. I'll get my wallet."

"No, no. Don't worry about it." But Philip Bentley ignored my protestations and stumbled off down a hallway. I took a step deeper into the apartment, looking around at the gloomy room—it felt like being underwater—and wondering whether I might dare pull open a shade in hopes it might improve the Bentley state of mind, but in the end I wasn't brave enough. The old man returned with a twenty and held it out to me.

"That's too much."

"It's a pittance. Not nearly enough. You rescued me."

I shrugged, took the bill, and shoved it in my pocket.

"Can I offer you a cup of coffee?"

Seeing the disappointment in his eyes as I began to make my excuses, I couldn't help accepting. After I'd done so, I wondered if I'd misinterpreted and he'd actually been counting on my refusal. There was silence as we waited for the water to boil and the old man spooned out coffee. The clock ticked. Sitting across the table, I watched as the plunger lowered, pressed slowly down by the withered hand, the grounds forced to the bottom of the glass cylinder. Was Denise awake and wondering if I'd ever return?

"French press," he said, testing these words on his tongue as he stared into the cloudy brown liquid. "Sounds delectable enough to be banned in Boston, doesn't it?"

"I want to be a writer," I responded.

My grandfather slowly raised his eyes and met mine.

"Really? The artist's life? I tried that. Can't say I'd recommend it."

I laughed nervously. "You did fairly well."

He looked around.

"Did I?"

He poured the coffee.

"What's the secret to being a successful artist?"

He set the cup before me. "Don't quit your day job and don't get married."

I chuckled.

"What's so funny?"

"You did quit your day job. Being a minister. And you got married. I wouldn't be here if you hadn't."

The old man pondered this. "Is that true? Much is dependent on marriage, but is *your* existence? Maybe, but not in the way you think. I'd never have stayed a minister if I hadn't got married and had to support your grandmother. But you likely don't know that your real grandmother was a girl named Judith in the church choir in Horizon. So I'd never have met Judith if I hadn't stayed a minister. Pretty girl. Pale as a ghost. Had a wonderful voice. Ethereal. Killed herself after the baby—your dad—was born. Your grandmother insisted on adopting it. A little bastard like his father. Your grandmother pretended she didn't know it was mine. She liked to pretend. It's what she did best. I'm guessing she never told your father. Didn't think it was any of his business who his mother was, I guess." He sighed. "So my advice sticks. Stay away from women. Or have you failed on that score already?"

I opened my mouth and closed it, my mind lurching as this revelation twisted my life into an unfamiliar contortion.

He smiled. "Who's the lucky girl?"

I stared at him dumbly another moment, thinking of my grandmother, before I found my tongue.

"Denise. A stock broker. Works in my office."

"You're a stock broker?"

"No. I'm just a messenger. A courier. But I've only been

there a few months. It's a foot in the door. I'll be selling before long."

The old man nodded, staring into the coffee.

"Sounds like you've managed to get some other body parts into some other openings as well." He paused to suck at something between his teeth. "A stock broker. A woman of means. Wish I'd been as wise. Might have made all the difference. Money's the only sensible reason to marry. Not that it's likely any other woman would have had me."

"It's not about her money."

"Well, that's not true." The old man raised his trembling head, widening his eyes. "There was Judith, wasn't there? From the choir. Your real grandmother. I wasn't bad looking back then. Not that you'd know it now. Can't stand to look at myself in the mirror. Back then my face wouldn't have shattered your lens. She considered me quite the catch. The minister's wife's husband. Women can never get enough of another woman's property: you'll discover that now that you're another woman's property. And I had enough between the legs to satisfy any woman. Just wasn't ever satisfied by *them*."

"You're saying my grandmother isn't really my ... grandmother?"

Philip Bentley eyed me suspiciously.

"Did your father tell you that?"

"No. You did. Just now."

He considered this and seemed to accept that it was probably true.

"Isn't really anything to you. An imposter. She's barren as the prairie that raised her and in which she'll be buried in

not too many more years, and may the Lord who died and
was buried two thousand years before her but refused to stay
in the ground—may the original King of the Zombies have
mercy on her soul. You've got my blood, my poor young
man. I see myself when I look at you. Not a single solitary
drop of her in you. Can't get blood from a stone."

We sat staring in opposite directions, me thinking about
the old woman who'd made me change my clothes when I
got home from school and then wouldn't let me go outside
until I'd tidied my room—understanding for the first time
why my grandmother had always seemed to resent my father,
my mother, everyone in the world. I stared into one of the
gloomy paintings, black dripping down the canvas.

"They're worth nothing. Might as well put them out with
the garbage. Tried getting a gallery interested but they just
wanted pictures of prairie towns or horses or the same old
thing. If I'd done more of those, they'd probably have found
other excuses not to be interested. Really they just wanted
the ones I did back in the thirties and early forties when I was
only just learning. Juvenile and entirely derivative. But those
are worth something substantial now. Naturally, I sold them
all years ago for next to nothing when people could still see
they were juvenile and completely derivative. When I first
painted them, nobody wanted those either. After I'm dead,
someone will probably discover these and they'll be worth a
fortune. Just wait and see. Or maybe not. Maybe I'll simply
be forgotten." He took a sip of his coffee. "Guess I won't
bother waiting around to see."

"I own some stock in a company that could help you with
that."

My grandfather carefully set down his cup.

"Help me with what?"

"A company traded on the VSE will freeze your body and thaw you out once they've found the cure for what ails you."

My grandfather considered this a little longer, staring at his own shaking hand.

"I've heard of that. Cryonics. That is an interesting idea. What is it that you write?"

"Stories. Poems. I started a novel."

"Are they any good?"

"I don't know. I think so. I like doing it. Writing."

The old man cleared his throat as if to prepare to pass along some very important advice.

"You'll never know for certain. Never."

December 2, 2012

I'm sitting at the dining room table opposite Philip Bentley's painting, the product of his shaking hands, but not part of the Bentley vernacular. I'm seeing the painting anew, Mary Abraham: through my nineteen-year-old eyes, at the same time as I see it through these fifty-year-old eyes. One of those strange ugly rectangles hanging on the wall of that Stanley Park apartment. The grandfather he … *I* had only just met.

Not much point selling it for only five thousand. If I do it's bound to be worth fifty in five years or less. Sheena's flight is booked for two weeks from now, and I'll have her to host, along with Mom, who is coming a couple of days later. No one hires in December. I'll start looking for a job in January.

I spent the morning contemplating the gun. Too many people insist on seeing beauty in a gun. Burnished metal. Perhaps it is more beautiful than the painting. Compare it to Sheena or Julia and its ugliness is undeniable. What would the two of them think of the gun? I'm not brave enough to use it, so why do I constantly feel the need to hold it in my hand? I've considered tossing it in a river, but it's part of history, a gift from my grandfather. It wouldn't be right to simply throw away the past.

This afternoon I managed to intercept Sid in his favourite bistro down in the financial district. The pressed-linen host led him to his usual table in the back corner near the windows—vaulted ceiling, dark hardwood walls with polished brass fixtures—where we'd had dozens of business lunches over the years, and when he was seated, I slid onto the leather banquette across from him.

"Bentley?" Sid said, still in the process of slipping off his gloves. "How are you? What are you doing here?"

"I want to talk to you. You don't return my calls."

"I'm sorry. There's not really anything to talk about." He unwound the eggshell blue woolen scarf (chosen to match his eyes, their colour enhanced by the shade of his contact lenses) from around his neck and placed it on the banquette next to him.

"Let's talk about Vancouver. I've been thinking about Vancouver a lot lately. Denise called the other day."

He raised his chin slightly and curled the corners of his mouth without parting his lips. Sid rarely showed his teeth.

"Really? How is Denise? She must be about a hundred and ten by now. That was a smart move, Bentley. Beth's getting up there, but she still looks pretty good for her age. How is Beth?"

"Sheena wants to go to school in the States. New York City. I'd like to help her."

"Sounds expensive. Tell her sorry. It's about time somebody pricked her balloon. That's one of the precious fatherly duties."

"It's about time somebody pricked your balloon."

He sat back and contemplated this statement with a smirk.

"I don't owe you a thing, Bentley. You got everything you deserved. If you don't believe it, get a lawyer. The company will be paying lawyers for your incompetence for years. Under the circumstances, we were more than fair."

He stretched an arm out along the back of the banquette and smiled, still without showing his teeth. Considering the violence of what he'd just said, he looked all too relaxed. He still had that tousled boyish hair he'd had when we met. If anything, age was only making him more handsome.

"You murdered my grandfather and your wife. The same day. You killed them both."

"Murdered? Me? I killed them? Amusing. And what about you? Did we do that? It was both of their wishes. It was a suicide pact. And anyway, they aren't even dead, Bentley. They're waiting to be reborn. Their action was chosen by them both to best facilitate their progress."

His claim was based on a belief that being frozen before death makes the body more viable for resurrection. Interrupting the body before the descent into death should allow the nanobots to be better able to turn back the deterioration of the sullied flesh. The problem for those in the cryonics business is that freezing living people is defined by the law as murder. I was there to remind Sid that I know where the bodies are buried. Or rather, stored.

"I don't need the money for me," I said. "It's for Sheena."

"Whatever you say. Is this blackmail?"

"I have been doing a little writing. It's an exposé of Argyle. I think you're really going to enjoy it."

"Ah, fiction! Good luck with that. I'm sure it'll be very entertaining. Send my lawyer a draft when you're happy with
it. Looking forward to it."

"Isn't that all there is to do in life, really? Look forward to
things? I've been thinking about that a lot lately. Vancouver.
Toronto. New York. Looking backward. Looking forward.
What do I look forward to now? I'm a desperate man."

Sid's smile widened so that I could actually see his white
teeth.

"My father taught me how to deal with desperate men.
Take a few ounces of lead and put it through their brains.
That generally salves their desperation. It's not personal,
Bentley. It's business. Count your blessings. You've got a lovely
wife and those two beautiful girls. So much to be grateful
for. Why would you want to throw all of that away? You really
don't want to make me angry. If you've learned anything
over the years, you should have learned that. But instead,
after almost killing my daughter you come in here and start
telling me that I should help your daughter. I've got to get
going," he said, though he'd only just arrived. "You should
talk to someone. Professionally. Goodbye."

He offered his right hand, but I did not draw my own
right hand—which was clutching my grandfather's Browning Hi-Power—from my overcoat pocket. Sid smiled at this
act, which he misinterpreted as a feeble snub; an act that may
have saved his life. I only say *may* because my hand was shaking so badly that I *may* have missed and killed someone in the
next booth. That's the reason I stopped myself. That's what I
tell myself, liar that I am.

"Take care of yourself," he said, winding on his scarf and picking up his gloves.

I watched him walk out the door and stride off without glancing back.

April 1986, Vancouver

"Denise asked me to ask you over for dinner."

Standing with Sid at the corner of Dunsmuir and Howe, waiting for the light to change, watching a woman in spiked heels across the street dangling a bill to a beggar as she sashayed past, I made the offer. A mist hung low over the city, so that it was like we were standing in the clouds.

"Do you think she knows him?" Sid asked.

The beggar snatched the bill as though he feared the woman was about to retract the offer. The woman just kept walking, her hips swaying like a model's on a fashion runway.

"Who?"

"That woman who gave the guy the money. Didn't you see? I think she's slept with him. Maybe years ago. Before he got the drug habit." Sid wiggled his eyebrows. He was wearing his Burberry trench coat and I had on the yellow rain shell that he said made me look like a fisherman.

"She didn't even look at him."

"No. He used to be something. Or somebody. And now she won't even look at him. She trampled what little dignity he had left by giving him that money, but he couldn't turn it down. He needs that money. He needs."

The light changed and we stepped off the curb.

"If you say so. Denise asked me to ask you over for dinner."

"Oh? Isn't that lovely? The little woman asked you to ask me over. An invitation to witness your domestic bliss. A peek into your sanctuary of sacred sex and home cooked meals."

"I haven't even given up my apartment. Will you come?"

"Well, I'm not so sure. What are we having?"

"Steak. I'll do steak on the barbeque. Do you like steak?"

As we passed the beggar, Sid leaned down and dropped some change into his cup.

"God bless," murmured the man, eyes raised to us hovering over him in the clouds.

"You're not very observant, are you, Bentley? I'm vegetarian."

—

"I met Ezra Pound's son in the showers of the YMCA in London, England." My grandfather spoke before turning to look out the window at the dishevelled man cleaning it with a squeegee. We were sitting in the coffee shop on Denman where we first met the day of his accident, but we were at a different table, away from the window and near the back wall. The man was washing the windows despite the fact that it was raining.

"Pardon?"

I'd been flipping through *The Georgia Straight* as we talked, and my grandfather had pointed out a photo of Madonna, who was about to release a new album, and he asked if I thought she was attractive. When I shrugged, said I guessed so and mentioned she had the same hair cut as Denise, my

grandfather brought up the meeting in the shower with Ezra
Pound's son.

"Pardon?"

A peculiar smile played on my grandfather's lips, his head
trembling in its way as he gazed at the squeegee man and the
damp afternoon traffic crawling along Denman.

"Well, I suppose that makes me a bit of a 'starfucker',
doesn't it? Kind of?" He turned back and looked me in the
eye. "Isn't that the expression?"

I looked away, no idea how to respond. The woman behind the counter leaned against the wall, talking to a cook
who was perched at the order window. It was impossible to
tell if they were bored or desperately in love.

"He asked me for 'tea' at his mother's apartment a few
times and I went, but I can't pretend I really liked him. Terrible snob. Constantly making fun of my rural roots. Rural
rooooot." He smiled at whatever was going on inside his head.
"Not nearly as good looking as his father. Had this terrible
adolescent wispy moustache. You could imagine him with a
long pink tail. The only attractive characteristic he had was
that he was the son of the great poet. Meanwhile, Daddy was
off in Rome, spouting anti-Semitism and Nazi propaganda on
Italian radio. Fraternizing with the enemy. Very famous. Infa-
mous. I had no problem with Jews myself, but a lot of people
didn't like them. We were brought up to not like them. And
no one knew about the camps at that time. No one? No one
but the victims and culprits. Do you know his poetry?"

"Ummm? I think?" I was distracted by his musings on the
Holocaust and his shaking hand holding his cup so that the
coffee threatened to slosh onto the table. "'The Wasteland'?"

"I thought you said you want to be a writer? That's his pal Eliot. I saw *him* lecture during the war. Wonderful lecture. Wonderful poet. Apparently didn't think much of Jews himself. Neither he or his son ever showed up in the showers at the Y … that I know of. Did Eliot have a son? Pound did *The Cantos*. Not that I ever read *The Cantos*, to be honest. I don't think anybody's ever read *The Cantos*. But that's what he's most famous for. Anyway. I can only think of a few poems I know. 'The River-Merchant's Wife.' The one about winter coming that sounds like Chaucer waiting in the cold at the bus stop. The haiku about the Paris Metro. *Petals on a wet black bough*…. Can't remember it exactly."

Noticing me staring apprehensively at his raised cup, he tried to set it carefully on the saucer and spilled his coffee. A brown stream came snaking across the table. I grabbed a napkin and dammed its progress. When I looked up, he was staring grimly into my eyes.

"Really? Ezra Pound's son? In Montreal?"

"You're not listening! In London, England." He shook his head in exasperation. "I didn't go to Montreal until after the war. I was in England during the war. I joined the army after we moved to Saskatoon. That's how I escaped your grandmother. The woman you thought was your grandmother."

And escaped my father. Now that he'd spoken the words, the old man looked a little embarrassed about gloating over the abandonment of his wife and child. The two of us have that in common if nothing else: both escaped Philip the younger. Maybe Sheena thinks I was trying to escape her. Of course, I couldn't speak of this, Sheena having not yet been born. Instead I asked, "Did you fight in the war?"

"I never saw action. Outside the London Y. Ended up living in that wonderful city for most of the war, watching the Hun reduce it to rubble. *Refusal to mourn the death of a child. After the first death, there is no other.* I can remember some of that one. *Never until the mankind making. Bird, beast, and flower. Fathering and all humbling darkness tells with silence the last light breaking.* Dylan Thomas. You know?" I shook my head, embarrassed by my exposed ignorance. "Pitiful. You need to read. If you want to be a writer, you need to educate yourself." He shook his head in disgust. "I was there right through the Blitz."

"That must have been scary."

Philip Bentley's wrinkled face opened into a fond and innocent smile that I hadn't seen before.

"Best time of my entire life. Wouldn't trade those years for the whole world. Sounds perverse, but it's true. I've often thought I should feel guilty about yearning for those war years when so many people were suffering. Babies burning, and I'm longing to bring it all back. There always seems to be babies burning somewhere." He shook his head and flashed the wicked grin that I easily recognized from my mirror. "There's just so much to feel guilty about in this terrible world. But in the end, how do you put out a baby once someone's set it on fire?" I didn't attempt an answer. "Are you planning on a baby with your new love? How is that going?"

"Ummm … Denise is fine. I'm a little young for a baby."

"You think so? Yes, you're only a baby yourself. Are you a breast man?"

I did not deign to respond. My grandfather laughed.

"Never got over suckling away at your mother's nipples." It was impossible not to hear contempt in this comment and the hurt must have shown in my face because my grandfather was suddenly chastened and apologetic. "Nothing wrong with that. Makes you normal. It's a lot simpler being normal. Unless you're not. Trying to be normal when you're not isn't very simple at all."

He lifted his shaking hand and raked it through his hair.

"You want another coffee?" I asked.

—

Looked up Ezra Pound's son. He did live in London during the Blitz, but he was only fifteen, maybe sixteen, when he left for the US in 1942, and he was likely not Ezra Pound's son any more than I am Mrs. Bentley's grandson.

—

"Is it okay if I bring a date tomorrow?"

Sid came out with this as though the idea had suddenly occurred to him as he was sorting through and planning his afternoon deliveries, placing them in chronological order. We were alone at the messenger desk, the buzz of the office going on around us: the clerks at their terminals, the odd client at the glass, speaking through the metal grill, Billingsley on the phone on the other side of his glass wall.

"Well, I don't know. Who do you want to bring?"

"A woman."

He smiled coyly, his mouth zippered tightly closed. He wore his designer jeans and his *War on 45* D.O.A. T-shirt: "Repent! You Fucking Savages! Repent!" Billingsley had warned him that the T-shirt was not appropriate for the office, but Sid ignored him.

"Not someone from work?"

"Of course not. I wouldn't date anyone from work. That would be stupid. Do I look stupid?"

He looked like he had some surprise he wanted to spring and I refused to give him the satisfaction of asking for clues. "I'll ask Denise."

"Oh, come on. You're not gonna make me come alone? It wouldn't be fair. The two of you outnumber me."

"It's dinner, not a wrestling match."

"Really? No wrestling?" He glanced to either side of him, apparently looking for eavesdroppers, before leaning in close and whispering in my ear. "The thing is, I suspect the two of you are planning on murdering me. Dead men don't talk. My guess is you don't want any witnesses who might let it get back to MacMillan that you're fucking his squeeze while working for him. Isn't that why you invited me in the first place?"

I sighed.

"Bring your date. We'll kill her too."

"Great. We'll be there at seven. She's also vegetarian."

He grabbed his briefcase and scampered off on his afternoon route. I walked across the office and stood looking down at Dunsmuir Street, the cars like tiny toys sluicing along in the rain, pedestrians hidden by a floating rainbow of umbrellas.

.

December 12, 2012

Is it our genes, those tiny soft machines, that make us so selfish as to choose our own comfort over what's best for the world?

Sid would say so and insist science was in his corner. Altruism is almost exclusively directed at those who are close genetic relatives and against those who are different. We look after our own. As Sid has lectured me many times, it's been proven by George R. Price's mathematical equations. Later, Price found God and tried to prove wrong his own equations by giving away everything he owned to drunks and strangers of any creed or colour who he met on the streets and brought home. He killed himself by slitting his carotid with a pair of toenail clippers. A scientist, a martyr, a saint. I would do well to follow in his bloody bare footprints (he gave away his shoes), Mary Abraham, but I am not nearly so brave.

I was thinking this, and perhaps you were reading my mind. You had great difficulty looking me in the eye. You had unzipped your burgundy parka so that I could see, with a bit of puzzling misplaced disappointment, that you were wearing a ubiquitous and very western beige sweater. No saffron sari under there. You *were* wearing a lovely purple silk scarf.

"Thank you for meeting me," you said. "I was not expecting your call. This has all been very difficult."

You right hand gripped the handle of your coffee cup, which sat steaming on the table between us.

"Have you finished your Christmas shopping?" I asked you, searching for a topic to lighten the tension before I realized that I may have put my foot in my mouth: I don't even know for sure whether you celebrate Christmas.

"Pardon?'

But you have met Christ. Presumably that means you celebrate his birthday? A personal acquaintance. With you I am one degree of separation from God. Your very name is Abraham. I decided again it would be best not to follow this path with spoken words. You were waiting for me to repeat my question: amid the din of the shoppers surrounding us you did not seem to be sure you'd heard me properly.

"I haven't done any Christmas shopping yet and I need to get started. I've never had so much time, but I still haven't done a thing. Can't seem to get myself motivated."

"You must be concerned about money …"

"No. No. No. I'll be fine. Don't worry about that. We'll be fine."

"Is Ms. Adams, your wife, a partner in Argyle?" That she remembered Beth's name took me by surprise. I had shown her Beth's photo on an Argyle brochure the first time we met and mentioned that we were married. She must have done further research.

"No. She's not a partner. I'd rather not talk about Beth."

You nodded, your dangling amethyst earrings bobbing with the gentle motion of your head. "When I met you on Queen Street near the beach you said that you'd promised her not to talk to me. I find that very troubling, considering that I'm now here, and I want to understand."

I looked at the table between us; the ring my cup left a moment ago. Shoppers all around us were resting with their packages, checking their lists, plotting their next moves. I'd chosen the place without ever having been there before—a spot so far from my regular routine there was little chance anyone I knew might appear and see me sitting there across from you. Between the ghost of your husband and the ghost of my grandfather.

"It's personal. It has nothing to do with Argyle. I'd rather not say anything more about it, thank you."

I glanced up and you were watching me, your coffee cup close to your mouth, a bemused expression on your purple lips, which matched your scarf and earrings. In your eyes I could see a furious recalculation.

"I see," you finally said, a weariness in your voice. "You are, I'm sure, in shock. I'm very sorry. I can't even say how sorry I am about your losing your job."

"It's not your fault."

Your face was pale, your purple lips making the shape of an O. You looked almost hurt that I was not giving you credit for ruining my life. It took a few seconds for the vowel to emerge from between those lips: not once, but twice.

"Oh? Oh? Is it? No? I appreciate your trying to spare me responsibility, but you've already made clear that it was my fault."

You leaned a little in my direction and I imagined reaching across the table and touching you as an expression of comfort and reassurance, but I did not move my hand.

"I'm sorry. I was upset and must have misled you. It was business. A business decision. They're moving in a new direction, away from human reanimation. They don't like the margins in our division. Nothing to do with you. You're in a good position to negotiate a refund. One of the things they most fear is negative media attention. They're hoping to keep the whole thing as quiet as possible."

"Refund? They've already paid Thomas a settlement. Joseph's son. My stepson. He's agreed to the settlement. All I want is to properly bury Joseph's remains as Joseph has asked me to do, but Thomas knows this and he's managed to convince them to keep Joseph's head. He insists it was Joseph's wish."

I didn't follow. Sid settled and still agreed to store the head for future reanimation? To be awakened, presumably in a cloned body, only to discover he has nothing in his bank account? It has all been spent by his son and his descendants. Robbed by a future now past.

"But you're his wife."

You sipped again, your lips leaving their mark on the white cup when you'd placed it again on the table.

"I am his second wife. Thomas is the eldest son. His mother passed on when he was still a teenager. He has always resented me. He claims I am guilty of erasing her memory. But it was Joseph who erased her memory to deal with his grief. Not me. I have no memory of her, except as a void in Joseph.

I've tried to heal that wound in Thomas, but it has proved impossible. Thomas is the eldest son. His rights supersede my own."

"No, they don't. Hire a lawyer. The courts in Canada will not see it that way."

"I'm not interested in lawyers."

"But Argyle wants to keep this all quiet, so if you were to threaten them with going public ..."

You shook your head, the amethyst earrings swaying. "My intention is simply to bury Joseph. To bring him lasting peace. Just as your grandfather wants."

You looked into my eyes, daring me to show some sign of mockery or doubt.

"Does he? Apparently. I understand. I've never had any desire to be frozen. Thawed."

"But your wife does, I assume, since she is in the advertising. Is she happy with this decision?"

You had leaned closer again, your eyes searching my face for some signal. Every time you mentioned Beth, you leaned closer.

"Very happy. Happiness is sometimes a difficult thing to define. You say that my grandfather is not happy."

You sat back, studying me, tickling your earlobe with your index finger.

"Does that surprise you?"

"A little. I didn't know him as a child, but I moved to Vancouver, where he lived, and we got to be friends. Of a kind. No, it doesn't surprise me that he'd be unhappy. It does surprise me that he'd visit you. Now that he's gone."

"We are never completely gone. I believe you know where Joseph is. And your grandfather. Will you take me to him? Please?"

The couple beside us were both staring into their phones, alone together at their table, having separate conversations with their electronic devices.

"Yes. Okay. I'll try. After Christmas."

You nodded.

"After Christmas would be fine."

And so we have entered into a contract, Mary Abraham. Once Christmas is over, I am bound to escort you to The Beautiful Place.

December 17, 2012

Sheena's flight was late. I should have checked the status before leaving home but didn't, and so Julia and I were sitting in Arrivals for more than an hour, watching joyful and tearful reunions while eating salt and vinegar potato chips. Eventually the board said her flight had landed but so had a dozen others and Sheena wasn't responding to my texts. Considering her reliability, I wondered if she would actually come wandering through the constantly opening and closing electronic doors or if we'd be waiting and wondering for hours more and finally have to give up and go home frantic and one daughter short.

"Are they from Vancouver?" Julia asked about a couple wheeling along their pastel suitcases, the umpteenth time she'd asked the same question in the last twenty minutes. I studied them, judging their left-coastedness.

"Hard to say. I hope so."

"Why don't you ask them? Ask if they know where Sheena is."

"I don't think we'll bother them. We'll be patient."

"I don't feel like being patient."

She kicked the concrete pillar I was leaning against, pressing her forehead against its cool surface and staring down at her toe striking it again and again. The doors slid open for the millionth time and Sheena emerged, staring blankly in front of her own toes, so that I couldn't help but see the echo in their postures, these two daughters of mine with different mothers, both so intent on the floor at their feet.

"She's here," I told Julia, squeezing her shoulder. Julia whirled, took a moment to spot Sheena, then charged up to the railing waving her arms wildly.

"*Sheeeeeeeeeeena!*"

My elder daughter lifted her chin at the call and couldn't help but flash a smile before she noticed the crowd of people watching and, with a hint of humiliation and betrayal, replaced the expression with a scowl. We met her at the bottom of the arrivals gauntlet and Julia embraced her, waist-height, making Sheena look all the more uncomfortable.

"Merry Christmas, *Sheeeeena!*"

"You're gonna give me a hernia."

"Dad got me a wooden toboggan last Christmas. Do you want to go tobogganing?"

"Tonight?"

"We need snow. It's supposed to snow tomorrow. I hope."

"I texted you and you didn't answer," I said.

"Phone died." Sheena patted the offending machine in her pocket. She was always forgetting to charge it. I held myself back from pointing this out, claimed my own limp hug and escorted them toward the car, Julia chattering nonstop and Sheena silent except for a few painfully extracted responses.

"It's great to have you here," I said, as I stowed her suitcase in the trunk.

"Yeah? I guess so."

When we got home, I made some hot chocolate, which Julia requested and Sheena silently accepted. After we drank it, sitting around the dining room table under their great-grandfather's painting, Julia and I escorted Sheena down to the pullout couch in the basement (which I'd already made up for her) and she collapsed in a heap, claiming exhaustion. We said good night and I put Julia to bed.

My girl is home. I can see Denise in her face, the way she wrinkles her forehead to show disdain for my remarkable stupidity, and in her walk, and even in the way she lifts mug to mouth and blows, which I suppose is one of the sources of Beth's antipathy to her. Beth does not want to be reminded that I had a life before Julia and her.

Beth is still out at her story session, so for tonight we've avoided the tension of their meeting. I can only hope that they'll both be on their best behaviour. For Julia's sake. Mom will be here too. It's Christmastime. My only wish is that the spirit helps us all to fumble through.

December 18, 2012

It's snowing heavily and Julia is ecstatic. I accompanied her to school, watching her catch snowflakes on her tongue, and then, despite the snow, continued on my morning stroll on the boardwalk beside Lake Ontario. The gusty east wind made the snow against the skin like needles, so I walked westward, wind pushing me, looking out across the expanse of grey water toward Buffalo, New York. The gale had the water churning, throwing whitecaps at the beach. The waves make a sound that gets in your blood, calming your heart-beat. *It was her voice that made the sky acutest at its vanishing.* I like walking most when no one else is out. People are so easily deterred. There's magic in being in one of the largest urban sprawls in North America, in a part of the city that is often flooded with people, and walking alone. You can pretend that you've escaped civilization and might walk on across the watery grey plain without sinking away to where thy father lies.

Only a crazy prairie boy likes walking by the lake in the snow, I guess. We know how to dress properly. Long johns. Tuque. Parka. Wool socks over cotton. Good boots.

Beth did not appear until after midnight last night. By then I had turned out the light. I heard her unlock the door, clomp up the stairs into the bathroom for her ablutions, before I felt her slip into bed. I pretended I was asleep and soon she was snoring peacefully.

Today she's locked in her office, and though it's past noon, Sheena still has not emerged from the basement. Beth is swamped with final rewrites for the Christmas special, so I've been picking up the slack, doing the shopping, making all the meals, and she almost seems to appreciate the effort. Despite Dr. Mengele's diagnosis, our marriage may have more than just a few gasps left.

We have Julia's Christmas concert tomorrow night. Mom's flight is tomorrow afternoon, so Mom will witness the performance. If the weather doesn't interfere. Knock on wood. I have promised Julia that we will toboggan when she gets home from school. I'm hoping Sheena will be up by then and will accompany us, but I can't say for certain, her body being on Vancouver and teenaged time. "Haven't been a teenager for a while," she would remind me.

Sheena has brought Vancouver with her, spilling out of that tiny wheeled suitcase and uncoiling my long path from there to this present moment.

May 1986, Vancouver
When the buzzer sounded, I answered and heard Sid's, "It's us." I pressed the button to release the lock and allow them inside.

"Go start the vegetables on the barbeque." Denise rushed in from the kitchen, straightened the flower arrangement on the coffee table for the fourteenth time, and pointed the way to the balcony. "I'll greet them and bring them out to you."

I stood waiting on the balcony, sipping a margarita while repeatedly brushing the vegetables with olive oil infused with garlic and hot peppers, exactly as Denise had demonstrated. I owe any culinary skills I have in large part to carefully following Denise's orders. My own cooking until that time had been meat and potatoes, but I took instructions well. The sun felt good and the snow on the mountaintops sparkled against blue sky. Six floors below, fellow residents and tourists (according to local politicians and media, hosting Expo 86 had granted Vancouver the status of a "world-class city") passed unaware that I watched them, and I thought of the way a hawk glides, scanning the earth for movement of possible prey far below. I used to watch the hawks while summer fallowing, and see them plummet from the sky to strike gophers that ran to avoid the cultivator, venturing too far from their holes.

From within the apartment, Sid's voice interrupted my memory and then another man's voice, followed by Denise's voice responding with an enthusiasm that was completely uncharacteristic of her, and a moment later I heard a woman's voice. There was something curious, something surprisingly mature, even matronly, about the woman's voice. I felt that it would be polite to go inside and welcome them, but was worried about veering from Denise's last command.

The balcony door opened and Denise led the procession out to me.

"Honey, you know Sid. And this is Arabella Wiseman!"

The balcony was narrow, and Sid—clad in a brilliant white suite—and Denise separated us, but Arabella Wiseman reached awkwardly past the bodies of our respective lovers (I remember wondering if she was really Sid's lover) and touched my hand.

"Pleased to meet you."

She was greying, in her late fifties. Sid was twenty-two. But she was worth many millions. I could not speak and so dumbly clasped her hand. Her grip was almost nonexistent, her hand cold and painfully thin. Denise raised her eyebrows in a look obviously meant to urge me toward some polite greeting.

"I thought I heard another voice," I finally said.

"Pardon?" Arabella asked. She was pale, anemic, looked weary, and was not dressed the way I'd expect a millionaire to dress: a black pinstriped pant suit. It did look smart, well-cut, expensive, but seemed not nearly enough.

"Arabella's bodyguard," Denise explained.

"My security," Arabella corrected.

Of course. Multimillionaires come with entourages.

"Do we have enough food?" I asked Denise.

"Oh, don't worry about Bill," Arabella Wiseman said. "He lives on raw meat. I threw a steak to him in the car."

"Looks good," Sid said, motioning to the barbeque. His white silk suit shimmered like mother-of-pearl in the evening sunlight. Not your average messenger's suit. Not your average anyone's suit. "Unfortunately, Arabella's on a special diet."

"I know it's rude," Arabella smiled apologetically, "but I've brought along my own dinner. I assure you it's entirely necessary. Otherwise, I wouldn't think of such a thing. You see, I've been invaded by something very dangerous and, consequently, my diet is very strict."

"Oh!" Denise said. "Invaded? You should have let us know."

Arabella's eyes had an odd elliptical shape, like a hawk's.

"No, no. It really is too much trouble to expect you to find something so specific for me when it's nothing to bring it along." She hoisted her Gucci bag with visible effort. "So please, please, please, don't be offended."

"It's not contagious," Sid added.

I nodded, slightly confused: I thought he meant the food she'd brought.

"Cancer," Arabella smiled. "It's only cancer."

I kept nodding until the word reached somewhere deep inside me and stopped my head from moving. There was nothing I could think of to say.

"Cancer?" Denise said. "Terrible!" Sid and Arabella didn't respond. When the silence became uncomfortable Denise asked, "Can I get anyone a drink?"

—

The vegetables turned out excellently despite the excess olive oil. To complement them, Denise had prepared rice in chicken stock (wondering if this was okay for vegetarians and, if not, whether it would be noticed) with bits of dried apricot, and also eggplant Parmesan, all of which Sid ate with an enthusiasm that made me nervous for his beautiful suit. Somehow, he deftly managed to shovel in food without dropping so much as a grain of rice on himself. Arabella had a bowl of some sort of greyish-green macrobiotic paste. I couldn't get over how very real she was, this woman with such an unimaginable heap of money; this woman in the clutches of a terminal illness. The shock of the materiality of her physical presence at our table made it difficult for me to form words. The two women carried most of the conversation, Arabella playing the gracious guest and Denise the fawning host.

"So you two met ... how?" Denise asked.

"Madison—Sid's father introduced us. You know Madison? Through MacMillan?"

Denise smiled uncomfortably so that all her teeth showed. "Of course. Yes. I do. MacMillan has been something of a mentor to me."

"I can't say that I like MacMillan," Arabella said.

"Well, no," Denise said. "Who does? He's a pig."

Arabella smiled widely, "Isn't he?"

They talked about the weather and Imelda Marcos' shoes and Ronald Reagan and the Contras and the Russians in Afghanistan and how fortunate it was that here in the West the corporations had successfully wrestled power from the politicians, until the table sank under an uncomfortable silence that Arabella finally assaulted with, "Sid and I are having a baby."

Everyone looked at Sid, who did not confirm or deny.

"My goodness," Denise said.

"Isn't it wonderful? We are so excited."

She reached over and took Sid's hand. I choked on some eggplant and tried to expel it, pounding my own chest. Denise offered me my water glass. I kept coughing.

"Is that ... wise?" Denise asked, still holding out the glass to me, but addressing Arabella. "Considering your condition? The cancer, I mean."

Arabella nodded at Denise's concern, her eyes resting on me. She waited until I'd gulped the water and had the coughing under control before she said, "I won't actually be carrying the baby."

"Oh?" Denise turned to Sid, her eyebrows raised.

"Me neither," Sid grinned. "I'm only bonded to carry cash and securities. We've found a lovely young lady to have the baby. A student. You gonna make it there, my friend?"

"Fine. I'm fine," I croaked. "Something went the wrong way."

"Well," Denise said. "What will they think of next?"

"We're living in the future," Sid proclaimed, heaping another helping of vegetables and rice onto his plate.

"It's even more remarkable than you think," Arabella leaned across the table toward Denise. "I'm the CEO and principal shareholder of a company called Argyle."

"Oh!" Denise said. It was a company we had discussed, because I still had a few shares of the new issue. Denise had sold hers already and had urged me to do so before the stock plunged, which was a normal pattern for new issues on the Vancouver Stock Exchange. "I had no idea that was you. Did you know that, honey?" Still unable to speak, I shook my head.

"My involvement is not widely known. From the beginnings of Argyle we've looked for ways to use our technology and our equipment and our science to broaden our impact on humankind. I founded the company in the early seventies, and considering that I was already forty and had never had children, I decided to freeze some of my eggs before it was

too late. A woman has only so many eggs. My husband was
not able to have children and I wondered, when he died, God
be with him, if someone mightn't come along with whom I'd
wish I'd been able to share my genes." She smiled and turned
her eyes to Sid, who blushed. I swear that he actually blushed.

"You froze your eggs?" Denise repeated.

"It's an important innovation and I believe that in time it
will become quite a good revenue stream. We really couldn't
survive with cryonics as our core business. Not yet, anyway.
So we've had to explore the potentialities of our technologies
to diversify into more lucrative areas that will subsidize what
is essentially a labour of love."

"Arabella just got a huge contract with the defence department in the US of A," Sid added in a stage whisper.
"Announcement's not until late Monday morning. If you're
looking for an interesting *buy* first thing Monday morning."

Denise leaned forward, her cocktail dress revealing a little
cleavage. "What does the Pentagon want you to freeze?"

Arabella pushed herself back very straight in her chair. "I
can't even pretend to know the answer to that question.
Viruses, I suspect. There's always the possibility of our enemies using biotech weapons against us. I believe they're using
our technology in the development of vaccines. I can get you
five thousand shares Monday morning, but unfortunately no
more. And you'll have to promise to hold onto it for at least
six months."

"Vaccines?" Sid asked mockingly. "Doesn't the defense
department develop weapons? Maybe even biological weapons? Or have I got that mixed up?"

"Sid!" Arabella scolded. "Please, shut up!"

"Sorry," Sid said, waggling his eyebrows. "What happens in Damascus stays in Damascus."

"I can assure you that if *I* believed for a single instant that they were planning on using our facilities in such a way, I'd never have become involved. When my husband was killed, may God have mercy on him, I got out of the business of mass murder. Argyle is interested in furthering life on this planet, not ending it."

She pivoted her raptor eyes from Denise to me, as though daring us to disagree.

"Of course," Denise said. "You're bringing a child into the world. Five thousand shares would be great."

"Exactly," Arabella said. "And I am most confident that the Pentagon's activities are directed toward defending the world against the threat of a global pestilence that could quite conceivably be set off by the Soviets or some rogue dictator."

"Congratulations," I said. "When is the baby due?"

Arabella picked up her napkin from her lap and dabbed her ashen lips.

"Well, we haven't actually implanted the egg yet. We're still monitoring the conception to be sure it all *takes* properly. There are so many variables to assess. But it will almost certainly be very soon. You are probably envisioning the eggs as being fifteen years old, which makes the whole thing seem all the more tenuous. But that's the beauty of our science. It's as though Madison has gone back in time to meet my younger self. Or, more correctly, I've carried my youth forward with me. We're very confident."

Sid raised his chin to bless the table with a look of beatific satisfaction made even more saintly by his ethereal suit (it was almost as if he were wearing a cloud) and a moment later raised his glass.

"Madison?" Denise asked.

Sid nodded. "That's my name: Madison. After my father."

Denise pondered Sid's name.

"And what does your father think? About the baby?"

Sid smiled, set his glass back on the table, picked up his fork, took another mouthful and chewed appreciatively, seemingly enjoying the food and company without the slightest misgiving. No one spoke for far too long.

"We aren't telling people yet," Arabella said. "We would appreciate your discretion."

"Of course," Denise said.

"A toast to the new baby," I burst out, raising my glass.

Sid raised his glass. Arabella picked up her sparkling water and Denise lifted her wine.

"Cheers! To Argyle!"

We drank and ate some more, and talked about the market and Colonel Gaddafi's wardrobe and the mining of Managua harbour and the Mexican drug cartel and Expo 86 and the consequent inflation of restaurant and food prices, until, after we'd entered another awkward silence, Sid fumbled out with, "Do you ever visit your grandfather, Bentley?"

I looked around.

"What? Yes. The odd time."

"What's this?" Denise asked.

"His grandfather. The famous painter. Arabella loves his work."

Arabella nodded enthusiastically.

"Yes. The great Philip Bentley. Sid's father has a beautiful one, and you must have seen that show on Emily Carr and her contemporaries at the Vancouver Art Gallery?" Both Denise and I shook our heads. "Oh! Sid's father took me. There were only two Bentleys, but they absolutely stole the show. He really is quite an extraordinary talent."

Denise shot me an accusing glance. "So I hear. I still haven't had the pleasure."

"Oh? I believe I've heard he lives fairly close. Just a couple of blocks away," Arabella added, pointing vaguely in the correct direction.

"Yes, but I've never been invited," Denise said.

Arabella touched a finger to her nose. "I had understood that he is reclusive."

"That's right," I said. "Very shy."

"I'm sure he'd be pleased to meet Denise." She reached over, took my hand, and said, "My dear boy, Sid tells me that you believe you can sell."

Denise looked at me. I looked at Sid. Sid looked at Arabella. Arabella was still looking at me.

"I'd like to try. I'm writing the securities exam next month."

Arabella released my hand and spread her napkin in her lap again.

"You should. You should try. You have a lovely personality. I've only just met you and I trust you, and there's really nothing more important in sales. It's all about trust. But, if I may be so bold as to give you a little advice, I don't believe the Vancouver Stock Exchange is the place for someone of your … particular talents and demeanour."

Arabella looked at Denise. Denise looked at Sid. Sid looked at me.

"She's right," Sid said. "Don't you think she's right, Denise?"

Denise picked up her napkin and wiped her lips. I hoped she might rush to defend my talent. I was sure that, once I got the hang of things, I would do just fine.

"Well, that's a good question. Sometimes I wonder if the Vancouver Stock Exchange is right for my particular talents and demeanour."

Arabella waved a dismissal.

"Oh, come on, Denise," Sid said. "You have the edge. Your Bentley doesn't. They'll eat him alive."

Denise considered this statement, twirling the stem of her wineglass between her fingers, and finally turned to me.

"Arabella is right. They'll eat you alive."

I looked at my plate, the smear of olive oil on china.

"We all have a purpose in life," Arabella said. "In my fifty-seven years I've discovered that the thing we must try to do is to answer our calling. The secret to success is to keep our minds open and listen, so that when that call comes, we hear. I think you'll do that. You seem like a good listener. Do you miss Saskatchewan?"

"Saskatchewan…?"

"I'm looking for a prairie representative for our sales staff at Argyle. Manitoba and Saskatchewan. We've got one man handling all three prairie provinces at the moment, but he's only barely doing an effective job in Alberta, where he lives, and he seems to want to convince me that Manitoba and Saskatchewan don't actually exist. I'm not so certain. Sid tells me that you're from Saskatchewan. It does exist, doesn't it?"

She grinned a little wickedly, narrowing her eyes so that a shiver ran through me. I recall being strangely thrilled by the sensation. Sid had started shovelling food into his mouth again.

"I think so," I said, all at once not entirely certain that Saskatchewan did exist.

"I am looking for an experienced salesman, of course. Since you're from there and know people and probably understand better than most the kind of thing that would appeal to the prairie demographic, I wanted to call on your expertise. Do you know anyone offhand who might be good for the position?" Once again Arabella patted my hand affectionately. Her skin was alarmingly cold.

"Experienced? I'll think about it. I grew up on a farm. I actually didn't know all that many salesmen. I do know that a lot of my dad's generation, which would probably be your market, are a little squeamish about spending money on … anything. They never got over the Crash of '29 and the Dirty Thirties."

I couldn't look them in the eye as I gave this little speech, and so I talked to my plate, staring at the last forlorn grains of rice, and when I stopped talking all I heard was the bubbler in the fish tank and the drone of the city going on all around.

"The Dirty Thirties! Like your grandfather's paintings!" Arabella finally burst out. "You see how much you know about Saskatchewan? That's why I'm asking you. Think about it. Take all the time you need. I'd be pleased to hear any thoughts you have on the matter. Does your father have a big farm?"

"No. One thousand nine hundred and twenty acres. Small. For Saskatchewan. Three square miles."

"Three square miles small! It strikes me that you grand-father might be a good friend to Argyle. A famous painter. An extraordinary talent. This is the kind of man we'll need in the future to help us build a new and better world. If he were willing to do a testimonial, there'd be no charge for our services. Could you pass that along to him? And tell him that I'd love to meet him?"

I looked into her elliptical eyes and got a dizzy feeling, like she was looking down at me from far overhead.

"All right. I can do that."

"Thank you," she said, once again, very briefly, placing her icy fingers on the back of my hand.

December 19, 2012

Sheena and I took Julia tobogganing last night. Got snow in our faces and down our necks. A few exciting spills, one when we found ourselves closing in on an oak, trunk padded with straw bales, and aborted our run to avoid the collision. Altogether exhilarating and my fifty-year-old bones survived the trauma, though I'm feeling it today. Hot chocolate afterwards, and I went to bed with a sense that everything in the world was fine.

Was awakened by shouts: Beth and Sheena and another voice I didn't recognize. I pulled on my bathrobe and hurried downstairs, soon confirming that the noise was coming from the basement. As I headed down the basement stairs, I could see Beth standing at the foot of the pullout couch and hear Sheena shouting, "This is my room! Could I have a little privacy? Get out of my room!" Sheena and another young woman were in the bed, the duvet pulled to their chins to protect them.

"This is my home!" Beth responded, gesticulating to indicate the space around us. "You cannot invite strangers into my home without my permission and fuck and smoke dope with them in my basement!"

I switched off the light, in hopes that darkness might lower the volume.

"Can we please keep it down? Julia is sleeping."

Beth hit the switch and we were all bathed again in stark diode-emitted light.

"Get out of my house," she said directly to Sheena's companion, "or I'll call the police."

"Fine!" the woman shouted and flung off the covers to reveal her naked illustrated body: I caught a glimpse of a peacock's head between her breasts before I turned and retreated back up the stairs. A moment later Beth followed me. We stood shuffling in the dining room, her glaring at me, while we listened to the murmur of voices from the basement and finally the clomp of the young woman climbing the stairs, pulling on her boots, and exiting by the back door.

"You go down and talk to your daughter and let her know that this kind of behaviour is not acceptable. I'm going to bed."

"All right," I said, not about to argue with her at 3:15 in the morning. She stomped up the stairs.

Sheena was propped against her pillow, weeping, the duvet wrapped around her. Wanting to comfort her, I considered embracing her, but imagined she was still naked under the duvet, and so I perched on the foot of the bed. She continued to cry, her tangled hair covering her face, and I sat there, silent, not knowing what to say or do. I noticed a book on the coffee table that I'd never seen before, so I figured it must be hers: The *Tibetan Book of the Dead*. I picked it up and opened it in the middle. *The First Method of Closing the Womb-Door* were the first words I saw.

> In that matter meditate; but even though this be found inadequate to prevent thee from entering into a womb, and if thou findest thyself ready to enter into one, then there is the profound teaching for closing the womb-door. Listen thou unto it:

I closed the book and held it up to her.

"You reading this?"

She wiped her eyes, looked at the book in my hand, and nodded.

"Good?"

She shrugged.

"What's it about?"

By now she had stopped crying completely. She sighed and wrinkled her forehead to indicate the stupidity of my question. "Preparing for death."

Her puffy bloodshot eyes held mine.

"Is that something you feel you need to do? Prepare for death?"

Her eyes widened and she gave a dismissive snort. "It's something everyone needs to do," she said.

I nodded. "I suppose you're right. Me more than you."

We sat staring into one another's eyes. I was hoping she'd say something, but she refused, and I finally gave in.

"I'm sorry. I didn't know you had friends in Toronto."

She snorted again. "We just met."

"Where did you meet?"

"Online."

"I see," I said. "Is that safe?"

"Depends how you define safe? She didn't seem to be the violent one."

"Violent? Beth was pretty upset. Look, we're all in this together, so there needs to be some house rules."

"Don't even start. The rules are clear. It's her house. I will not be inviting anyone into it again."

"Our house."

She raised an eyebrow. "Whatever you say. Actually, come to think of it, I did read a passage in here that made me think of you. It sounded like something Argyle could use in their marketing. Maybe Beth could recite it on one of their television ads. Let me see if I can find it." I handed her *The Tibetan Book of the Dead* and she began leafing through it until she found what she was looking for. She smirked at me and began to read: "Then the Lord of Death will place round thy neck a rope and drag thee along; he will cut off thy head, extract thy heart, pull out thy intestines, lick up thy blood, eat thy flesh, and gnaw thy bones; but thou wilt be incapable of dying. Although thy body be hacked to pieces, it will revive again."

She clapped the book shut, awaiting my response.

"Lovely. Now I'm really looking forward to dying. Maybe we should get some sleep."

She threw herself back on her pillow and closed her eyes.

"Sounds like a plan. Please turn off the lights as you leave."

Watching her lying there, the bird's nest of her sweaty hair reminded me of her call from her bed that morning so soon after I'd been fired. If she hadn't called, would I have pulled the trigger? I walked over and kissed her on the forehead.

"Gross," she said.

"I love you."

"Love you too."

I heated some milk in the microwave, made Ovaltine, and sat down at the dining room table, gazing into my grandfather's painting as I drank. I needed both the sleep-inducing magic and the extra pause before I went to bed, hoping that by some miracle Beth might already be asleep.

She was not.

"Did you talk to her?"

"I did. She said it wouldn't happen again."

"It most certainly will not," she said, as though she had already arranged to prevent it through the sheer force of her will. She predicted that Sheena's friend and her henchmen might return before morning to murder us all. I said nothing and eventually she ran out of steam and switched off her lamp, settling on her side of the bed.

"Good night," I said.

"Merry Christmas," she said.

—

The day began relatively calmly, which I must begin to take as a warning.

Beth had another story meeting with Winston and his people and was out the door early, reminding me that it was Julia's Christmas concert this evening. I walked Julia to school, telling her that Grandma would be there by the time she got home, and that we'd all be going to her concert. She skipped along jubilantly, kicking up snow, singing carols, dancing so that she barely touched the earth. Apparently she'd slept right through the shouting.

I came back from my walk to find Sheena at the dining room table, perched in lotus position on her chair, eating a bowl of Julia's sugary cereal.

"You're up early. Good morning."

She chewed a while, considering.

"Is it?"

That made me think of you, Mary Abraham.

"Grandma comes today from Saskatchewan, and it's Julia's Christmas concert tonight."

She contemplated this information.

"Guess it must be then."

"Are you okay?"

"Fine. I'm just wondering how much more of this homophobic bullshit I'll have to put up with while I'm here."

"Beth is not homophobic. She just doesn't want you inviting total strangers into the house. It's not safe."

"Right."

"She's not homophobic."

"I know. Some of her best friends are faggots."

"I'm sure she would have no problem with you inviting friends."

"Good to know. I'll do my best to develop some friendships out there on the street."

"Do you want to come with me to the airport to pick up Grandma?"

"Sounds like a blast. Maybe I'll meet some friends in the ladies' room."

—

I remembered to check and Mom's flight was on time, but nevertheless Sheena and I ended up standing and waiting (leaning on my favourite concrete pillar where I had leaned two days before with Julia, watching the doors slide open and closed, Sheena next to me carefully studying her phone with a wrinkled brow) for so long after the plane had landed that I began to worry that something must have gone wrong.

The intercom called my name, telling me to go to the airline information desk, where a woman told us they had mom and her luggage and she would lead us to her.

"She stood up during the flight and demanded to get off the plane. The flight crew and even the co-pilot came out, which is quite extraordinary. They were all trying to convince her to sit down. She refused. She kept insisting she wanted to get off."

The woman told me this as though I were the one responsible for this cataclysm.

"Holy shit," Sheena grinned. The woman was clearly not amused by her delight, and silently added it to the list of Bentley transgressions.

"I'm sorry," I said. "She must be quite confused."

"If we'd had to land the plane in Winnipeg the cost would have been her responsibility, but fortunately they were finally able to convince her to take her seat."

"How could they have landed the plane without getting her to sit down?" I asked.

The woman did not answer. She led us to an elevator and eventually to a room somewhere in the bowels of the airport, and into a small office. There was Mom, hunched behind a desk in a crowded, cluttered room, slightly dishevelled, looking confused and frightened. Another airline employee, a middle-aged man, recounted her sins once more and expressed the airline's concerns that she was in no condition to be travelling on her own. The fellow talked as if she were not in the room or was not capable of understanding what he was saying.

"You okay, Mom?" I interrupted him and she nodded in an unconvincing manner. She looked as though she'd aged a decade since I'd seen her last summer, her skin a mottled grey.

"Hi, Grandma," Sheena waved. Mom looked even more confused, as she obviously did not recognize her granddaughter.

"I'm sorry for your trouble," I said to the two airline employees. "Thank you for looking after her so well."

The man forced a smile. "You're welcome. If your mother is planning on taking her return flight, she'll need to be accompanied by an attendant."

"We'll cross that bridge when we come to it," I said. "Merry Christmas."

I helped Mom to her feet and the employees escorted us back to the elevator and to Arrivals, from where we found our own way to the parking lot. Once we had her in the car, buckled in the front passenger seat, I asked her again if she was okay.

"I'm fine. I'm sorry about that."

"It's okay, Mom. What happened?"

"I'm very sorry. I saw that you had to bribe them to get me out of there. That was a lot of money. Where did you get all that money?"

Sheena snorted from the back seat and I shot her an over-the-shoulder frown. She was enjoying this more than was appropriate.

"I didn't bribe them, Mom. You're mistaken. Why did you want off the plane?"

"That was a lot of money," she shook her head sadly. "It was terrible. The pilot was just a teenager and he was stoned on some drug."

Sheena couldn't stop laughing, and Mom turned to look back at her, the gravity of the situation not leaving her face. Sheena forced herself to stop.

"Don't worry, Grandma. I'm not stoned."

Mom clearly was not convinced.

"Where are we going now?" she asked me.

"We're going home, Mom."

"Home?"

"We're going to Julia's Christmas concert tonight. She's really excited that you're coming."

"Oh? That's nice. Christmas." She nodded. "Merry Christmas. That was a lot of money you paid them." She craned her neck to look around, something clicking in her mind, and all at once we were transported to Vancouver in 1990. "Sheena! Is that you? Your hair looks wonderful that way. Where is your mother?"

Sheena beamed a smile. "Goodness knows. Great to see you, Grandma."

May 1986, Vancouver

"Why would I want to meet this lady? I like my privacy and, anyway, I'm not particularly interested in women. Happy to meet your wife-to-be on the other hand." My grandfather hefted a tomato from the vegetable stand. "Wonder where this comes from?" Peering at the label, he couldn't make out the words, so held it up to me for assistance.

"Hothouse. She's a fan. And she's also very rich."

My grandfather nodded, disappointed. "Probably the first time it's ever been out of doors. Oh, well. Hothouse dwellers shouldn't throw stones. Money used to interest me a great deal, but no longer. I've got as much as I need until I'm dead, and it's not much use afterwards."

When I'd arrived at his door a half hour earlier, Philip Bentley had complained that he didn't have any coffee to offer and was in fact running out of groceries and wondered if I would be willing to escort him on a shopping trip. It seemed like the right thing to do. There was no rain at the moment, but the sky was overcast, and I hoped we could finish before it began to fall. My grandfather set the tomato back on the pile and, with palsied hands, struggled to rip a plastic bag from a roll. I attempted to assist, but was met with a glare.

"Denise definitely wants to meet you."

In the middle of trying to find the opening to the plastic bag, my grandfather halted his struggles and stared, bemused, at me.

"Pardon? Who?"

"Denise? My … girlfriend? If that's okay with you?"

Philip Bentley studied me carefully.

"I'm not sure. I'd have to clean the place. The woman isn't

coming in until next week. I'd have to have food. I suppose I could cater."

I looked at the sidewalk and saw a tomato had rolled off the pile and been trod upon, its seeds spilling out across concrete.

"We could meet somewhere. At the Sylvia?"

I glanced up and saw that he was carefully considering this plan.

"The Sylvia is nice. Just so long as you're not ashamed of the old faggot."

"Why don't we meet for brunch at the Sylvia?"

He frowned.

"Maybe just coffee. I don't like eating in front of anyone I don't know well. I'm sure it's entertaining watching me spilling food all over myself but ..."

"Coffee at the Sylvia next Saturday?"

For a moment he looked annoyed that he'd been interrupted, but a second later he nodded his assent.

"That sounds fine. I'll be on my best behaviour."

He finally managed to get the plastic bag open and drop a couple of tomatoes inside.

"Even hothouse tomatoes have doubled in price for Expo."

—

Built in 1912, the Sylvia is an ivy-covered boutique hotel overlooking English Bay. It is still there, so far as I know. It was only a few blocks from Philip Bentley's apartment and from Denise's and from my apartment. As Denise and I walked toward the Sylvia that morning, it was my apartment that stifled our enjoyment of the sunshine. She insisted that

I should give my landlord my month's notice. I hadn't slept there in weeks. Why continue wasting money? These were wasted dollars that I was stealing from my future self. From my children. From my grandchildren.

"I need it for studying."

"Studying, my ass. Or maybe studying someone else's ass?"

"Just for another month or two. I'll give notice the first of July."

"Don't be so sure. You may need your little love nest by Canada Day." I saw a shiver pass through her. She'd insisted she didn't need a jacket, though she was wearing a red sleeveless blouse and, despite the sunshine, it was still spring: a cool breeze was wafting off English Bay. "You think I'm standing still, waiting for you to make up your mind? Think again."

"I never said I hadn't made up my mind."

I shed my jean jacket and offered it to her. She pulled it on.

"You don't have to say. It's obvious."

I didn't respond. It was true that I was deeply conflicted about giving up the apartment, the four hundred square feet of the earth that was mine and mine alone. It was more of a commitment than I felt ready to make.

"Why didn't you mention Arabella's offer to him?" Denise changed course, leaping back into the middle of an earlier conversation. In the past few days, we'd gone over my last meeting with my grandfather many times: Denise thought helping him buy groceries was a nice touch, but wasn't pleased that I'd done so little to move the cryonics conversation forward.

"I told him she wanted to meet him, but he said he wasn't interested."

"That won't impress Arabella into giving you that job. If you want to be a salesman, you have to make him interested."

"I thought it was better to soft pedal. I thought we could bring it up today. I don't want a job in Saskatchewan."

"You mean you thought I could do it for you."

"Anyway, she said she was looking for someone with experience."

Across the water, freighters were slipping between the University Endowment Lands and West Vancouver toward the Pacific Ocean. Ahead of us, we could see the Sylvia, ivy almost completely enveloping the russet brick building.

"Of course she's not going to hand it to someone who can't sell. Why would she do that? She wants you to sell yourself."

"I don't want a job in Saskatchewan. I'll mention the show at the Vancouver Art Gallery—that Arabella saw it and she loves his work. Maybe he'll meet her."

"He's an old man who's been flattered all his life and can see right through that schtick."

"He hasn't had as much flattery as you'd expect. I don't think he's had his fill."

"He's got pictures hanging in the Vancouver Art Gallery next to Emily Carr. Isn't that more flattery than any of us are likely to get in our lifetime? Even I know who Emily Carr is."

"But before you met me you'd never heard of Philip Bentley."

"Now I have."

Philip Bentley had arrived early and was waiting at a cozy table by the window looking out at English Bay, a coffee already before him, his head and hands shaking even more noticeably than usual. He caught sight of us and struggled to his feet as we rounded the bar and approached, offering a quivering hand to Denise. She took it, then dropped it and clasped him in her arms to give him a firm squeeze, her cheek against his chest. Not knowing what to make of the blatant aggression of this woman in a ridiculously oversized jean jacket, he gave me a worried look that was still there on his face when Denise pushed him back to arm's length.

"Oh, I've alarmed you. Don't worry, I'm not making advances. You're the first of the Bentley family I've met and I'm so excited!"

My grandfather opened and closed his mouth twice before he finally spoke.

"I'm not even sure I can properly be called family. I've only just met the young man." He was avoiding her insistent eyes, lowering himself back into his chair. "Seems like a nice enough fellow. Can't very well be related to me."

Denise laughed a little too gleefully, then was suddenly serious. She pulled off my jacket, draped it over her chair back, and seated herself, waiting for me to say something. I couldn't think of anything. For a few moments Denise and Philip Bentley studied each other suspiciously.

"I need a coffee," Denise finally said, trying to get the attention of the waiter.

We discussed whether the sunshine would hold and how the persistent rain might dampen the spirits of Expo 86. My grandfather had overheard someone in the waiting room at his doctor's appointment the day before saying that there were investments being made in an attempt to control the weather in order to ensure a successful fair. "With the Russians. And look at the sunshine today." Denise was skeptical. They both tried to prompt some sort of comment from me. I shrugged and smiled. The coffee came and the waitress topped up my grandfather's. He raised his cup to his lips but his hands were shaking so badly that he simply set it back in the saucer without venturing a sip.

"Parkinson's?" Denise asked.

He gave the question silent consideration, turning to look at me, the presumed betrayer.

"My grandmother had it," Denise explained. "So I'm familiar. Looks like you need a little more dopamine this morning."

In defiance of her comment, Philip Bentley raised his cup again and successfully sipped without spilling a drop before carefully placing the cup back into its saucer.

"No, actually. My doctor tells me that I'm getting too much dopamine from my pills, which accounts for my psychotic episodes. We're alike that way. You two look as though you're also getting too much. Did you know falling in love spikes the dopamine levels in your brain? Sex too. Not that there's a difference. Between falling in love and sexual arousal. Is there?"

He was looking directly at me when he spoke the final two words, but it was Denise, adjusting her sleeveless blouse, who answered.

"There's definitely a distinction. Ask any prostitute."

Philip Bentley narrowed his yellow eyes and aimed them at Denise.

"I don't get much chance to talk to prostitutes these days, but if you say so."

Denise nodded, but did not speak for some time. The family at the next table were talking about their visit to the aquarium and the splash the killer whale had made.

"My! Isn't this going well?" Denise finally said to me. "Your family is utterly charming."

What could I say? They'd already successfully made an argument of the weather.

"Don't mind me," Philip Bentley offered. "I apologize if I seem cranky. I'm just an old painter who can no longer paint. I am constitutionally cranky. And you somehow managed to fumble onto the very subject of conversation I like least. My disease. I'd prefer to discuss yours."

Denise glanced out the window toward a sailboat skimming slowly by in the light breeze of the bright morning.

"What about cures? Do you ever think about that possibility? It's a way of putting a more positive spin on the discussion of diseases."

"The cure for love? Or Parkinson's? I know the cure for love. Time. Doesn't work with Parkinson's."

"Are you sure? It wasn't that long ago that people thought they'd never find a cure for polio. But time passed and they did."

"A vaccine, not a cure. There'll be no vaccine for Parkinson's and, anyway, I've already got it. I'll be dead before they find a cure, so not much good their science will do me."

"You could have yourself frozen so that you're still around when the discovery's made," Denise said.

He took these words in, looking from her to me.

"Ah, yes. I have heard of that. I suppose you're selling this cryonics company the boy was telling me about."

"Not at all. I did buy a few shares recently, but mostly I'm just interested in the idea behind it, and how it might help you. Being family and all."

"Did you do well on your investment?"

"Very well, so far. Seventy-five per cent increase in less than a week."

"My goodness! Sounds like it's time to sell."

"Agreed! You need to teach some investment sense to your grandson."

Denise clapped me on the back of the head with an open palm and I glanced around, embarrassed, to see if anyone was watching. No one was, except my grandfather.

"Oh, I'm sure you'd be a much better teacher. On the other hand, it's a bit ironic, isn't it, to be such a short-term investor in such a long-term product."

"While the money is on the table, you should take it and walk away. If you can. That's my investment strategy. That's my nature."

"I see. Well, I think you're wise in this case. I'm too cynical to allow myself to believe in fairy tales about freezing people and bringing them back to life. I'd be just as far ahead turning back to Jesus. I was a minister once, you know?"

"No, I didn't know that. Did you know that, honey?"

I nodded. "That was a long time ago."

"Fifty years ago. I've long since lost my faith in second comings."

"Are you comparing science to religion?"

"I guess I am. They both ask an old man to believe in the future."

Denise leaned across the table and clasped his tremoring right hand, holding it still.

"What have you got to lose?"

Philip Bentley's face paled as he stared down, horrified, at her hand clasping his. No one spoke, awaiting an explosion. Finally, none having come, Denise released him, and he withdrew his hand to safety, beneath the table.

"I suppose you're right," he said, focussing across the room, searching for the waiter to rescue him. "Apparently I have already lost all dignity."

December 20, 2012

Everyone was on their best behaviour for Julia's Christmas concert last night.

Once we were home from the airport, I told Mom to relax on the couch while I made pasta to go with the Bolognese sauce I'd left simmering toward integration and perfection on the stove. Mom would have no rest, though, and was soon trailing me around the kitchen trying desperately to be helpful, but only succeeding in getting in my way. She needed a job and so I got her to cut up the strawberries. Spinach salad with strawberries is a particular favourite of Sheena's. At least it was the last time she was here, and if it's not any longer she didn't say anything to give it away, eating without complaint and without picking a fight with Beth, who tried hard to keep Mom talking even though she seemed to want to remain silent.

"Has it been cold in Saskatchewan?"

"Sometimes."

"Was it cold when you left?"

Mom looked around her, as if for clues.

"I don't remember. Where is Denise?"

Beth frowned, pulling at the strap of the red cocktail dress she had chosen for her concert entrance. "She couldn't make it, unfortunately."

Sheena did her best not to smile too hard. We hadn't spoken of what happened at the airport, deciding that would be our little secret. Julia saved us from the awful silence by breaking into "Jingle Bells."

After supper Julia got dressed in her elf costume and we trooped up the street to the school, Mom's arm locked to mine for support. She obviously had no idea where she was or what she was doing here, but she rolled along with it as if this were how she spent all her evenings.

The concert proceeded numerically through each grade's performance, youngest to oldest, "All I Want For Christmas Is My Two Front Teeth," to "Carol of the Bells." Julia's class sang "Frosty the Snowman," "Jingle Bells," and "Deck the Halls."

We walked home in darkness, Mom's body slumping heavily against me; she was more than ready for bed. Beth and Sheena were quiet and Julia still singing, still trying hard to pretend she believes in Santa even though she no longer does.

"A sleigh," she said as we passed a Santa pumped full of air in front of a neighbour's house. "A sleigh pulled by flying reindeers. Who thought that up?"

"Some desperate starving writer," Beth answered.

"Like my mom," Julia added.

"Oh, your mom's not starving and has plenty to be grateful for," Beth said. "For instance, she has you."

Julia's mother was a writer, but her father was not included in that disreputable assembly.

Mom put one foot in front of the other. I joined in on the refrain of the carol that Julia began to sing: Fa la la la la, la la, la la.

May 1986, Vancouver

Denise was working late, having drinks with a client, and so after some studying for my securities exam and working on the novel and packing some boxes in my apartment, I went over to visit my grandfather. It was a sunny evening, so I coaxed him out for a walk along the seawall. The trees and the water made me feel I'd escaped the city, even with the steady stream of bicyclists and joggers and dog-walkers and lovers streaming past on the narrow lane of pavement and the heavier freighter traffic chugging by on the water and the vehicular traffic humming white noise in the background. We shuffled along, Philip Bentley so unsteady that every few steps I thought he might fall and I'd reach out and grab his elbow. Attempted aid was met with an annoyed chant of, "I'm fine. I'm fine. I'm fine," until I relented and released him.

"You ever think about painting anymore?"

"Why in hell would I want to do that?"

"I don't know. You're an artist."

"I'm not. Never was. Sounds so superior. What kind of arrogant fool would go around calling himself an *artist*? I was never anything but a painter, and I'm no longer one of those. How do you paint with *this*?" He held up his right hand and we watched it tremble, a gnarled branch in the breeze. "I actually did try. Those ones on my walls at home. Did them in my studio in Montreal. Thought maybe something interesting might happen if I gave in and let the shaking take over. Figured maybe Parkinson's would unlock the genius I apparently locked up somewhere after I did those ones back in the thirties and forties. But it didn't work. It was just too frustrating not being able to put down what I intended— what I saw in my mind. I was doing abstracts, so you'd think it wouldn't make any difference. But it did. Much as you'd like there to be, there's nothing abstract about a body that won't stop shaking. It's concrete. About as spiritual as a pile of shit."

He shoved his hand in his pocket and would have toppled over if I hadn't grabbed him by the arm.

"I'm fine. I'm fine. I'm fine!"

I released him and we walked on in silence, my grandfather watching a young man in Gore-Tex approaching us on roller blades, arms sweeping side to side to maximize momentum, the scent of sweat and cologne hanging for an instant in his wake. My grandfather turned to me and said, "You don't know what a gift it is to be young. The young never do. Drink it all down. Like Baudelaire says, 'One should always be drunk. With wine, with poetry, or with virtue, as you choose.'"

"I *am* writing."

My grandfather pursed his thin lips quizzically.

"What are you working on?"

"I've started a novel."

Philip Bentley came to an abrupt halt. "If I had a hat, I'd take it off to you. That's quite a marathon, writing a novel. Might take you years. Can't imagine working on a painting that might take years. Sistine Chapel. I hope you're reading

lots of good ones. You've read *Gatsby*, I hope? And *Lolita*?" I
nodded, though I hadn't read *Lolita*. I could see that he could
see I was lying. "Good. That's what you want to aim for. Aim
high. A novel. I guess you took my advice, then, and got rid
of the woman?"

"Denise really liked you."

"Really? Well, I can't say I like her all that much. Maybe
she grows on you?" He looked me up and down, searching
for signs of a growth. Finding none, he resumed walking. "I
suppose she's attractive. If you like that sort of thing."

"We'll have you over sometime."

"Really? I don't think so. I'm planning on getting a life."

A seagull landed on a rock at the water's edge and scanned
the beach for something to consume.

"Arabella Wiseman wonders if she could visit you and
look at your abstracts. She's a big fan. She saw some of your
pieces in the show at the Vancouver Art Gallery."

Philip Bentley stopped again, just as suddenly.

"The name sounds familiar."

"The woman who runs Argyle? The cryonics company."

The couple directly behind had to skirt us, avoiding a cyclist
coming from the other direction.

"Listen. I told you I'm not interested. As it stands, a few
people know I'm a guy who painted some paintings about
a century ago, though they probably couldn't say what the
paintings look like. I don't want to spend the next hundred
years known as the loony Canadian artist who had himself
frozen."

"All right. I understand. I'm only telling you because she's
a fan and she said she wanted to see your abstracts."

"I see." He turned and looked across the water toward a freighter docked at the huge yellow sulphur pile in North Vancouver. "She wants to buy one? She likes abstracts? She would actually appreciate the work?"

A strange dizziness overwhelmed me, a sense of déjà vu, my eyes blurring, and I almost grabbed my grandfather to steady myself. He gave me a long deep look and I got the feeling I was being painted and placed in a frame.

"She's dying," I said.

My grandfather nodded sagely.

"Aren't we all?"

December 22, 2012

Had not been out for my walk for two days, having been staked indoors by hosting duties: attempting to entertain Mom and Sheena and Julia while Beth locked herself in her office. Mom lay down for a nap after lunch, Sheena was not yet up, and Julia went tobogganing with friends, so I made a break for some air.

I was walking up our own street, back from my lakeside stroll, when a black limousine pulled to the curb just ahead of me. The front passenger door opened and a burly man stepped out and opened the back door, motioning for me to get inside. I turned around, thinking there must be somebody behind me, and saw there was not. I should have retreated toward the lake; instead, I approached warily and peered into the back seat of the car. There sat Sid, smiling.

"Bentley. Good to see you."

"What do you want?"

"Wanted to say hi. Get in."

I attempted to dodge around his henchman, who grabbed me by the arm.

"Get in," the ogre repeated his master's order.

"No, thank you. I'd prefer to walk."

He stood looking down at me without releasing my arm.

"I don't really care what you'd prefer," he said.

I considered a suitable response but, looking into his reptilian eyes, thought better of it, and slid into the back seat. He sat down beside me and pulled the door closed.

There I was in the middle of the long black leather seat, between Sid and his goon. I hate the middle seat. The driver pulled away.

"All ready for Christmas?" Sid asked.

I didn't respond. Sid was looking his best, his hair coiffed perfectly with those wayward cowlicks spilling over his forehead, as if he were on his way to some holiday party.

"How's the writing going?"

"Last time I was in the back seat of a car like this was with Arabella," I said.

"Really? Did you want to make a confession about that? Did you fuck my wife in the back seat of her limo?"

"No. She wanted to fuck, but …"

The goon looked to Sid as if he were awaiting permission to beat me to a bloody pulp. Sid just laughed without showing his teeth.

"Sounds like Arabella. Is that one of the stories you've written up in your book?"

"Not to that chapter quite yet. Kind of busy right now with Christmas."

"Yes, I suppose. You have company, I hear. Both your mom and Sheena. How is your mom doing?"

I met his eyes.

"You hear?"

"I hear things," he smiled. "Beautiful family gathering round the home hearth, I heard. Do you hear?" He grabbed his earlobe and pulled it playfully.

"I'd like to get out," I said.

Sid kept smiling his thin-lipped smile, but finally nodded to his brute, who tapped the glass to signal the driver. The car stopped and the goon opened the door and stepped out. I slid out and placed my feet on the pavement solidly before I stood.

"Merry Christmas, Bentley," Sid called. The goon got back in, closed the door, and the car pulled away.

December 1986, Vancouver

You are probably wondering, Mary Abraham, about my rather provocative and indelicate reference to Sid's frozen wife, Arabella Wiseman. I know it sounded crass, but I was recalling an actual event. I'm not sure if that makes the comment any more forgivable.

Once upon a time, in that long ago holiday season, Denise informed me that I had been invited to MacMillan's Christmas party as her other half. She felt it was too risky for me to go because she'd told MacMillan I was a writer, a University student, grandson of the famous artist, Philip Bentley, and MacMillan wasn't aware I actually worked for him. But I insisted on going and Denise relented.

Instead of a suit, Denise picked out a tweed jacket with patches on the elbows and a pair of khaki cotton trousers. According to her, this was what a young writer might wear if he were invited to a party and wasn't sure what to wear.

I wasn't entirely convinced, but was relieved she hadn't suggested a cape and beret. The party started early, at four in the afternoon, because middle-aged brokers generally pass out before ten, owing to the fact that they have to get out of bed so early. The nine o'clock bell that opens trading on the stock exchanges in New York and Toronto rings simultaneously at six a.m. in Vancouver, so the brokers were generally in the bar by shortly after two.

MacMillan had insisted that Denise should get a ride with him directly to the party when they finished a late meeting. I could find my own way on public transit and meet them there. She hoped I might get unnerved and change my mind about going, but I said that was fine.

I took the bus after work, just in time to get caught in the traffic bottleneck in Stanley Park on the approach to Lion's Gate Bridge. While the bus inched forward, I stood crushed against a teenager whose backpack was pressed into my chest. Out the window, the park beckoned in shades of green and grey and black that reminded me of my grandfather's abstracts. I had an urge to force my way to the door, abandon the vehicle and charge into the woods, offering my body and blood for consumption by the wildlife within: raccoons and skunks and swans. I resisted the urge, swaying, trying to think of nothing as we inched forward and braked, inched forward and braked.

When I'd reached West Vancouver and it was finally time to pull the cord for my stop, it was after five and it was raining. It was always raining. I checked the map Denise had drawn for me and climbed the steep street. MacMillan's estate sprawled along the edge of a cliff overlooking Burrard

Inlet. Wrought-iron gates opened to a driveway of Tuscan red interlocking bricks. The doorbell chimed the first few bars of "We Wish You a Merry Christmas." To my surprise, Mrs. MacMillan answered the door herself. I had seen her once or twice in the hallways at Universal but, of course, she didn't recognize me.

"Come in, come in. You're someone new."

I tried to introduce myself but she wasn't listening— seemed to be stoned on something, possibly Valium, that made her voice sound like a late-night FM deejay on an MOR radio station. She took my overcoat and examined my tweed jacket, rubbing a lapel between two fingers. "Oh, it's a horrible thing, isn't it? I suppose it was your father's?"

I stammered for a moment and came out with, "My grandfather's. Philip Bentley? The painter?"

She nodded a serious nod, her hairspray holding her hair steady as a helmet.

"I'm the same. You'll notice a few ghastly knickknacks I keep just to have a piece of the family around. But clothing—I'd not have considered clothing. I suppose you can smell him on it." She buried her nose in my chest and took a deep breath, then made a sour face. "Pleased to meet you," she said and I'd agreed before I realized she was speaking to my jacket.

Mrs. MacMillan hadn't married MacMillan for his money: her father had even more than his. According to Denise, Mac-Millan and Mrs. MacMillan had not shared a bed since the newspaper story about their six-figure wedding was freshly decomposing in the landfill. Their three children, who were all away at private schools in the East, were not seen by her as evidence to the contrary. The only thing they had in common was their interest in saltwater aquariums. As Denise put it, "They only stay together for the sake of the fish."

The fish were everywhere: there was a tank built into the bar, a tank inside an oak console television, a huge tank over the mantelpiece, even a freshwater tank under the floor in the centre of the sunken living room. Walking on water appealed to me more than I would have expected, Mary Abraham. I stood staring down into the eyes staring up at me from the mirror reflecting the electric oranges, reds, and yellows of the tropical fish.

A pretty server in perfect white linen blouse and a short black skirt offered me a glass of champagne and I accepted. "I'm Candy. Anything else you need, just let me know," she said with a wink. I thanked her and looked around for Denise, who was nowhere to be seen.

There were a few brokers from the office, but most of the guests were elderly—friends of Old MacMillan (everyone called MacMillan's father Old MacMillan, but not to his face), who was holding court in the corner behind the white grand piano. Word was Old MacMillan's cancer was in remission. A thin layer of white hair combed painfully across his pate only partly hid his skull, bone yellow. As he talked, he flailed his arms as though warding off a swarm of angry wasps.

The brokers I knew from Universal, rapt in conversation, took no notice of me. I stood alone in my corner, contemplating the nearest tank of fish, shimmering fins more breathtaking than butterflies. Candy stopped again and I downed what was left of my champagne and took another glass. "Oh, you're thirsty," she said. "Why are you standing here all by yourself?"

"I don't really know anyone."

She leaned closer and whispered in my ear, "No loss. Dull bunch."

Mrs. MacMillan floated up and locked arms with me, and Candy skittered off with her tray.

"I really must apologize, but I need to go to bed. I have to get up very early tomorrow for an appointment with my urologist."

I glanced at my watch: 5:30 in the afternoon.

"Ohhhh. I hope it's nothing serious."

She didn't seem to understand. "I like urologists, don't you? Surgeons are such egotists, but urologists always have such lovely personalities." She had a way of gritting her teeth when she smiled.

"I … don't think I've ever met a … urologist?"

"No? Oh, you *must* get to know one. They really are priceless." With that, she dropped my arm and whisked off. I barely caught up to her before she could escape.

"Excuse me. Would you happen to know where Denise Davis is?"

"Who?" Mrs. MacMillan turned abruptly to face me, her eyes so wide that I might have just asked if I could touch her breasts.

"Denise Davis. I was supposed to meet her here."

For the first time, Mrs. MacMillan attempted to focus on me, but the effort made her eyes cross. She put a hand to her forehead and looked at the floor. "The Davis woman? Well, my husband hasn't arrived yet. I suppose she's with him. Isn't she always?"

And then she abruptly closed the door between us.

I considered leaving, but instead tossed back my glass of champagne and went looking for Candy. She had disappeared. MacMillan, on the other hand, had manifested himself on the other side of the room, wearing a black Italian suit with narrow lapels and a Santa Claus tie. He stood on his fish tank, smoking a cigar, making vague motions at the heavens, talking to an older man in a blue Italian suit who I assumed was one of Old MacMillan's buddies, and to a tiny woman who had her back to me.

"Oh, look! Isn't that her?" one of the brokers asked another, motioning toward MacMillan and the woman.

By the time I'd crossed the room, MacMillan had loosened his tie and unbuttoned his shirt far enough to show off his good luck charm: a polished nugget that dangled against his pale freckled skin like a deformed egg. As I edged into the circle, MacMillan was analyzing the latest machinations of the market, waving his cigar so that the ash spilled onto his fish tank floor.

The woman was Arabella Wiseman. Her posture revealed her fatigue, but she still had that curious strength her body managed to carry despite her lack of flesh. Our eyes met and she smiled but quickly averted her gaze so that we would not distract or interrupt MacMillan. When he reached the punchline, she chuckled appreciatively before stepping over to me.

"Mr. Bentley! It is such a pleasure to see you." She gripped me in her arms and squeezed so hard that it felt as if she were hanging on for dear life. Over her shoulder I could see everyone at the party suddenly centring their attention on me, watching her display of affection with studied interest, measuring it in dollar value, whispering. She stepped back and presented me: "Have the two of you met Mr. Bentley? Madison Hedges and Gus MacMillan."

MacMillan's eyes narrowed, but before he could speak Sid's father interrupted: "Philip Bentley's grandson, I presume? My son has told me about you, but we haven't had the pleasure," he offered both his hands and clasped mine warmly. "I'm a big fan of your grandfather's work. I have one in my dining room. A marvellous thing. Makes me think of my own childhood: how little we had back then and how happy we were despite it, and how much we don't appreciate what we have now. I sit and look at it every morning while I'm eating my cornflakes. Makes me feel young, and that takes some doing these days."

"*Angus* MacMillan," MacMillan corrected without offering his hand. Instead he sucked hard on his cigar so that it glowed brightly and Arabella took a step back, looking a little nauseous.

"Watch out for *Angus*," Madison Fairmont Hedges II patted me affectionately on the shoulder. "Word has it he has recently been rejected by a young lady, and that has soured his generally sunny mood. Not that that should be a problem for a blissfully married man, such as himself. Isn't that right, Gus?"

"Of course," MacMillan smiled darkly. "Nothing more blissful than marriage. I like to call it *The Love Coffin*. Climb right on in, enjoy yourself." He tapped the ash from his cigar. "How did classes go today? Have exams started?"

"No," I said. "Yes. A few. Fine."

All three stared at me, MacMillan's cigar smoke twisting off in slow coils.

"And how do you know Arabella?" Sid's father asked.

I opened my mouth and then looked to Arabella for guidance.

"His grandfather introduced us."

"Arabella! You never told me you knew Philip Bentley," Sid's father scolded. "You *must* introduce me."

"I'm sure his beloved grandson would be happy to do that, wouldn't you Mr. Bentley? We met fairly recently. Professionally," she said, and Madison Fairmont Hedges nodded knowingly. I nodded too. MacMillan looked bored. "So I can't say I know him well. But I already feel as though I've known this young man for many years. He has an old soul."

Everyone waited for my response—some evidence of my spiritual wisdom.

"I don't know…," I shrugged. Nothing else entered my head, and so I turned to MacMillan and asked "Where's Denise?"

"Oh. The little missus and I went out for a couple drinks, but she didn't feel so well, and I had to take her home." He turned to Arabella and Sid's father: "She said all she wanted was her bed. She does so like her bed, that girl." He sucked his cigar.

"There is a pernicious bug going around, I hear," Arabella cooed soothingly.

"Is your grandfather still painting?" Sid's father asked.

"No," I said, picturing Denise with MacMillan writhing in our bed. "He has Parkinson's. His hands shake too much." Madison Fairmont Hedges II frowned sadly.

"He's done some abstracts," Arabella said.

He looked even more disappointed.

Arabella gave her glass a little shake to make the ice cubes tinkle. "I went to see them. In his apartment. They're very good."

"Really? Well, I'm not much into abstracts, but it would be great to have a look. Here's my card. Give me a call and we'll set something up."

I took the embossed rectangle and thanked him.

"Wonderful." Arabella said. "I'd love to be included, if your grandfather doesn't find me too boring." She glanced toward the group of Universal brokers ogling her over Mac-Millan's broad shoulders.

"The vultures are descending, Arabella," Madison Fairmont Hedges II said. "You may want to make your escape." He drifted over to intercept the group and MacMillan followed, his cigar smoke trailing like exhaust.

"Don't mind Gus," Arabella patted me on the shoulder. "He's always rude, even if he doesn't hate you because you've got something he hasn't. Just watch out he doesn't sneak up behind you with an icepick. In fact, now that you've made your brave appearance, I'd vacate the premises. Just to be safe. Better safe than dead, as the philosophers say. Do you have a car? I'll give you a ride."

She narrowed her eyes on me and I felt that shiver once again.

"Oh, no, that's okay ..."

"Not at all! I insist!"

"It's too much trouble ..."

"No trouble at all."

A bodyguard followed us to the door, murmuring into his walkie-talkie. Someone found our jackets for us. Outside, the rain was still coming down. The bodyguard led us out and another man on a walkie-talkie met us on the Tuscan driveway with an umbrella to protect Arabella. The limousine glided into place before us just as we reached the curb, and her man opened the door. Almost a simple black Lincoln Town Car, but stretched a little so that there was a seat facing backwards toward the seat facing forwards. She gripped my arm snugly as she settled in and I slipped into the seat facing her. The bodyguard closed the door and got in up front.

"Would you like a drink?" she said, motioning toward the bar fridge. "Help yourself."

"No thanks."

Despite the distraction of my surroundings, thinking *Fuck her*, meaning Denise.

"You're sure? If you change your mind just help yourself."

The car began to move. We rode in comfortable silence for a minute or more.

"Oh, look!" Arabella pointed off toward the horizon: a full moon was breaking through into the twilight. "Isn't that romantic?"

When I didn't respond, Arabella smiled sadly.

"It is…," I managed.

There was another silence, the world sliding by, ocean below, street curving along the edge of the precipice, everything a bit jumbled by the way the champagne made my brain threaten to float up through the top of my skull.

"But what need does a young man have for romance with an old woman?" Arabella asked. I coughed, bewildered, confused, lost.

"I'm sorry. I'm tired."

She turned to look at the ocean, the moon hanging delicately above the lights of the city, close enough to the horizon that I wished it might tumble from the sky.

"I'm absolutely exhausted, but when you reach my stage of being you learn not to allow feelings to get in your way. You're worrying about what MacMillan was intimating he'd gotten up to with your Denise."

She wanted to ambush me, and so I roused myself to meet her.

"Is she mine?"

"Of course not. She never was and she never will be. But, if it makes you feel any better, she's not MacMillan's either. She despises MacMillan." Arabella sighed. "You could not have helped hearing Sid on the subject. It's all the biological imperative. Spreading your genes. Try to look past the clinging and see your way to what matters. Life is a gift. It will not last forever. Don't get hung up on petty jealousies. Don't be in denial of your mortality. Peer into the eyeholes of your own skull. You're a writer, I hear. Recite some poetry for me."

Those eagle eyes were looking right through me.

"I'm afraid I'm not much good at reciting."

"All right. Well, then, kiss my inner thighs."

I blanched. "You, ah, met my grandfather?'

"Yes. His illness gives us much to understand one another. Your grandfather is ill and old and wants to be immortal, of course."

"Wants his art to be immortal."

"His art. His self. One is an expression of the other. Thank you for telling him about me. He is going to be an important spokesman for our brand. You've made a major contribution to Argyle and you should know that we are in your debt."

She smiled, this tiny woman in the back seat of her huge car. What was it about her that I found attractive, Mary Abraham? In a funny way, you remind me of her. You're very different, of course, but you are the two most serious and powerful women I have ever met. She was like the goddess Kali: she might have been holding a severed head in her hand, her tongue extended.

"I don't want to move back to Saskatchewan," I finally said.

"Why not? I was there last weekend. A beautiful place."

"I'm writing my securities exam next week."

She tilted her head slightly.

"I'm impressed. You're turning me down. No one turns me down. Do you know that? Not even that egotistical arse, MacMillan, who already has more money than he should ever need. You are a truly remarkable young man, Mr. Bentley. You've made a dying woman very happy."

She smiled a painful smile and I nodded, fearing, from the way she was tilting her head, gazing into my eyes, that she was about to try to kiss me.

"You need someone experienced," I said.

"I need you. I don't need anyone else in the world but you, Mr. Bentley. And do you know why?"

I was nodding my head and kept nodding until I realized that I did not know why.

"Why?"

"Because you don't need me."

She jerked suddenly away, gazing out the window and into

the darkening sky. "There will never be another moon like this one. Could you hold me? Please?" I opened my mouth but couldn't speak. She leaned forward and grasped me and I awkwardly raised my arms to enfold her, cradling her thin body to my chest. She raised her chin and kissed me, a tender kiss that brushed my cheek, her lips even colder than her fingers, and then she slumped back into her seat, looking as though the effort had almost killed her.

"You've hurt me," she said, her eyes squeezing shut, savouring the pain.

"I'm sorry."

Her eyes slowly opened and I could see her see me sitting there across from her in her mobile fortress. "Thank you," she said. "For hurting me."

Then the car began to slow and stopped and the door opened and Candy, the server from the party, scooted in next to me, across from Arabella.

"Mr. Bentley, this is Candy," Arabella said.

"Hello?" I said, and Candy smiled.

"We've met," she giggled. The car started to move again.

Candy pulled her skirt higher so that I could see she was wearing no underwear. She was unbuttoning her white linen blouse.

"No …"

"Kiss Candy, Mr. Bentley. Don't be scared. You can't hurt her. You know you want to kiss her. Do it for an old dying woman. I will enjoy watching you kiss her. Consider it one of my final wishes. Pretend she's me. A younger self."

"I can't …"

Candy straddled me, unclasping her bra.

"Of course you can. Sometimes you have to learn to take what's right in front of you."

Candy ground her crotch into my lap and moaned, her breasts in my face.

"I want to come. You make me so wet. Please, make me come. Look into my eyes while I come."

Candy's azure eyes were wide as the prairie sky.

—

The moon had climbed higher, skimming its way behind a sheen of thin cloud. Six floors above I could see Denise's living room window. I'd asked Arabella to ask the driver to let me off at the end of the block. I stood looking up at the window for a moment before going inside, wondering if Denise was looking down at me.

I called her as I entered the door and a moment later she emerged from the bedroom and threw herself into my arms, weeping.

"Were you at MacMillan's all this time—what did that prick tell you?"

"I left right after he got there. Where were you?"

"What did he say?"

"A couple drinks—he said you had a couple drinks."

"God, he's a bastard. I'm sorry, honey. I just couldn't face it. I know how much it meant to you. Forgive me? We went to Checkers and he started acting like such a goddamned pig—I couldn't spend another second with him. I love you. I just couldn't stop thinking about how much I really love you and I said to myself, 'So what the hell am I sitting here with this prick for?' Did anyone at the party recognize you?"

"Nobody," I said, disentangling myself and directing her toward the couch. She clung to my arm. I needed to take a shower. Denise sighed and leaned into me, her head resting against my chest.

"I can smell MacMillan's cigars on you," she said, and then she raised her chin and looked into my eyes. "Were you down at the ocean? You smell like the ocean."

December 23

After the ride in Sid's limo, I was overcome with fear and fury knotted into a lovely noose. I walked home and wrote my account of the MacMillan Christmas party before Mom woke, transcribed it from my diary into a Word document last night after she went to bed, then read it over this morning, and before I could reconsider, sent a copy to Sid.

This is what is referred to as revenge porn, Mary Abraham.

Ten seconds after pushing the send key I was overwhelmed by terrible fear and regret.

I'm peering out windows, trying to spot hit men or ninjas about to attack.

Time and again it is my own body that entraps me and turns my life into a living hell. As I grow older, the great weakness of lust is eclipsed by anger and both are contained in my flesh as much as in my mind. Not that I underestimate the weakness of my mind, but it's the way my body overwhelms my mind's resolve that has been my endless downfall.

I've made Mom a cup of tea and Sheena has just got up and is slumped in a chair drinking coffee. Julia is out tobogganing.

Without me there to protect her from whatever stranger approaches.

"I'm gonna check on Julia. Want to come?" I ask Sheena.

"I just got out of bed. What's wrong with you?" Sheena asks. "You're wound a little tight today."

I say nothing, but know that she can sense the blood and brain matter and the gun, an arms-length away, in the top drawer of the credenza, where I have placed it close at hand.

Mom sips her tea and looks from Sheena to me. "Where is Denise?" she asks.

December 24, 2012

This afternoon, grey sky threatening more snow, we were heading to Beth's parents. Beth and Sheena were on their phones, Mom sitting between Julia and Sheena in the back, wondering what planet she had landed on. The black limousine I had my eye on accelerated past us.

A jumbo jet appeared so low it looked like a bird perching on a wire. Julia squealed and Mom looked quite worried. Sheena and Beth, staring into their phones, did not notice. Beth's phone rang and she answered, "Tony! Merry Christmas!"

"How many people were in that plane?" Julia asked.

"Maybe two or three hundred," I said.

"What? What do you mean? Oh my God. Oh, Tony. Oh my God!" Beth squeezed her phone so hard her knuckles were white.

"Three hundred?! Was that the biggest airplane in the world?"

"No, not nearly …"

I did my best to pay attention to Julia and eavesdrop on Beth while navigating the holiday traffic. Unless Beth was overreacting, something was very wrong. I suspected overreaction.

Or inappropriate empathy. Like the time he called Beth and not his lawyer when he got arrested for beating up his girl-friend.

"Which hospital? I can't come now, Tony. I wish I could, but it's Christmas. As soon as I can. Tomorrow."

She cooed at him a little longer before she said goodbye. I glanced at her. She held her head in her hands, massaging her scalp, not looking at or speaking into her phone for the first time since we'd left our driveway, tears tracing down her cheek.

"Tony's in the hospital. They're not sure what it is yet." She gasped a little, trying to catch enough breath to say the word she had to say. "They think it's ... *cancer*. They think it may be in his brain."

"Oh," I said.

Sheena stared into her phone.

"Is another one coming?" Julia craned her neck to see higher into the sky.

"I'm worried about Denise," Mom said.

—

Beth's family has a habit of making toasts, something un-imaginable in my family. It's too public a stance, too falsely formal for the Bentleys, the suspicious territory of show-offs like salesmen and politicians and preachers (such as my grandfather had once been, it's true, and I ended up a kind of salesman, but both my grandfather and I were something else at our core). Beth's father had never spread the word of God but was the former owner of the local Buick dealership, a calling he saw as equally spiritual. He'd sold the business a couple of years before I met Beth, and Beth's parents live in comfortable retirement in a new subdivision where all the huge houses look the same and face the street with yawning double garage doors. There are no sidewalks.

At Christmas Eve dinner, Beth made a toast, saying how grateful she is for me, even though I sometimes drive her crazy, and she wanted me to know that she was standing firmly by me through the difficulty of this time. Sheena lifted her eyebrows and puffed out her cheeks in a way that indicated she might vomit. I raised my glass while wondering why, if Beth was standing by me, she could not stand to feel my touch. Beth's father shouted out, "To the undertaker!" and Mom flinched with alarm. "Don't let this pull you down, boy! It's a hidden blessing. You were in a dead-end line. I see a new and better road opening up for you!" With this pronouncement he downed his glass of wine.

He has always called me *the Undertaker*, telling me that, *No thanks*, he was in no need of my services: he was doing a fine job of pickling himself. He was right about that.

"And I'd like to make a special toast, if I can…," Beth's voice caught, and the table went silent, everyone waiting to hear the real point of her speech. She took a deep breath and charged on: "To Tony. I want him to know that we're all thinking of him today."

Her father was already refilling his wine glass with the cheap Pinot Grigio in the blue bottle with the dragonfly, but he paused and set the bottle down heavily.

"I will not toast that asshole!"

"Henry! Would you please shut up!" Beth's mother said, though she didn't like Tony any more than her husband did.

"Well, why is *she* toasting that asshole? He used to beat her up, for Chrissakes…!"

"Grandpa! Don't swear!" Julia burst into tears, sprang from her chair, and fled from the room.

Sheena looked accusingly at me, as if I were the one making a scene, and Mom stared at the table, clearly feeling it was all her fault.

"Now look what you've done, and at Christmas," Beth said to her father, standing up to follow Julia and motioning me back into my chair. Beth's mother grabbed her husband's wine glass before he could. Every so often she had these brave moments where you could glimpse a bit of Beth in her, though mostly her husband had worn her down to a cheerful acquiescence.

"You're not having any more. Try to be a little more sensitive. The man is ill. He may well be dying."

"I don't give a damn. If he were here I'd kill him myself. Give me my wine!"

Beth's mother looked to me for support and shook her head, embarrassed. I slouched a little more deeply into my chair. What could I do at his table? She hated the way he inevitably ruined her idea of a perfect Christmas by getting drunk and disorderly, but it was not my place to scold him. Even if I did, it would only make things worse.

"Give me my *vino!*" he demanded. "I want to drink another toast to my son-in-law, and a damned fine son-in-law too, despite the fact he's temporarily a stay-at-home bum. Considering some of the trash the little girl's dragged home over the years, he's well ahead of the competition." He looked to my mother, offering her part of the credit. Mom smiled and nodded fearfully. Beth's mother sighed and set his glass down in front of him, picking up her own glass.

"Thank you for making my little girl happy," she said.

Mr. Adams nodded assent, apparently satisfied, and took a deep drink. I sipped my wine and avoided Sheena's eyes.

—

We were married right here at Beth's parents' place, out in the backyard, on a warm day in June the year after Julia was born. Beth worried for months that it would rain. It didn't. She also worried about walking across the lawn in her heels and so practised the manoeuvre repeatedly and finally settled on a pair of ivory slip-ons with very little heel. She bought a simple dress, traditional white (ivory actually), but not particularly traditional for a wedding gown in any other way: bare shoulders, tasteful décolletage, simple classic cut, just past knee length so that it revealed her lovely calves. Coco Chanel would have approved, her friends agreed. She also chose the flowers and the food and the decorations and everything else except the wine, which was left to me—I picked a red I like from Corbières and Pinot Gris from British Columbia and real Champagne, though I thought it overpriced. I could have found a Crémant that was equally interesting.

I also suggested one of the musicians, which became a small bone of contention.

"Since your parents have the piano, my grandmother would like to play one song during the ceremony. Just one song."

Beth took a very deep breath and let it out as a heavy sigh.

"You know I think your grandmother is lovely, but please talk her out of it. I'm counting on you."

"Why? She's not good enough?"

"Her playing is lovely for someone who is practically a hundred years old. I have Maria playing cello. Maria plays with the Toronto Symphony Orchestra."

"She'd like to play just one song."

"It only takes one song or one speech to ruin a wedding. That's all anyone will remember. My father wanted to say a few words and it has been forbidden. If I can control my family, I don't see why you can't control yours."

"She's not going to play "You Light Up My Life." It'll be Beethoven or something."

"Beethoven played badly is still bad."

"Did she play badly when she played for you? I thought she was very good!"

"She's not quite steady, honey. There are gaps that shouldn't be there."

"Fine. You tell her she can't play."

Beth swept her hair back and placed her hand on her hip.

"She hasn't been told that she *can* play, *has* she?"

"She has offered to play. She has expressed interest in play-ing and I suspect that the reason she has expressed interest in playing is because when you met her you made such a fuss over her playing. You encouraged her. I'm not going to be the one to tell her she can't. You'll have to do it."

She took another deep breath.

"Listen, honey, I'm sorry. I understand what you mean. If that's what happened, I'm sorry. Your grandmother is a lovely woman and I don't want to hurt her feelings, but I'm afraid it ultimately might be embarrassing for her. Playing after Maria. Could you please tell her that you don't think it's a good idea?"

"I won't!"

With that tiny show of will, I turned and marched from this very room.

I understand now that I was the ass, Mary Abraham. It was her wedding day. She'd been planning it for months. She wanted it to be perfect.

—

Old Mrs. Bentley at the piano reminds me of my grandfather. Does he actually want to be buried, Mary Abraham? The freezing really has succeeded in keeping him alive, poking his trembling fingers into my life in a way that Grandma never could. There is still no cure for Parkinson's. I'm fairly certain that's why he decided to do what he did: what they convinced him to do. He held out the hope that he could be brought back with hands steady enough to paint a masterpiece.

Everyone else is sleeping. Well, probably not Sheena. She is likely sitting up reading *The Tibetan Book of the Dead*, listening for reindeer on the roof. I suppose I'd better get to bed before Santa arrives. I'll be in trouble if I scare him away.

If I were diagnosed with cancer would Beth react with such terrible grief?

December 25, 2012

It was still very dark when Julia wrestled us from bed.

Beth's mother was already up and had made coffee. Mr. Adams and Sheena were still sleeping, but Julia knew from past experience that she was allowed her stocking without everyone present, so she was not overly concerned until she'd pulled the mandarin orange from the toe.

"Where's Grandpa and Sheena?"

Mom looked around. "Where's Denise?" she asked.

Beth, in her chiffon leopard peignoir, puffed out her cheeks and exhaled.

"Denise is in Vancouver, where she has lived for many long years. This is my parents' home you are visiting. I am Beth. I am your son's present wife!"

Mom and Julia and Mrs. Adams were all quite frightened by this outburst. No one spoke.

"You can open one present before they get up," Beth said to Julia.

Julia studied the bounty heaped under the tree. "It's okay …"

"He's tired," Beth's mother said. "Best if we let him sleep a little while longer. It might put him in a better mood. We can go ahead. We'll just keep a few things to open with him."

"Serve him right," Beth said.

"Mommy!"

"I'm sorry, honey."

"Don't worry, sweetheart," Mrs. Adams, wrapped in her pink bathrobe, reassured Julia. "I'm sure he won't mind."

"But what about Sheena? We need to wait for Sheena," Julia said.

Beth looked at me accusingly and rolled her eyes.

—

The Saturday we were married was sunny, the sky a crystalline blue the colour of Beth's eyes. Not much smog. Beth's father had driven her and baby Julia out the night before, so I wouldn't see her before the wedding, and I drove out with Sheena the next morning.

"You sleep okay?" I glanced in the rear-view mirror at my newly teenaged girl (unimaginably more mature than when I'd last seen her at Easter) in the back seat.

"Fine."

Sheena was unusually quiet, even considering she was working on a pencil sketch of the Hindu goddess Kali standing on her husband, Shiva, a severed head clutched by the hair in one of her six hands. I wondered if I could detect a sense of mourning—an awareness that the significance of this day for her was that there was no longer any chance of her parents ever reuniting. We were passing Pearson airport, and a passenger jet flashed suddenly before us, the landing gear visible. I pointed it out but she only glanced up from her sketch for a moment and said, "Wow," without much enthusiasm.

My parents and my grandmother were staying at a motel in Bolton, glad to avoid having to come into the city. They were all in the same double room to save money, though I had offered to pay for a decent hotel and anyway, they were not really short of cash. They'd just never learned to spend. My father answered the door when I knocked. Already dressed in his best suit and a bolo tie, he smiled warmly and shook my hand but his eyes moved downwards, unable to meet the eyes of his only son, the surviving boy who was supposed to take over the farm but instead had left him an old man with no one to hand his life to.

"You look nice for a second-hand husband," Grandma Bentley proclaimed. Already in her finery, a bright floral-patterned dress, she was well-prepared, she assured me, for what might well be her last public performance. My father smiled and my mother straightened my tie, assuring me that I looked "like a new Dodge." Sheena sat quietly in the corner, shading in shadows on her sketch. The entire gathering, even my grandmother, exuded a tinge of mourning.

This went beyond their unspoken discomfort over our waiting to marry until after Julia was born. Denise was family, while something about the woman from the television made all of them feel just a little uncomfortable. The way she asked so many times how long Sonata 19 would take to play, wanting Grandma Bentley to define it to the second. "The woman is an artist herself. She should know that it will take as long as it takes to get to the end. I like her well enough, but she has a bit too much of the East in her."

When I walked into the Adams' house Beth's mother handed me baby Julia and a bottle and sent me into the guest bedroom so that Beth could finish arrangements without me seeing her. One of the most important details was listening to Grandma Bentley rehearse. I was glad not to be present for that. As I was burping Julia, a cloth on my shoulder to protect my suit from spit ups, she somehow managed to pee on me. Marking her territory. Perhaps she was concerned about the arrival of the elder half-sister and the mysterious retreat to the grandparents' dwelling. After changing the diaper and handing her over to Sheena, who took great joy in her new little sister (even put away her sketching pad) never having had a sibling before, I tried to wash my shirt and dried it with a blow dryer. It wasn't really too serious: a small yellow spot that my jacket concealed.

At eleven in the morning I was standing in the backyard near the pool, in front of the small gathering of invited guests, mostly family, sitting in plastic chairs. I was talking rather informally with the Unitarian minister, the woman who would marry us. We discussed the weather, how we had been blessed with such a perfect day, while the guests listened intently, as though this were part of the ritual. My grandmother began playing the sonata, then stopped and started again. The piano had been rolled out on the concrete patio and Beth's friend Maria stood beside Old Mrs. Bentley, turning pages. The careful notes carved a wavering pattern in the suburban morning, melding with traffic and birdsong. When it was through, everyone applauded politely. A moment later Maria's cello etched a few solid notes of Bach and Beth appeared in her perfect dress on her father's arm, stepping out through the glass patio doors. A murmur of approval rose from the women. The men smiled and responded with silent appreciation. When she reached me, Beth released her father and took my arm.

I was in the middle of the verse from Yeats—"and loved your beauty with love *false* and *true*"—gazing into Beth's shining eyes, when a voice distracted from the proceedings. Everyone turned to see Tony stepping through the patio doors with Rachel on his arm, he in his white tuxedo and she in a red cocktail dress. "He looked like some silly rock and roll singer and she looked like something out of Revelations," Grandma Bentley said later. I thought this was a bit ungenerous. The dress was actually quite tasteful: something I could imagine my grandmother wearing herself in the sixties. The couple took their seats near the back while proceedings continued. Rachel later insisted it was her fault they were late, but I blamed Tony.

After the ceremony, the party spread from the yard into the dining room and spilled into the garage, which had been designated as the smoking lounge. The bride was a smoker, so the focus of festivities ended up being there. Beth's father kept it so clean you could eat off the painted grey floor. He was manning a cooler of beer and taking nips from a bottle of whiskey, glowering at Tony and muttering to himself. When I went over for a beer, my new father-in-law made it clear that he was "only stopping myself from beating the prick to a bloody pulp" because he did not want to ruin his daughter's day. I, having not yet been told of the beatings (which, Beth told me many years later, were a couple of physical altercations where she gave better than she got, once actually counter-attacking Tony with the shards of a broken wineglass so that he had to have stitches in his chest), assumed Mr. Adams was still upset about Tony's betrayal of Beth when, in the third season of their relationship, he'd slept with a somewhat prominent Hollywood actress during the Toronto International Film Festival. He was outed the following morning when a newspaper published a picture of the couple leaving a festival party.

"It's not a big deal," I said. "They were just a bit late."

The old man raised his wild highland eyebrows. "Late, all right. He'll be the late Tony Lee-Knight when I'm through with him."

December 26, 2012

I dropped Beth off at the hospital on our way home, explaining to Julia as we sat in the car watching her mother pass through the revolving doors, that she had to visit Tony, who was ill. Julia said she knew, but wondered what Tony had caught, and I told her the doctors were not yet certain. Mom looked even more than usually confused.

"Where's Denise?" Sheena said, chuckling at herself.

We drove on home in fluttering snow. Sheena and I unpacked gifts and luggage; I surreptitiously scanned the street for men watching from long black vehicles. Once inside, Sheena headed for the basement, Julia went up to her bedroom and played quietly with her presents, and Mom followed me around, assisting me in the folding of laundry and helping me to start dinner. The phone rang and I didn't answer, not wanting to speak to Beth—to carry half of a conversation that could only be about Tony. When I checked the message, she said that Tony was so depressed she couldn't leave him yet, and so she would not be home until late.

I got Mom and Julia to bed and crawled in myself.

Beth woke me to explain the diagnosis is an aggressive non-Hodgkin's lymphoma that has already spread to the brain. It is also in his spinal column, which is why Tony has been having so much pain in his back: tumours pressing on nerves. The treatment will be chemotherapy and will begin as soon as possible. I wasn't really interested in the details, pretending to listen but not really hearing much at all. What grasped my attention was the fact that the pretty talent agent had dumped Tony when she heard the diagnosis, presumably not wanting to be saddled with the responsibility of a dying man. Dropped him like a hot potato, Beth said, but I thought a hot branding iron was more appropriate. Why would you pick up a branding iron except to brand something? And if the branding iron had no proper handle and you were not wearing gloves, you'd end up getting branded. Who could blame her for the natural impulse to let go? Beth only understood branding as a marketing concept (having never smelled the singe of the cow's hair when you pressed the red-hot metal into her flesh) and made it clear that she felt the young woman's reaction was shocking, though she did not want to judge. She had already begun gathering a support group on her iPhone on her way home in the cab. After she finished debriefing me she went to her office to carry on with the job. There were all the old friends, all the old girlfriends, to contact. She didn't want Tony to be alone.

—

After the wedding party at her parents', Beth's friends carried on celebrating here in our Toronto home. Somehow my mother and Grandma Bentley got wind of the plan, and

before we knew anything about it, Beth's mother had gener-
ously offered to drive them into the city and to our front door
for a taste of the après-party, and then back out to their motel. Sheena insisted that she wanted to attend too, and seeing
that there was no one left to look after her, aside from my
dad, we couldn't very well argue with her. Beth's father had
already passed out in his recliner in the living room. Philip
Bentley Jr. wasn't interested in any more festivities and drove
his Dodge Monaco (Mom, Dad, and Grandma had driven all
the way here for the wedding) to the motel room, where he
planned to get some sleep.

Grandma Bentley and my mother perched politely on
our couch, watching the party unfolding around them:
drinking, dancing, marijuana smoking, and the general hilar-
ity induced by these ingredients. I decided it would be best
to distract them with a tour of the house, which Grandma
Bentley had never seen, and led them up the stairs to see
Beth's office. When I opened the door to present the master
bedroom, Tony was sprawled across the marriage bed snort-
ing cocaine from a mirror resting on Rachel's lap. I closed
the door. Grandma Bentley and my mother gazed up at me
with slightly embarrassed expressions, trying to pretend they
hadn't seen.

"And the baby's room is this way," I said, leading them
down the hall.

—

It reached midnight and the party got louder and threatened
to spin out of control, Beth's friends flailing their bodies to
the music on the stereo. I pleaded with Beth's mom to take

Mom and my grandmother home and insisted that Sheena
go to bed. I escorted her up the stairs to her room, the baby's
room, where Julia lay sleeping.

"I'm not tired," Sheena said.

"It's late. You're exhausted."

"I'm not."

"Get into your nightgown."

"It's too noisy."

"Get on your nightgown. Good night."

"Will you lie down with me?"

This had been our normal routine when she was younger,
but she was almost fourteen and she had not asked me to lie
down with her for at least a couple of years.

"Okay. Get on your nightgown and brush your teeth."

I lay there next to her, an arm across my forehead the way
my father used to lie on the couch after lunch or listening
to the radio at night—was perhaps lying at that moment in
a suburban motel room too many miles away. I listened to
the party throbbing through the walls, recognizing a voice
every now and then crying out above the general din, and
wondering how I could possibly expect Sheena to sleep, but
in a few minutes she was under, one hand clutching my shirt,
her breath tickling my ear. I lay there feeling her breathing
until I almost surrendered to sleep myself.

—

There is a moment I will never forget that evening at the
after-party on the night I married Beth: this one moment in
the evening that stands out in a strange way from all of the
others.

When I came down the stairs from putting Sheena to bed, most of Beth's friends were quite drunk or stoned—were singing and dancing or huddled together discussing the past or the future, the stereo blasting—and my mother and Grandma Bentley, firmly in the present, were looking weary and uncomfortable as they waited for Beth's mother to get ready to leave. I sent Beth over to prod her mother toward the door, but when she got there they launched into a moment of their own, shouting into one another's ears, hugging and crying, and I saw it was not safe for Beth's mother to be driving anywhere.

Standing with an empty wine glass on the edge of the celebration, pondering whether or not it would be too impolitic for the groom to drive them back himself, I furtively studied my mother and grandmother. They slumped on the couch, silent, witnessing the decline of Western civilization. In the middle of all the commotion and all of her weariness, Grandma Bentley all at once noticed the painting by the husband who had abandoned her, hanging over the credenza in the dining room. She'd been sitting there all night, so it was strange she had not noticed it earlier, but I could see by the way she suddenly stirred and rose that the painting had only caught her attention at that exact instant. She struggled to her feet and crossed the room, weaving through dancers and drunken revellers, intent on a closer look. At last she stood only a couple of feet away, studying the painting from close up. A mess of black and grey splotches of thick oil paint doing its best to suck all of the energy from the room. You could see she was mesmerized. I elbowed my way toward her, wanting to save her from falling in and disappearing forever.

"It's something, isn't it?"

Tony had also noticed her advance and, because he was standing on that side of the room, had got to her before me, resting a hand on her shoulder, yelling into her ear loudly enough that I heard his question as I arrived on the scene. At first, Mrs. Bentley did not seem to hear him or be aware of the fact that the man in the white tuxedo was shouting into her ear, but at last she tore her eyes from the painting, and with a profound expression of betrayal, looked straight into his eyes.

"How could he possibly make me look so ugly? I don't look anything like that. Do I?"

Tony stared blankly for a moment, glancing at the painting and back at my grandmother, before shaking his head three times, glancing at me, and rushing off to Rachel.

"Do I?" my grandmother asked me.

"No," I said, as we both turned back to the painting. "Not at all."

But I was lying.

I suddenly saw her in the way the black paint met the canvas, smearing off to grey in the thinning drips. She was there, staring back at me, her eyes accusing me of every sin I had ever committed and, for the first time in my life, the painting made sense.

But only for that moment. For the fifteen years since that evening, I've looked for her, but have never found her again. She is gone.

—

Eight years ago, Grandma Bentley reached one hundred and three years of age before succumbing to pneumonia while Beth and Julia and I were on vacation in Cuba. Being so far away and in the middle of a holiday, I did not return for the funeral. My mother understood, and my father never spoke about such things. The very fact we were in Cuba, supporting Castro with our tourist dollars, must have infuriated him, though it likely wouldn't have bothered my grandmother, who was not particularly political.

She has crumbled to dust by now, Mary Abraham, and is content to remain in her grave.

December 28, 2012

This morning I told Beth I had an errand, left Sheena to watch Mom, and met you by the lake, on the other side of the urban agglomeration, in Mississauga, in a park I had never before visited, never even heard of—we might as well have been on the other side of the earth from my neighbourhood. The majority of the people sharing the park this chilly morning were born, like you, in Southeast Asia and looked to me a little lost in that wintery urban wilderness. Probably just my projection. Across the lake to the east, downtown Toronto hovered over the water, the CN Tower marking its place, and my eyes scanned the shoreline further east to where I knew my home would be, my wife and my mother and my daughters. Disorienting to be searching for it across the water.

"In Saskatchewan. I'm not comfortable saying more. I'll take you there."

"You're certain that's where it's located?"

"Yes."

Today you wore a puffy blue down-filled parka and a knitted cap with a brim to shade your eyes. You walked beside me along a gravel path through the leafless grey trees, our feet crunching the thin layer of snow that had fallen the night before. You were weighing my proclamation against my emphatic earlier claim that I didn't know the location.

"You call it the Beautiful Place. In Buddhism, Pure Land is ruled by the Amida Buddha. Amitabha. It's a peaceful garden where all who reach nirvana gather."

"Like Heaven?"

"Like Heaven, but here on earth. Here all around us. Right now. You could just tell me where it is and you wouldn't have to be involved."

I watched your breath plume from your lips.

"No. I'll take you."

You nodded, peering up at me from below the brim of your cap, waiting, but I did not say more.

"When do we go?" you asked.

"I'm not sure. We talked about early January, I know, but my wife has a colleague who is suddenly very ill, and I'm not so sure about leaving right away. She's overwhelmed by what's happening with him and I'm obviously going to be looking after Julia whenever she's away."

"What sort of illness?"

"Cancer. Brain."

"That doesn't sound like it will be cleared up quickly."

"No. On the other hand, I have my mother here for Christmas and I'll have to take her home. She can't fly on her own. Maybe when I take her, I can take Julia along. My mother still lives on the farm in Saskatchewan where I grew up. The only thing is, I also have my elder daughter Sheena here, and I doubt she wants to go to Saskatchewan."

You stopped abruptly at a bench beside the trail, brushed

the snow aside, and sat down. I nervously seated myself beside you. For a while you did not speak. When you finally did, you spoke so softly that I had to lean closer to hear.

"I think it is time to let go." You paused, clenching and unclenching your gloved hands to get your circulation going. *Let go.* "Minding the wishes of ghosts. I don't even believe he was there. Or your grandfather. I had wished that he could be there with me and he was. I realize how much stress I have put you under."

"It wasn't your fault…," I began to protest, but found I did not have the energy and did not want to risk talking you out of your conclusion. We sat listening to a crow squawk, the sound making it even colder on that bench by the great lake. Were there crows in the Pure Land? "I suspect you're right, though. You do need to move on. Honestly, I don't see what good can come out of rescuing his head."

We sat listening to the crow and meditating upon the dead man's head.

"Yes. It is only a way of hanging on to him when it is time to let go."

The walk back to the parking lot was weighted with an even deeper silence than the walk into the woods. The way you would not look at me, your tense strides through the snow, made me suspect that you'd hoped I would not accept your reprieve. It was only a test of my commitment to your plan, and when you discovered I had none, you released me. But then I suspected you were testing your own commitment as well.

In the parking lot, I said goodbye and held out my hand to shake yours, but you pretended not to see the offer as you opened the door of your vehicle. "Goodbye. Thank you for everything," you said, and before I could respond you slammed the door closed. I waved to you as you drove away and you lifted your hand half-heartedly.

As I pressed the ignition of my Lexus, a long black limousine braked behind me, blocking my escape. The door opened and Sid's goon emerged. I reached for the gun in my glove compartment. He opened the back door of the limousine and Sid got out and approached me. I did not open the glove compartment or my window and so he tapped, smiling, and motioned me to lower it. I obeyed

"Bentley! Fancy seeing you here! What are you doing in this part of the world? So far from home?"

"Nothing. Just driving around. You enjoyed the new chapter?"

"Ah! Exploring the city. It is a wonderful mix of worlds, isn't it? Wasn't that Mary Abraham I noticed driving away just now?"

I considered asking him again about the chapter I'd sent him, but decided against it.

"Yes. She wanted to talk."

"Really? What did she want to talk about?"

"Nothing. She said she was going to let it go. She's had enough. I've had enough. Nothing to worry about, Sid."

"Really?" He sounded genuinely surprised, which I took as some sort of victory: it's difficult to make Sid sound surprised. "I hope you're telling me the truth, Bentley. I must tell you that I was very disappointed to see the two of you here. Very disappointed."

"Were you?"

"Very very disappointed."

"Are you threatening to kill me, Sid? Why don't you just do it? You'd be doing me a favour. I've been thinking of doing it myself, but I just never get around to it."

Sid spit on the pavement before looking back into my eyes. "First you disappoint me and now you're asking for favours. It's the holidays. Go back and share it with your wife and your mother and your daughters. Be grateful for what you have. Don't disappoint me again."

He strode away and slipped into the back of his limousine. His goon closed the door and gave a long glare into the reflection of my eyes in my rear-view mirror before he got into the front of the car. A moment later the juggernaut glided out of the garden.

———

Mom always liked to read but is having double vision, so I'm reading *Howard's End* to her. I have no idea whether she is actually following the story, but she seems to enjoy hearing me reciting the words. Julia was there in the living room listening too, when her mother came in and interrupted.

"You should go and read to Tony. He'd like that. You could take your mom along and read to them both at the same time."

I gave her a long empty look and Mom joined in. The two sets of eyes unnerved Beth and she fled the room after kissing Julia on the top of the head.

Tony is still in hospital awaiting his chemotherapy treatments. Beth's schedule of constant visits from friends and ex-girlfriends has apparently been very successful and Tony is seldom alone. A nurse comes in during the days, but Tony can't afford to hire someone to be there around the clock. He needs the care group because he feels too fragile emotionally to be alone for many hours. Beth's night is tonight.

We decided to go to a kids' movie while Beth was out. Beth objected. "Can't you wait until tomorrow night and we can all go together? We are a family. Remember? I don't know why you have to exclude me. Tony is very ill. He may be dying. Can't you find a little compassion in your heart? There is a heart in there, isn't there?" she asked, trying to make the words sound light, as if she were only teasing, tapping her finger on my chest.

I looked to Sheena and she raised her eyebrows.

"Okay. We'll go tomorrow."

To placate me, this evening while Beth was away at Tony's, Julia told me she'd go to a movie with me the next time Beth went to see Tony, but I'd have to promise to keep it a secret.

"Cross your heart and hope to die?"

I made the X to mark the spot.

—

Beth wept as she filled me in on Tony's latest as she was getting ready for bed. I was already tucked in.

"He looks terrible. Practically a ghost already. There's this thing sticking out of the top of his skull that they implanted there for administering the chemotherapy doses. It's hard not to stare at that spot. He looks like Frankenstein. Or his monster, I mean. He's still fighting, though. Blames it all on heavy metals that corporations have pumped into the environment. They're killing us all, he says. We have to take action to stop them."

She blew her nose. Her sniffling and the sound of the television filled the silence until she found the remote and clicked it off. I had been watching the weather forecast, so I raised my eyebrows to her, noticing for the first time that she had changed her nail polish from black to a red that matched her lips. She sighed, a deep and mournful inhalation and exhalation, as if she were doing her yoga.

"There's something I need to tell you. It's only because he's like a child. He's like Julia is sometimes when she has a nightmare. He's afraid of dying. He's living a nightmare. He sleeps with the light on. He's afraid to sleep alone. He asked me if I'd lie down with him, just because he's so frightened. So he wouldn't be alone. He's afraid he's going to die alone."

I looked up at her, but she was staring into her hands lying open in her lap and would not look at me.

"I understand," I said, rolling away from her and closing my eyes.

December 29, 2012

This morning Mom watched me scrawling in this journal and asked what I was doing.

"Writing," I said.

"I should introduce you to my son," she said, her crooked grin widening so that I could see the dark spaces where her teeth were missing. "He wants to be a writer. His grandfather was an artist. He lives in Vancouver now."

"I'd like to meet him," I said.

I watched her watching me, the lines of her face shifting slowly from the joyful expression to one of shame as she slowly realized the mistake she had made. She recognized me, her son, sitting there before her. I didn't know what to say, how to comfort her, so went back to my scrawling.

—

I came in the back door from a walk on the boardwalk and found Beth at the dining room table at my laptop, reading. She looked up at me.

"You have a message from Mary Abraham," she said. "She wants to know if you're okay. She's very worried about you.

She dreamt about you last night. She wonders if you can meet her. Again."

"Oh."

She lifted my laptop and hurled it against the wall. We both stood looking for a moment at the hole the corner of the machine had punched in the drywall, and then at the thing itself, lying splayed on the stained oak floor. There was a problem with the screen. Compromised. The screen had been. Beth pointed to the door.

"Get the fuck out of my house."

I nodded. "I'm sorry."

"I said get the fuck out!"

"I'm going."

"And take your mother and your daughter with you!"

The events that followed are hazy. I know that I must have gathered Mom and Sheena, and recall a shouting match, Sheena repeatedly telling Beth to fuck off, and Julia insisting that she wanted to come with us, further infuriating her mother, who told her if that's what she wanted, she should go. The next moment I remember clearly is pulling the car out of the driveway, Sheena comforting Julia in the back, apologizing, as though it were her fault, and Julia reassuring her that it was okay. Mom sat next to me in the front, looking only slightly more confused than usual.

I drove a few blocks to a cheap hotel on Queen Street and checked us into a room with two double beds. Not too cheap. Not one of those motels in Scarborough. Close enough that Julia can walk home if she chooses.

Which is where we are now: Julia, Sheena, and Mom

watching *The Wizard of Oz* on television while I sit here at the desk by the window looking out at the cars in the parking lot, writing down what I can remember, bemused by what I already cannot recall. There is a movie theatre across the street, so we've decided to go see our movie this evening, the way we had originally planned, but excluding Beth. We're all pretending that what we are experiencing is part of some large mysterious plan.

I'm considering the echoes, the way my life repeats itself, making it clear that fools like me never learn a thing, or persist in learning the same lessons over and over again.

Follow the yellow brick road. The tin man always had a heart.

December 1986, Vancouver

Candy in Arabella Wiseman's limousine is clearer in my memory than the drive from my home to this hotel only a few hours ago. What does that say about me, Mary Abraham? About this heart and brain?

A few mornings after MacMillan's Christmas party, Denise didn't feel well and phoned in sick. When I got home from work she was curled on the couch in the living room in her flannel nightgown, a grim expression on her pale face, her short black hair sweaty and spiked like she was the lead singer in one of Sid's favourite punk rock bands.

"Feeling any better?"

"No. But I figured out what's wrong with me. Pissed on a stick. Turned blue."

This was my first hint of Sheena's impending arrival. Denise scowled as she told me, daring me to make an incorrect response.

"Oh," I said.

Apparently, I did not get it right.

"Don't worry. I'm going to exterminate the little parasite, bleach out the entire place, and post a warning sign in there: 'Trespassers will be crucified upside down'."

I look at Sheena watching Dorothy trying to get home, her arm draped around Julia, and then look up into the corner of our hotel room and see the filament of a spider web drifting in the currents of the air. I might have been my younger self looking away from Denise's burning eyes, up into the corner of Denise's apartment, and seeing the same spider's web.

"We'll talk about it," I said.

"No, we will not. Nothing for you to talk about. None of your fucking business. I spent the day reading your diary." She motioned to where my journal was lying on the coffee table. I had not noticed it there. I picked it up and met Denise's eyes.

"I was curious. Do forgive me."

"It's private!"

"It certainly is."

Her eyes were sunk in hollow dark pits. She bit her bottom lip as if trying to draw blood. All I could do was shake my head.

Denise took a deep breath, her face pale as a corpse. *"Look into my eyes and make me come.* Anyway, it doesn't matter. I hope you enjoyed the Candy. Capital C."* Her pupils seemed to quiver. "At least if you were going to fuck her little friend while she watched you could have accepted her job offer. You fucking coward. Why don't you grow up?" She sprang up from the couch, took two steps toward me, stood on her tip-toes, spat in my face, and backed away. *Pas de deux.* She took two steps back, looking very ill, waiting for me to react in the way she'd imagined I would react. She had been preparing herself all through the long day, but was still somehow not prepared as she watched the globule of spit dangling from my nose. I could feel her whole body had gone numb and her mind was inside out, pressing an impression into my mind. At that moment I was more her than myself. I wiped my face with my sleeve. "You bastard," she said. The television was on, mumbling away, unaware, the way televisions will. "I'm going to kill your miserable child."

She spun away and headed for the bathroom, left the door open, so I followed her inside before she could close the door.

"Get the fuck out of here! Get the fuck out!"

"Denise!"

She started to cough uncontrollably.

"I need a glass. Get me a glass of water," she gasped between coughs.

I went to the kitchen to fetch the glass. When I returned the door was locked.

"Let me in." The sound of her coughing had stopped. "I want to talk to you! I have something to say to you!" No response. I set down the glass and kicked until my foot went through the door and reached through the hole and opened it, marvelling at how remarkably easy it was to do—the remarkable thinness of a door. Denise sat on the toilet, staring at the floor as though she hadn't heard me coming. She didn't look up.

"I love you," I said.

"Love," she said, finally raising her eyes to me. A shiver went through her body like a snake passing over her grave. "You make me want to puke. Get out of my apartment."

I stood there looking down at her perched on the toilet looking up at me. "You know what I'm going to do? I'm going to burn those bloody pages." I went and got my journal, found a box of matches and lit one as I walked back to the bathroom. The match burned my fingers and I dropped it into the sink, shaking my hand.

"Very impressive. Give it to me."

She held out her hand. After a second's delay, I handed over my journal. She opened it and started reading. I was all at once dizzy and collapsed against the vanity, weeping, begging her not to read it again. She sat there reading, cold as the outer planets, never showing a sign that she was even aware of my presence. I was invisible. The journal was real. If I were to reach out, my hand would go right through her. When she finished, she handed it back to me.

"Go ahead. Burn it."

I took it from her and opened it, flipped to the offending pages, then flipped right past. I tore a ream of blank pages from further back, folded them, and set them on fire. When they were about to burn my fingers, I dropped them into the tub and we watched the flames consume them until there was only a froth of carbon lying there on white porcelain. She looked up at me.

"Fuck off and die."

I slumped against the wall, slid to the floor and sat there weeping for us and for our unborn child. She snapped off some toilet paper, wiped herself, stood up, and stepped over me to get out the door. I pulled myself to my feet and followed her to the bedroom, where she was curled in the middle of the bed.

"You're really going to throw everything away over nothing at all?"

"If you think it's nothing you're bound to keep on doing it for the rest of your life. You'll never grow up. Why can't you be a man?"

"I love you."

I clasped my hands as if I were praying and dropped to my knees. I'd barely been to church and had never prayed in any posture except as ordered by a teacher or minister in some assembly, but at that moment, Mary Abraham, this seemed the only thing to do.

"Just go away and leave me alone."

"What about you? What about you and MacMillan?"

"I don't give a fuck about MacMillan. Leave me alone."

"How do I know it isn't MacMillan's baby?"

"I don't give a fuck whose baby you think it is. It's nobody's baby."

I buried my face in the bedspread, my hands still clasped.

"You can't do this."

"I can do anything I fucking want."

She struggled up from the bed, but I stepped in front of her and placed a hand on her shoulder.

"Don't touch me!" she screamed, batting the hand away. I put one hand on either shoulder. "Don't touch me!" she screamed again and smacked me in the nose with the back of her hand. The jolt shocked through my sinuses, and when I touched my nose and pulled away my hand, I saw blood. She tried to get past me but I blocked her and rested my hands on her shoulders again. "I said don't touch me!" She hit me again and then raked her nails across my face, pushing me out of the way, but I stepped in front of her and placed my hands on her shoulders once again. She hit me again and again, sobbing now, finally showing enough grief to satisfy me. I let her pass.

I could taste my blood. After wadding tissue into my nostrils, I took nothing but my damaged journal and walked out the door. I was not wearing a jacket. It was raining. I went back inside and put on my jacket and left all over again. I had no idea where I was going.

Somehow I have arrived here in a hotel on Queen Street in Toronto.

"I'm melting!" the witch says.

December 30, 2012

Though I was three minutes early, you were waiting. Another coffee was how, I had understood immediately, it needed to be. I'd suggested a place I had never been, near the subway line, where Sid or his henchmen would have difficulty following without revealing themselves. No one followed me, I am certain. I have never been more alone. As I approached the table you smiled a little sadly and raised your hand. Before you was a latte.

"I'll just get a coffee."

I stood at the counter watching the young barista make my cappuccino, her panty line visible through her tight black skirt. Changing the direction of my gaze, I saw you studying me. When the coffee was ready—the fancy swirl in the frothed milk looked something like an oak leaf—I added sugar, balanced it back to the table, and sat down across from you.

"All is well with you, Mr. Bentley?"

Unable to meet your eyes, I looked around for some threat or blood offering going on at a nearby table.

"I'm fine. I'm just fine."

"You are?"

"I am."

The burgundy parka was draped on your chair. Your sweater was western, though more colourful than last time, an olive green, and your ebony hair fell over your shoulders in a mass of velvet tendrils: how do I describe your hair without sounding like a romance novel? You looked into your latte.

"Two days ago, I was lying in bed when a wave of energy hit me. Pain. Such pain. I saw your image in my mind. I was sure it was your pain." You raised your kind eyes to me, awaiting some response, but I did not know what to say to you, Mary Abraham, a woman who could feel my pain when I could not even feel it myself.

"I'm glad I was wrong. I'm not often wrong about this sort of thing. I am relieved to hear that you're okay." You raised your chin further and looked up to the high glass ceiling. We were nestled in a space that was once outside a grand old bank, the more-than-a-century-old limestone wall close enough that either of us could reach out and touch the fossils in the stone. The architect had designed a tall atrium that joined the new building to the old building, and the ceiling was forty feet above us, glass, so that the winter-blue sky was visible, as if to remind us we were once outside a building. I looked up and saw a gull glide over.

"Sorry to have alarmed you."

You brushed your hair back over your shoulders.

"I should not have bothered you. Something told me that I should not contact you again, but I could not stop myself. Unlike me. But the pain was so real."

"I'm glad you did. I'm ready to take you to The Beautiful Place."

You looked me directly in the eye.

"What's changed? Your wife's friend found a miraculous cure?"

"No. I had a dream. I dreamt of your husband. It wasn't the first time. I keep dreaming about your husband."

"You do? I see." You reached into your black purse, took out a breath freshener, popped one in your mouth, and offered one to me. I shook my head, took a sip of my coffee, and wondered if you were trying to tell me that my breath was bad. "What did Joseph say?"

"He said he was ready."

"Ready?"

"No. Sorry. That was the first dream. This one I saw him in a coulee in our big pasture and he told me he wanted his head."

"Oh? That's what he said to me. You are having my dreams now."

"Roughly."

As I told you the dream, you sipped your coffee. Until you interrupted me.

"*What* is it you say was in this large pasture?"

"A *coulee*. It's a *valley*, only smaller. Bigger than a *draw*. Where the runoff eroded a path to the creek over a few thousand years. This was a particularly deep coulee. We used to find buffalo bones there, and Dad found arrowheads. The Cree, the aboriginal people who lived there, used to chase the buffalo into a kind of corral they built there, and ambush them."

"So you know this particular ... *coulee*. Could you please spell that?" You reached into your purse again, took out a notebook, and opened it on the table. I spelled the word.

"*Coulee*," you said. "An indigenous hunting ground."

"A small valley. There are tipi rings along the edge of the creek valley there. You can see for miles up and down the valley. They must have camped there so that they could spot game from a long ways off. Or enemies."

"And that's where you saw The Beautiful Place. What did it look like?"

"The Beautiful Place isn't really there. It was a golden pyramid in the dream. Like the Great Pyramid of Giza. But smooth and polished. Plated with gold."

"The Great Pyramid of Giza? Built by Khufu. By thousands of slaves. I've been there. Have you?"

I shook my head, thinking guiltily of Julia, wondering if you were about to offer embellishments, name a few of those slaves you knew before you met Buddha and Jesus; but you did not.

"Dad and my grandfather and your husband were all standing at the base of the pyramid, down at the bottom of the coulee, and your husband walked up the hill to me and told me that he wanted his head. That's when I noticed he had no head."

You nodded, your hair fell over your left eye and you swept it back.

"He approached you. Without his head. When do we go?"

I looked you in the eye before looking away, up at the ceiling, the blue sky overhead, no birds flying, but a few clouds floating, and I remembered lying on my back in the pasture as a child watching the clouds passing above me so fast it gave me vertigo; made me aware that the world was actually turning and that I was clinging, helpless, to the edge of the earth.

"Soon."

"Soon?"

"I need to take my mother home. I just need to talk to my daughter about ..."

"I see. I'll pay for the plane tickets."

"I think we'll drive."

"In the middle of winter? Drive halfway across Canada? What's the excuse you gave your wife?"

I shifted in my chair and looked into my coffee.

"I need to take my mother home. I need to put her in a home, or at least get her more care. My father died a year ago and she's not doing well. She still talks to my father."

You nodded again and repeated the ritual with your hair.

"Do you? Still talk to your father?"

"No. We never talked much when he was alive, so maybe it's time to start."

"Maybe." You took a sip of your coffee and set the cup back on the table. "And what about your wife? Do you talk to her? What does she think about this trip of ours?" I didn't respond. "I must make it clear that I'm not willing to travel with you if she doesn't know and approve."

"You don't need to drive with us. You can fly and we'll pick you up at the airport in Regina. Though I'm concerned that Sid might be watching you and he'll follow if he finds out you're heading for Saskatchewan."

"I asked about your wife. Not Mr. Hedges. I don't really care what Mr. Hedges thinks about our trip."

"Maybe you should. Mr. Hedges is a dangerous man."

"I asked about your wife."

"My wife and I are in the process of separating."

Your features all at once melted away, your red lips puckering, the blood leaving your face, your shoulders collapsing as you leaned closer to me and you said, "No! I thought so!"

"It's for the best."

"I'm sorry. I knew something terrible had happened. Your grief hit like a tidal wave. I knew it was you. I'm so sorry."

I looked at the table, my hands gripping my coffee cup.

"Not your fault. So we're going?"

"We're going to the Beautiful Place. Joseph thanks you."

I forced a smile. "I hope my grandfather thanks me too."

December 1986, Vancouver

I stared, hypnotized, at the name typed on white paper shielded under yellowed plastic, *Philip Bentley*, but couldn't force myself to reach out and press the black button beside the name. After standing for several minutes concentrating, attempting some kind of extrasensory connection, I finally whirled around and began to walk away, but couldn't make myself do that either: after only half a block I slowed and eventually stopped, stood in the middle of the sidewalk so that a dog walker had to edge past me, the corgi sniffing my shoes, recognizing some forgotten love, before being yanked away. A moment later I was drifting back toward the building.

I had nowhere else to go. I couldn't very well go to Sid or anyone else at Universal Securities. Perhaps I could have gone to Billingsley, but I had no idea where he lived, and it might just as well have got me fired. After almost half a year in Vancouver, a seething mass of people—the West End was one of the most densely populated area in all of North America, according to Sid, more people per square foot than Manhattan—I had not a single friend I could call on and there was nothing left for me to do but throw myself into the arms of my family. Going to my grandfather was at least preferable to running back to the farm. I gazed at the name for another thirty seconds before stabbing a finger at the button.

There was no response for quite some time. Feeling a strange relief, I'd already turned to walk away when the voice came crackling out: "Hello. Who's there?"

I whirled back, took a deep breath, and spoke my name into the grill. There was no response beyond the low buzzing of electrons flowing, scattered remnants of the Big Bang. I thought I heard an intake of breath, but it might have been nothing more than white noise.

"Well … what a surprise."

The lock buzzed and I pulled the handle and stepped inside.

When I got to his door, it was open slightly, the chain still on, and I could see two yellow eyes peering out through the crack at me.

"I was kind of wondering what became of you. Not that I wasted all that much time wondering, to be honest. Don't worry yourself about that."

"Yeah. Sorry. Things got a little busy."

"Busy? Count your blessings. Some mornings I wake up and pretend to be busy. I like to make a list of things I don't really have to do and then don't do them. The only days I'm busy is when I have a doctor's appointment to check on the inevitable state of my inexorable demise. Nice to see you."

There was the sound of the fumbling of the chain and the door opened a little further so that I could clearly see his face, loose jowls quivering in the dim light. He looked even older than a few months earlier, when I'd seen him last.

"Nice to see you too." I resisted the urge to ask about his health.

"Haven't you got the rosy cheeks? Little boy cheeks. Must have got a bit of sun somehow. I can't stand the sun, but so often here I wish the days were brighter. Doesn't that just about sum up the human condition?"

"I know what you mean. The rain gets depressing."

We stood nodding at one another until he pulled the door open wide.

"I was about to get ready for bed. I'm tired pretty early these days."

"Sorry! I should have called."

"If you're here, you might as well come in for a drink or a cup of tea or something. I've got a bottle of red wine open. Rioja. Had it with supper and wasn't too bad. Or Scotch?"

"Thanks, but I don't need anything."

I stepped through the doorway and stood shuffling in the shadowy corridor, closet on one side and narrow black decorative Japanese table on the other. He closed and bolted the lock. "I need to ask you a favour."

My grandfather cocked his head and lifted one eye with suspicion. "Oh?" he said. "What happened to your face?"

I touched the marks tracing across my cheek, as though

feeling the wounds might help me better remember the nails piercing my skin.

"Nothing. I need a place to stay for a little while."

"Oh?"

"Denise and I had a fight."

"Oh!" He grimaced. "And you want to stay here?"

"Just for a little while. Would that be okay?"

"Well … the thing is…," he motioned toward the apartment, "there's not a lot of room."

"I can sleep on the couch. Just for a … few days."

The old man shook his head severely, the gesture reminding me of Dad scolding me about leaving a gate open.

"I'm not used to having anyone around. There's not even a guest room. I don't really see how it could work."

"You'll hardly know I'm here. I'll be at the office most of the time. Or out."

"I just don't see how … it could work."

I nodded, smiled acceptingly, and stepped past him to the door.

"I totally understand. Sorry to bother you so late." I twisted the bolt.

"Wait, wait, wait!" He put his hand on the door as if to prevent me from opening it, though he didn't have the strength to stop me. "You can stay here tonight. Okay? You can sleep on the couch tonight."

By way of offering him some chance to reconsider, I gave him a long questioning look before bursting out with, "Okay. Thanks! Thank you!" I re-bolted the lock. When I faced him again, the suspicion was back in those yellowed eyes. He raised a trembling hand and slid open the closet.

"Where are your things?"

He was looking at my damaged journal clutched in my left hand.

"I left … in kind of a hurry. I didn't really plan on coming here. I couldn't think of where else to go. Thank you. I'll have to go back and get some clothes tomorrow."

I took off my jacket. A clenched hand came down on my shoulder, steadying itself by gripping my flesh.

"There you go. You'll stay here tonight and you'll talk to her tomorrow. When she sees those marks on your face she'll feel terrible. Everything will be fine tomorrow."

He hung up my coat, led me into the living room, ordered me to sit, and pronounced that, under the circumstances, we needed a scotch. He poured us each a couple of ounces in heavy crystal tumblers. While I took my first sip of liquid fire, he put a classical recording on the stereo. "I've chosen something appropriate to the evening's festivities. It was traditionally sung by a castrated male." I flinched and, reflexively, clenched my thighs.

We settled across the coffee table from one another and I set the journal down there between us. The voice on the recording was so hauntingly high that it made me grit my teeth, images swimming through my mind of holding down calves while my father cut off their testicles with a jackknife. My grandfather went on for a while about how much he'd disliked Expo. Not that he'd actually gone, but he'd heard nothing but bad things. "Why would anyone want to pay big bucks to watch advertisements?" Dazed, I sipped a little more deeply, savouring the heat as it plunged down my throat to my stomach, nodding absently, falling under the cold anaesthetic of the alcohol and the blotches of black paint splotched on the canvases hanging around me.

"Is that your latest masterpiece?" He motioned to my journal on the table.

I shook my head. "Scribbling. I just remembered, I met another fan of yours at a party the other day."

"Pardon?" He looked annoyed at the mention of this unknown fan.

"He's a friend of Arabella Wiseman's."

"Oh. I met with her, you know? I liked her. She told me she might have bought a painting if she were not planning on dying so soon."

"She's an interesting woman. Her friend has one of your paintings in his dining room. One of the Main Street series. He's quite a collector and he really admires your work. He asked if you were still painting and I told him about these ones and he said he'd like to see them. He's dying to meet you. He gave me his card." I took out my wallet and flipped through the business cards until I found *Madison Fairmont Hedges II*, and handed it over. Philip Bentley studied it carefully.

"What kind of man would hide behind a name like that? With a number at the end? Sounds like a bad sequel. Redundant. There are only bad sequels." He glanced up at me and back at the card. "He must be rich if he has a Main Street. He'll hate these. I can tell by the baroque name and the design of his business card."

I raised my palms. "You never know."

"I do know. He might be interested in them as an investment, but it would be a pretty risky investment. These are so different from my juvenilia. In my naivete I may have managed to do something almost original. These are just failed Sobels."

"I think he likes risk."

"I'm not interested in being an investment. What was this fight about?"

"Pardon?"

"What was it you were sparring with your woman about? I hope she's not so badly disfigured as you."

The business card was extended to me between two quivering fingers. I saw an image of Denise sitting on the toilet, handing me the journal, her eyes the colour of apocalypse. I slipped the card back into my wallet.

"Nothing."

He shrugged dismissively. "Good. That means you'll definitely be home in your own bed tomorrow night."

"I doubt it." The old man sank back into his chair, looked away, forlorn, and leaned his forehead into the palm of his right hand.

"Other woman?"

"No."

"And do you … love … this other woman?"

"There is no other woman."

"Which is why you're not staying with *her*." He turned back to me, baring his jaundiced teeth like a dog preparing to attack. "So, no other woman. It can't really be that serious."

"She thinks there's another woman."

The soprano hit a note I had never heard before, that I had not imagined could be sung by the human voice; so high that it caused shivers to pass through my body like an electrical current. A moment later I had the strange sensation that I *had* heard it before, so long ago that I couldn't remember. My grandfather fidgeted, trying to find a more comfortable position in his chair.

"If she thinks there is another woman, you must reassure her. Don't worry her. If you love her. Do you love her?"

The ethereally high voice of the woman singing the part of the castrato overcame my grandfather's grumblings, and I closed my eyes. The voice polished the patina from my soul. When I opened my eyes again, my grandfather was staring at me, some drool trailing from the corner of his open mouth until he wiped it away with his sleeve.

"Do you want to call her?"

"Not really. Better to give her some space."

The old man lifted his scotch and peered into the crystal glass, divining the future in the ice cubes, before he moved the glass unsteadily to his mouth and sipped. The soprano's vibrato was pitched at precisely the same frequency as his tremor and so for the first time I could see the terrible beauty of those quavering fingers.

"I may have been wrong about you being in your own bed anytime soon. I'll get some sheets."

December 31, 2012

We have two double beds in our hotel room. I am sleeping with my mother for the first time since before I remember. The first night she lay in her quilted winter nightgown with her eyes open, glancing at me suspiciously as I crawled in beside her wearing my long johns and a long-sleeved T-shirt. Perhaps she was thinking of my father. I'm fairly certain no other man has slept with her since he died.

"Night, Mom," I said as I flicked off the lamp. She glanced over to the corner where Sheena was still up, staring into the glow of her laptop, her earbuds in, and then at Julia in the other bed, already asleep.

"Night, night," she said, closing her eyes to the noisy world.

Last night, after Mom fell asleep, our second night in the room, Sheena and I slipped out for a walk in the snow. I'd convinced Julia to go back to her mom's on the condition that she could come and be with us to celebrate New Year's Eve. I doubt that Beth will honour my commitment. On the other hand, perhaps she will. It will leave her a free agent to ring in the new year in her new life.

"What's the plan?" Sheena finally asked when we'd walked an entire block without speaking, snowflakes drifting down around us like the feathers of some ancient bird.

"I need to take Mom back to Saskatchewan. I need to sort out some care for her."

"I guess," she said. "I mean, we're going somewhere for a drink?"

"Yes," I said, trying to calculate which of the bars near our home was right for my daughter. Because it was less crowded, I chose the one with the beach theme over the one across the street with the English pub theme.

"We shouldn't be too long," I said when we'd ordered our drinks from the bored waitress in a tight red dress cinched by a thick black belt that Sheena studied carefully. "What if she wakes up?"

"You want to tell me to forget about New York, right?"

"No. Not at all. You'll go to New York. We'll figure it out."

"Oh, fuck off, Dad. Divorces aren't cheap. And you've got to put Grandma in a home. That must be expensive. Or does she have the money?"

"Don't you worry about that. You'll go to New York."

"How? What's the plan?"

"I'm sorry I brought you here."

She looked around the large, mostly empty room that smelled of stale beer, the retreating waitress taking the next table's order, the men slumped at the bar watching the hockey game, and a few other lonely parties at the tables doing the same (apparently thc bcach theme does not appeal widely at Christmas time). She was searching for the specific reason for my apology.

"To Toronto. I'm sorry it's been such a terrible Christmas."

"Whaddayou want me to say? Oh, that's okay, it would have been just as shitty with Mom? No, I think you managed to outdo her for once. Congratulations."

"I'm sorry."

Sheena ignored my apology, her hands locked on her knee, her fingers intertwined as though to keep them from strangling me.

"Who's the woman? The one Beth was screaming about?"

"Nobody."

"Fuck off, Dad."

I had never before noticed the way her skull revealed itself beneath her skin, and I wondered if she was eating enough.

"Do you want to get some food?"

"I'm not hungry. Who is the woman?"

"Her name is Mary Abraham."

I told my daughter about you, explaining that we are not lovers, that we will never be lovers, that our bodies were never meant to touch, that you are a messenger from the gods.

"You're taking her to The Beautiful Place to rescue her husband's head?"

"And your grandfather. The great Philip Bentley. Might as well pick him up while we're there."

She untwined her fingers and waved her hands in celebration.

"Wow. I'm coming too."

"Really? It's in Saskatchewan."

She laughed. "Of course it is. When do we leave?"

"The day after tomorrow. New Year's Day?"

She thumped her glass down on the table so hard whiskey sloshed on her hand.

"You're not taking me! You don't have a ticket for me! What the fuck do you expect me to do? Stay with Beth? Go back to Vancouver?"

I laid a hand on her shoulder to calm her.

"No tickets. We're driving. Sid won't expect us to drive."

"Driving? Fuck Sid. You do realize that he's more afraid of you than you are of him?"

She placed a hand on my hand and I felt her blood beneath the skin.

"Doubtful."

"We're driving all the way to Saskatchewan in the middle of the winter?"

"Through Canada. Sid won't expect that. You don't have to come. You could go down and check out Parson's and New York City if you want. I'll pay."

"And miss the trip with Grandma and the Messenger-from-God to rescue my famous frozen Great-Grandpa from The Beautiful Place? Fuck that!"

December 1986, Vancouver

"So how did it go today?" Philip Bentley asked with a tone that affected his complete lack of interest in my response.

We were watching television. It was only slightly earlier than I'd arrived the previous evening. I had returned a half hour before, pressed the button and been admitted, found the door open and the old man slumped in his chair watching *Miami Vice*.

"One of the few guilty pleasures I have left," he had said with obvious embarrassment, and I smiled in what I hoped was an accepting way.

"I've heard them talk about it at work. I haven't seen it."

For a long time neither of us said a word. I pretended to watch the unshaven men with their angular handguns and badges and diamond-studded earlobes and bright silk shirts but I was actually plotting my future. There were no vacancies in the building where I'd had my bachelor apartment, but there were some coming up nearby. But nothing available until New Year's Day. I was trying to figure out how to raise this: was it too much to ask to sleep for almost twenty nights on his couch? I'd killed the day wandering the streets and walking the seawall; had a greasy burger combo for dinner and to calm my stomach bought an apple at a greengrocer on Davie. I could go home for Christmas and put away a week that way, but then I'd have to face Dad's blank and furious eyes and Mom's interrogations.

"Interesting show. Dark side of the American city," my grandfather said when the credits were flowing past, a ubiquitous pop song playing. "I've seen a bit of that dark side myself. You wouldn't believe me. Not the kind of thing I should be telling an impressionable young fellow such as yourself. But you're not a child any more. You've seen both sides of the bedroom door." He paused, as though waiting for me to urge him to continue, and when I didn't he continued anyway. "I've seen the bottom dwellers who don't use bedrooms. Not quite the type they have on this show, but you've still got to dive pretty deep to find them. Size attracts them. I'm fairly big, by any standards. Sometimes I'd offer and then refuse. You wouldn't believe the things that go on in certain kinds of movie theatres. There are those who do, and those who like to have it done. I was one of the latter. That worked out well for me because size attracts them. You understand? Maybe you got my inheritance?" His voice faded away for a moment. Either he was savouring the memory or imagining my size, a thought that made me extremely uncomfortable. "I've never talked to anybody about this before. I have no idea why I'm talking to you about it now. My tongue's getting loose, along with my brain. So how did it go today?"

There was a commercial for some unidentifiable pharmaceutical on the television, featuring happily smiling people of various persuasions. "Not so well."

"That's too bad. Let me show you a relic of my checkered past." He struggled to his feet and went to the closet where he reached down a box from the top shelf. Considering the story, I was very nervous about what might be inside, and when he handed over the object, it was a handgun every bit as large and far more real than those we'd seen on the television show.

"Browning Hi-Power. My service pistol from the war. They were built right here in Canada. Toronto. At the Inglis plant. You know, Inglis? Home appliances. This is the only one of their appliances I have left in my possession."

I couldn't take my eyes off the dull black metal firearm lying heavy in my hands, and was not sure what to say.

"When I'm gone, it's yours. Okay? But you'll have to look after it."

"Thank you?"

Philip Bentley squeezed my shoulder, lifted the gun from my open palms and returned it to its hiding place in the closet.

—

Beth allowed me into the house to pack some things this afternoon. One of the things was my grandfather's handgun and the box of shells, still safely hidden under my dresser. I buried them in my suitcase between two sweaters.

There were papers spread out across the dining room table, which I tried not to inspect too closely. Strange how quickly a home can become foreign territory: my photos already removed from the bedroom and dining room credenza. I had experienced it once before, so there was something familiar in the alienation. We stood next to my grandfather's painting while I told her I was taking Mom to Saskatchewan to arrange care for her—that I'd already talked to the woman at the Prairie Sunset home in Broken Head and they said they'd need to do an assessment, so the whole process might take a while. Sheena had agreed to tag along.

"Well, that's nice. A father and daughter trip. Maybe you want to take your other daughter too. One big happy family."

She was looking her very best, hair meticulously fluffed and combed, makeup perfect, her lips matching her ruby earrings.

"What about school? It's going to take a while. Getting Mom settled."

"I don't imagine Julia will mind missing a little school. There hasn't been an hour gone by without her reminding me that she's going back to spend New Year's Eve with her sister and her grandma and her dad. She obviously wants quality time with you all. So here's your chance."

"All right then. That would be fine."

"All right. Happy New Year to you."

After I'd left, her red lips floated in my mind like an afterimage.

And so we're back in our hotel room for the celebrations. Mom is having a nap so that maybe she'll be able to stay awake past nine o'clock this evening. Julia and Sheena are both gazing into their phones. I have reservations at a French restaurant nearby. We will ring in the New Year with French food and wine, and tomorrow we will drive to Saskatchewan. What could possibly go wrong?

January 1, 2013

We are spending the first full night of the new year in Sault Ste. Marie, Ontario. Beyond the exotic French name that means Virgin Mary Cataract (Julia looked it up on her phone, cooing the pronunciation *"Sss-uuuuuuu,"*), we're not really sure where we are because we arrived in the dark and could not see beyond our headlights. Mostly our impressions are the whiteness of the snow in the moonlight and the tunnel of forest and red Precambrian rock on either side of the highway we've watched peel by all day, with glimpses of Georgian Bay now and then to our left. Our motel room is not much different than our hotel room in Toronto. Except that Mom is not here with us. When I explained our established sleeping arrangements, you apparently felt that sons should not be sleeping with their mothers, and insisted that Mom take the other double bed in your room, and so I have a bed to myself. You and Mom are likely already asleep. Sheena is studying her phone and Julia is using Sheena's laptop. They seem reasonably happy, despite the long, cramped day of driving.

My impression is that they have both fallen head over heels in love with you.

I have actually been in Sault Ste. Marie before. When I was eight and my brother Frank was ten, Mom took us on a road trip from Saskatchewan to Ontario to visit her family. My mother grew up on a farm in Southern Ontario. She'd come to Saskatchewan as a nurse to work in the hospital in Broken Head, which is where she'd met my father. Dad didn't come on that road trip. He didn't get along that well with Mom's family and so stayed home to tend the farm. Mom asked a friend, Alice, an English nurse, to come along for the long drive to help manage us boys. Sault Ste. Marie was a somewhat memorable stop because when we got into our motel room Frank and I started wrestling and bouncing on our bed and Frank went out of control—as usual—hit his head on the headboard, and had to be rushed to the hospital for stitches. Alice didn't drive so Mom had to take him, and I had to stay in the room and listen to the scolding of a stern Alice. She wasn't as harsh as she might have been, since I was her favourite. Frank was always the guilty party. By the time Mom and Frank got back she was telling me stories of the Blitz of London when she was a girl, sleeping in tunnels under the city while the bombs fell.

"You remember the last time we were in Sault Ste. Marie, Mom?" I asked her when everyone agreed that we should drive another hour and a half from Blind River, where we were having our supper in a truck stop. "We were jumping on the bed in the motel room and Frank fell and had to get stitches."

"Yes, Frank," Mom nodded, her eyes brightening. "I haven't seen Frank in a long, long time. I wonder how he's doing?"

I did not remind her that it had been she who had found him sitting in the feed trough in the barn, the rifle between his knees, a hole in his forehead, but a moment later I could see in her eyes that she had remembered. I reached across the table and touched her arm. Neither you or Julia had any way of correctly interpreting this squeeze, knowing nothing of Frank or how he was doing. Sheena turned and looked out the window into the Blind River darkness.

—

I'd checked out and managed to get everyone into the car before ten in the morning, which I viewed as a major victory on New Year's Day, and we'd picked you up at the coffee shop in North Toronto we'd agreed upon. We'd chosen it again from the Internet, close to the subway, close to the highway. Neither of us had ever been there before. The idea was to project seemingly random movements, in case Sid was watching. Despite the fact that it was New Year's morning and if he'd been watching at all he would know that I had been kicked out by Beth and was huddling with my family in a hotel on Queen Street, taken up by my own miseries and therefore obviously no danger to him, I could still feel him watching, his eyes following me in the crosshairs of his mind.

I was a bit nervous about how Julia might react to you, and so I'd explained that you were coming along with us because you were on your way to fetch your husband in Saskatchewan. That seemed to satisfy her. Sheena was curious and welcoming, wanting to catch a glimpse of the source of your faith. Sheena does not trust faith, but it fascinates her, and has always been a central theme in her art, represented by things like feathers, stone tablets, trees, jewels, and dust. She longs for the comforts of faith while having the tendency to sneer at the faithful.

Today you finally wore a sari, as I had longed for, vermilion, with a floral print at the border in a marigold shade. You had on your burgundy parka, but it was fairly warm for New Year's Day, so you had not zipped it up as we approached the car, where I had left everyone while I went to fetch you. My mother's reaction to meeting you was a new category of confusion. I opened the car door to introduce you and her face folded in a way that suggested she could not possibly absorb yet another scarlet woman introduced to her by her son, and this one with golden brown skin.

"Where are you from?" she asked.

"Toronto," you said.

"Oh? You don't look like you're from Toronto."

Sheena covered her face with her hands. You lifted your eyebrows and smiled.

"I am," you said.

After making your claim on Canada, you explained to my mother that you were originally from India. Your family, you said, had come from the province of Kerala, on the southern tip of that distant universe.

"Nice to meet you," Mom said.

You took Julia's hand next, telling her you were so happy to meet her. She studied you, obviously fascinated by your sari. Sheena had already raised her eyebrows to me in a way that I interpreted as approval. You took her hand next, and told me I was lucky to have such beautiful daughters.

I agreed. Sheena appeared a little distrustful of the objectify-ing patriarchal flattery, but at the same time could not help but look pleased.

We managed to wedge your bag into the trunk, and there was some initial arguing about the seating arrangements. I was intent on moving Mom to the back seat with Sheena and Julia, but you insisted you would sit in the back and got in between them. This thrilled both Julia and Sheena.

"Wait!" you said, as I was about to put the car in gear. "I have something for you. For everyone." You reached into your purse and brought out a small package, handing it over the seat to me. I opened the box, unwrapped the tissue, and found a small blue crystal figurine of a woman, seated like a Buddha, her left hand clasping one raised knee and her right hand cradling a vase to her belly.

"Thank you?" I said.

"Wow," said Julia. "Who is she?"

"Guanyin, the goddess of mercy and compassion. She'll be watching over us. She'll protect us on our journey."

I revolved Guanyin in my fingertips and finally let her rest in my palm. My fifty years on earth gave me nothing to help prepare a response to this declaration. This few ounces of glass would guard us from evil?

"Well? Do I put her on the dashboard?"

You shook your head. "She might fall and break. Give her to Julia. She'll look after her."

I handed over the goddess as directed and slipped the car into drive.

We were not yet out of Toronto when Julia, still studying the goddess, said, "I like your voice. You sound a little like

India and a little like England." In the rear-view mirror I saw Sheena roll her eyes.

"I suppose I do. Some of my teachers were from England. And my parents both went to England for their education."

You had taken off your parka, revealing the full splendour of your sari, the blouse, raw silk, matching the border.

"I'd like to go to India for my education," Julia said.

"I don't think the car will make it," I said.

Somewhere between Parry Sound and Sudbury you began teaching Julia and Sheena to meditate. I even wondered if Mom, craning her neck to watch from the front seat, might be taking in the lesson. The girls sat straight-backed, hands on their knees, while you told them to focus on their breath, the car suddenly so quiet that none of us could help but focus on your voice, wherever it came from, and on our breathing.

"What do you mean by 'empty'?" Sheena asked.

Emptiness, you said, is allowing your attachments to this world to fall away, so that you are connected directly to your own goodness, to the spirit of all existence, to God. Hollow yourself out and find fullness in your emptiness.

"Abandon your ego," Sheena translated.

I remembered Beth explaining this to me after a yoga class, advising me that it would be good for me to try meditation, as it might help with my insomnia. If only I could stop my racing mind at night, perhaps I might fall back to sleep.

Stop your monkey mind, you said to the girls, to us all. But I had to watch the road.

December 1986, Vancouver

My grandfather insisted he would make dinner for me my second night there.

I had spent the day looking for a new home, and was eventually escorted by a sad and balding superintendent through a bachelor apartment on Nelson Street. Four hundred square feet, except for the tiny bathroom, really all one room, but the kitchen separated into a galley by a partial wall. I liked the way that small wall demarcated the space where the cooking happened from the rest of the apartment. Somehow this seemed important to my future: different spaces to organize my mind, partition my thoughts and actions, position the posture and stance of the man I would become. The morose superintendent, scratching the mole on his forehead, said he would need a deposit by the following day to hold the apartment and I promised to bring a cheque. By the time I emerged into misting rain I had only a few hours to kill, walking the seawall, strolling the paths of Stanley Park, before I wandered back to my grandfather's apartment for the appointed dinner at seven.

Denise told me later that she had an abortion that day. I did not hold that against her: it was her body, and I certainly hadn't done anything to make her feel that I had any right to anything deposited there. Mostly, I was relieved.

It was over a year before she would become pregnant again with Sheena, but the lost child had whispered to me that Sheena was coming, that Julia was coming, and that there would be more losses along the way.

As I neared my grandfather's apartment, I planned how to approach the subject of the nineteen remaining nights on his couch. The dinner tonight was a promising sign, but I couldn't rule out that the formality of the occasion was meant to signal a goodbye: "It's been wonderful having you here, and I wish you all the best on your next couch." If that were the case, I thought maybe I could afford a room for two weeks in one of those decrepit hotels by the Granville Street Bridge. I wondered at the thickness of the doors, the trustworthiness of the locks, and at the desperation of the drug users who lived in those crumbling edifices. But with a plan and a secondary plan, I was feeling just the slightest bit proud of myself for my resourcefulness.

When I arrived, Grandpa was at the stove, paddling at a large saucepan with a wooden spoon. "This is a stew your grandmother used to make back in the Dirty Thirties. Only in the summers if we could manage to get special ingredients. Now you just walk down to the corner and all the fruits of the earth await you. I'll bet it's still part of her repertoire. Hope it doesn't make you homesick."

I washed my hands, set the table, and he served me a bowl of the stew with a chunk of crusty baguette, pointing out that it wasn't likely Grandma would have ever served crusty baguette in Saskatchewan. It was not.

"Bon appétit," he said, hovering over me like an ancient maître d'. He'd donned a black suit jacket over the striped blue dress shirt he'd been wearing while he cooked, which had been stained here and there by the bubbling broth. The stew was tasty, vegetables and beef and potatoes, but it reminded me more of Mom than Grandma. I really can't recall much about the meals Grandma Bentley made the times she looked after me or when we'd visited her apartment in Broken Head, except that, in a general sense, I preferred Mom's cooking. I do remember the tomato aspics and Tommy Douglas salads, the vein of lime green Jello running through, that she routinely brought to potlucks.

"I found an apartment not far from here."

His spoon halted before his mouth and his hand began to shake so violently that some broth and a chunk of potato spilled onto his place mat. "You did?"

"Unfortunately, it's not available until January 1st."

He set his spoon in his bowl, picked up the piece of potato with his fingertips, and carefully placed it on the edge of his bread plate.

"Of course. You'll stay here until then. That's not a problem." He coughed. "The worst part of this disease is that I can't risk eating in public anymore. Too embarrassing." He picked up his napkin to wipe off his fingers and wiped his lips, too.

"The stew's fantastic," I said. "Why don't I cook tomorrow night?"

"That would be wonderful. I hope. You can cook? You won't poison us?"

—

For lunch, at a truck stop near Sudbury, you ordered a spinach salad, asking the waitress to hold the bacon bits.

"Are you vegetarian?" Sheena asked. She had been frowning over the menu, brow furrowed, apparently trying to find the option that offended her least.

"I am. Only for the past several years. I still miss bacon. And fish. I particularly loved fish." You smiled warmly at my mother, who was listening carefully, and who had ordered fish and chips. Sheena ordered the spinach salad without bacon bits. Two truckers in the booth across from us were discussing the economy of Mississippi in comparison with that of Ontario.

"Fruit salad!" Julia said, clapping her hands in celebration. "I'm going to be a vegetarian too!" The middle-aged waitress laughed, shaking her head, and went off with our order.

"I think we made her day. Are bacon bits even made of real meat?" I asked.

"I'm not sure," you said. "Are they not?"

"You realize I was raised on a beef farm? My father had deep issues with vegetarians."

"Dad!" Julia said. Sheena clapped her hands over her face in exaggerated embarrassment. You smiled and looked at my mother, who was still listening carefully.

"Do you have deep issues with vegetarians?"

"Not at all. Are all Buddhists vegetarian?" The habits and beliefs of one of Beth's friends made me vaguely aware that they are not.

"Not all, but I am. Strictly speaking, I am not even Buddhist. I was raised Christian and I would still call myself a Christian. Though I had an argument with Christ a few years ago that led to my … discovery of Buddhism. Vegetarianism is part of my attempt to feel compassion for all sentient beings. I have since realized that it was my ego that led me away from Christ. And the habits of some of his followers. Even in my own family. I have sustained my relationship with Buddha."

"Do you have to pray twice?" Julia asked.

"Pardon?"

"Do you have to pray twice? To both of them?"

You considered this question carefully before you answered. "People have often imagined their gods at the top of a mountain. I also like to imagine them that way. All of the gods are really one god, on the top of that mountain. People just approach God from different directions, depending on which side of the mountain they are coming from."

While you spoke, Julia fingered the edge of your sari. Sheena had dropped her hands from her face and interlinked the fingers beneath her chin. I couldn't tell for sure whether there was irony in her crooked smile or not.

Mom's eyes had brightened as she listened to your words. She lifted her fork and studied the tines while she spoke.

"We were always told never to discuss religion. Or politics. Or the birds and the bees." She frowned, glancing self-consciously at Sheena and Julia. "But as I recall, that's pretty much all anyone ever wanted to talk about. Except the weather."

She smiled widely, showing all the gaps in her teeth, and looked out at the cars going by on the highway.

"Beautiful day," she said.

January 2, 2013

You bought a Virgin Mary figurine in the gift shop of our hotel this morning, Sault Ste. Marie printed on the base, and presented it to Julia in the car as we were pulling out of the motel parking lot.

"Mary joins Guanyin," you pronounced.

"And they're not on different sides," Julia said, contemplating the two figures, Mary in her right hand and Guanyin in her left.

"Different sides?"

"Different teams? They're on top of the same mountain."

Your face beamed warmth through the cold cramped car.

"Some believe them on different sides, but they are both on the side of compassion. They are sisters."

This morning you wore a blue sweater and a pair of jeans much the same as the ones Sheena wore.

"What was the argument you had with Christ?" Sheena asked.

I glanced at your faces side by side in the rear-view mirror, Sheena's lips set in a definite challenge and yours carefully pondering your response.

"I lost faith. I eventually discovered it was more an argument with tradition—with my family—than with Christ. A woman's place, according to my church, left no place for me. There were too many men standing between me and Christ."

"Too many men," Sheena nodded knowingly. "Your husband?"

"No, not really him. Well, maybe. He had no respect for faith of any kind, except science, which he insisted required no faith. He was a software engineer. He worshipped Ayn Rand."

"That must be how he found Sid," I said.

When you did not respond, Sheena found my eyes in the mirror. "Is that how you found Sid?"

December 1986, Vancouver

Monday morning, I had to go back to work at Universal Securities. Denise did not appear. Sid called me at the messenger desk. He was taking some time off to be with Arabella. He proposed we meet for a drink after work. Diesel and Sparks, the other messengers, sat listening, the office humming around us. I swivelled my chair so my back was to them. Sid suggested Checkers at 3:30 and I agreed, wondering what it was he wanted.

"That Sid?" Sparks asked as I hung up. "How's old Sid doing?"

"He's still sick. Chest thing."

Sparks crumpled a paper, threw it at the wastebasket, and missed.

"Faggot."

Impossible to tell whether he meant Sid or me or maybe even himself. For missing.

There wasn't enough time for me to stop at the apartment building to drop off my deposit and get to Checkers on time. Or I didn't think there was time, but when I got to the bar, Sid hadn't yet arrived. By the time he made his entrance it was close to four and I'd already ordered my second beer.

"How proceeds the battle?" he said, throwing his gloves down with great gusto and tossing his camel hair coat in one of the empty chairs. He wore jeans and his Clash T-shirt, the bass player destroying his guitar.

"Staying dry," I said.

He shivered, as though surprised that a T-shirt wasn't really appropriate for this time of year.

"Not easy right now. And after such a beautiful summer: a hundred days without a drop. In Vancouver! Those Russians certainly have developed reliable weather technology: I'll say that for them. But you look like you have allowed the rain to enter your soul. That's something my father taught me: never allow the rain to enter your soul. What happened to your face?"

"Cat got me."

"Hmmm." He rubbed his hands together to warm them. "Didn't know Denise had a cat. Heard a lot about her pussy." He settled himself into his chair like the accused and fictitious feline finding the right spot to perch, and ordered a hot toddy from Marlis, our favourite waitress in all the world: she was lovely in every way and always had a sunny disposition. "You want one too?" I shook my head, motioning toward my pint of beer. "You should. I swear, toddies are the only way I manage to survive the winter. Bring one for him too." Marlis looked to me to confirm and I relented.

We settled in, made a few unenthusiastic comments on the state of the city (the successes and failures of Expo 86) and of the world (President Reagan and his Star Wars initiative and the weather technology Evil Empire) and of Universal Securities (the other Evil Empire), before Sid leaned forward with a weary smile: "Arabella isn't doing so well."

"Oh, my goodness. I just saw her the other day. At Mac-Millan's party. She seemed to be doing … okay."

"She mentioned she saw you. I won't even ask what the hell you were doing there."

"How bad is she?"

Sid had caught the eye of an attractive young woman sitting at the next table and so had an incongruous smile on his face as he told me. "The cancer is moving into endgame. She can't get out of check. We talk about it that way." He unlocked his eyes from the young woman and turned them back on me, crossing his arms in a self-hug to warm himself. "The battle metaphor is more appropriate for life than it is for death. Death is a comrade across the table having a friendly game with you that you know damn well you're going to lose."

An image of Arabella, teeth gritted with pain, came into my mind.

"Sorry to hear that. You're okay?" I lifted a hand, considered reaching out, before letting it rest again on the table.

"Well … it's not like it's a surprise, is it? Surprised by death? You might as well be surprised when the sun sinks over the horizon. Without denial, we'd never be surprised. The animals are surprised, but not us. They never see it coming. Denial is our attempt to be like the animals. I got over denial a long time ago. When my mother went without saying goodbye. She was too afraid of hurting me. By saying goodbye. People are just so fucking stupid. Even mothers. I've known since then what I was getting into." The drinks arrived and Sid requested that Marlis put it all on his tab, including my beer. I protested, but Sid put a firm hand on my shoulder to silence me. When she was gone, he raised his glass. "But the thing I wanted to tell you is, Arabella's got one last pawn that's making a charge for Death's end of the board. And that pawn is about to become a queen."

"Cryonics."

"Of course. You know this. We delay the game indefinitely with cryonics. Until we've figured out our next move. But there's one small problem with cryonics—well, it isn't a problem with cryonics *per se*, but with the system as it stands. The problem is that it isn't legal to freeze someone until a doctor has pronounced the person dead. You see the conundrum. A cure for cancer is found and the body is regenerated, but how do you enact a cure on a body that's been pushed beyond the pale by the progress of the disease. Fortunately, Arabella has a doctor who is an expert in cryonics and who will sign the necessary documentation at the optimum time."

I swear I felt the hair stand up on the back of my neck.

"The optimum time?" I leaned closer. "You mean you're going to freeze Arabella before she actually dies?"

"She'd like to say goodbye to a few special people, so we're having a party tomorrow night. And we'd like you and Denise to come. And maybe your grandfather. Do you think he'd like to come?"

I took a sip of my hot toddy, attempting to hold my hand steady. "Is this a good idea? Should you even be telling me?"

Sid licked the centre of his upper lip. "That's a funny reaction. Am I telling you something you'd rather not know?"

"Well … maybe?"

"Because it's not above board?" Sid raised his eyebrows and leaned in close to give a stage whisper. "That's right. We're breaking the rules. We want to cheat our old pal Death. Isn't that dastardly of us?"

"I can understand … maybe … the two of you, and your doctor, wanting to do this for your own reasons. But I'm not sure why you want to bring anyone else into it."

"Because we want you to be part of our story, Bentley. Part of history. We want you to be our Saskatchewan representative. We think there's great potential in Saskatchewan. Hasn't death always been an issue there? I can't imagine any more pressing issue in Saskatchewan."

"I don't …"

"Don't give me *don't*. Do you really want to give your precious future to the Vancouver Stock Exchange?"

I took another sip and dabbed my lips with a paper napkin that said Checkers in black floral font on a red and white checkerboard. Sid pulled his lip balm from his jeans pocket. He applied it, rubbing his lips together to spread it evenly, and puckering them at me.

"I want to be a writer," I said.

"Great. That's a hobby. Unless you're a genius. Are you a genius?"

"I don't know yet. Maybe. I just want to write."

"Don't quit your day job. Didn't your grandfather work in advertising? Ask his advice."

"I have."

"And what did he say?"

"Don't quit your day job."

"You see? And the thing is, it's only going to get worse. It won't be long before machines will be writing better than any human."

"Machines?" I rolled my eyes.

"Yes. Artificial intelligence. Think of it this way, Bentley: How are you going to support that little woman of yours? You don't want her to be supporting you, do you? You realize that she doesn't want that? You realize that she'll lose all respect for you if she thought that's what you wanted."

Applying more lip balm, he was again studying the pretty woman at the next table.

"Denise and I have split up."

He turned to me and sat staring, the cylinder of balm arrested at his lips.

"What do you mean? What's going on?"

"We're having some problems. I'm staying at my grandfather's."

"Problems? We all have problems. Arabella is dying. That's a problem. That doesn't mean we give up on what's most important. Family. What could possibly be more important than that? You can't just walk out on your woman because you have problems."

"I'm not freezing her alive."

Sid didn't respond.

"I didn't dump her. She kicked me out."

"And why would she do that?"

I shook my head. Sid curled a foot up under himself and sat holding his hot toddy, hugging himself with his pale freckled arms, studying me with a perplexed expression.

"I'm sure she'd see things differently if you accepted Arabella's offer."

"It's not. No. I didn't … I don't want to talk about it. She kicked me out."

"Like hell she did. She's just pushing you away to make sure you'll come running back no matter how hard she pushes. It's a test is all it is, can't you see? You need to rush right back into her arms and hold her and tell her that you'll never leave her. Tell her that you'll never let her go."

"She's got MacMillan."

"She doesn't give a shit about MacMillan. You're throwing bullshit at me here, Bentley."

"What is this? I thought you'd be delighted. What happened to all your terrible warnings about Denise."

The young woman at the next table got up and pulled on her jacket, flashing her eyes toward Sid, before she pranced with her friends toward the door, Sid's eyes following her.

"You don't listen, Bentley. You started something, and once you've started something you can't just quit. You're not a quitter, are you?"

Marlis stopped to ask how we were doing and I watched her talking with Sid, who grasped her wrist lightly and released her. I wished I could touch her so easily. He ordered another round, and when she was gone he downed the last of his drink and set the glass on the table, motioning to my mug.

"Drink up, my friend. Fortify yourself against the rain in your soul. You know why you don't want to talk about the reason your lovely partner kicked you out of your beautiful new home? You're ashamed. I know you, Bentley. You wish you could go back to the way it was before. Because you want Denise. You want a family." I shrugged. "Of course you do."

I swallowed the rum-flavoured dregs of my cup, thinking of the fetus that Sid did not know about.

"Denise won't listen …"

"Of course she will. Talk to her. Tell her about tomorrow night. Let her know we'd like to see you both. Let her know that Arabella wants to say goodbye. For a while." Marlis approached with more drinks.

"And bring your grandfather."

—

I suggested a game we used to play on road trips when I was a kid, where everyone chose a colour and each time a car passed you got a point if the car was your colour. There were not many cars on a North Ontario wintery highway, though, so it was mostly too long a wait for another to appear, and Julia got upset that there were not enough red ones, her colour, so I traded her for silver. Gradually even Julia's interest dwindled away. You settled things once more with another meditation session.

After watching Lake Superior intermittently, we veered north toward Wawa, where we stopped for lunch. After we'd eaten, you insisted on driving. I told you I wasn't tired, but you'd seen me stretching my back uncomfortably and were adamant that you should take over for a few hours. I relented and switched to the back seat, Julia between me and Sheena. They were watching a Harry Potter movie on Sheena's laptop, each with one earbud. Mom was unnerved by the new driver, and kept twisting her neck uneasily to make sure I was still there behind her.

"I'm worried about your father," she said to me. When I didn't know how to respond, you did.

"What is it that worries you, Mrs. Bentley?"

"I think he may be a homosexual," Mom said.

Sheena took out the one earbud and put it into Julia's ear.

"What makes you think so?" Sheena asked when neither you or I had the courage to reply.

"I'm not sure," Mom said. "I just have a feeling."

"Your husband loved you," you said, and you reached out and with your right hand and took my mother's hand in yours, one hand on the wheel.

"Mary is right," I said. "Dad loved you, Mom."

I glanced at Sheena, who seemed on the point of adding something.

"It's in his blood," Mom said.

There was something in the way she said this that reminded me of my father. I had never before heard anything like this come from her, and she had certainly never expressed this worry to me. It didn't sound like her. Perhaps the dementia had carried her back to some current of my father's anger that lived on in her mind and she had turned that current, always directed against my grandfather, back against my father. In death he had abandoned her. I do remember an un-comfortable conversation years before, pre-dementia, when she told me that she had always had to be the instigator when it came to sex. It must have been her version of the birds-and-the-bees talk, though it came much too late, as I already knew all about sex. Or I thought I did, at least, and I had no wish to discuss sex with my mother or to picture my parents having sex. When she told the story then, she expressed it as some purity or shame in my father that made him want to pretend that they only had sex for her sake. Apparently he had aspirations of sainthood and did not trust his body.

"I'm not sure how well I knew the man," my mother said from the front seat.

Sheena scowled and bit her lip and I thought she would speak, but instead she turned away to the window to watch the blasted red rocks go by, the battered pines recede. She refused to look at me. A few miles later frozen Superior reappeared, sheets of blue ice piling up on the shore, and I realized it had always been there, vast, unending, immovable, except for the dunes of drifting snow.

January 3, 2013

We pulled out of Thunder Bay early, into the red sky of the morning. Sailor's warning. We finally left the lake behind, beside us all day yesterday, cold and looming like a lunar landscape, as we sped away into the heart of the great northern woods. We had not driven far, each of us settling back into our own space in the private world of our journey, windows fogging from five people breathing, when you produced yet another figurine and presented it to Julia. This one, in lotus pose, looked somewhat similar to Guanyin, except that she seemed more warlike, more powerful, and she wore a diaphanous robe, so that her breasts, even her nipples, were visible.

"Tara joins Guanyin and Mary on this third day," you pronounced.

"May I see?" Sheena asked, and Julia handed her over. "*She* doesn't look like a virgin."

You looked concerned by this observation. "No," you said, glancing at Julia. "She's from the Tibetan Buddhist tradition. She is joined to the male, both physically and spiritually."

Sheena handed her back with an expression of distaste.

"And what about Guanyin? Is she joined to the male?"

"Guanyin *is* a virgin. In one story she dies the night before her wedding. In another she is a princess who refuses the husband her father has chosen for her."

"What does her father do when she refuses?"

You paused before answering, as if weighing your words.

"He sentences her to death."

Sheena smiled bitterly and nodded, her hair still a little damp from her morning shower. "Maybe she's not a virgin. Maybe she just likes women."

She caught my eyes in the mirror when she said this. You did not respond.

—

When the snow began to sweep across the highway, obscuring and then revealing the car ahead of us, I began to tell prairie stories, attempting to demonstrate that this was nothing to me, that I had survived far worse.

"Remember the time we went to a movie, Mom, and a storm came up while we were in the theatre, and on the way home the blizzard got so bad that Dad made us roll down the windows because that's the only way we could see the edge of the grid road and avoid driving into the ditch?"

Mom thought about this, an expression on her face as if she were remembering, but she did not acknowledge that she did indeed remember.

"We made it home that way," I said, "even though we couldn't see ten feet in front of us."

"Will it get so bad today?" you asked.

"I hope not. I don't think so. If it does, we'll just have to stop for a while and sit on the side of the road."

Nervously, you began another meditation session with the girls.

December 1986, Vancouver

After my drinks with Sid, I didn't go to Nelson Street with my deposit for the apartment as I'd intended. It wasn't that I'd forgotten. Sid had made it clear what a foggy concept the future was, and I felt uncomfortable trying to fix on such a definitive course. Better to leave options open, I thought, as I wandered out of Checkers, weaving slightly because of the two beers and two hot toddies. Perhaps it was too soon to be moving on to a new life. Instead of putting down a deposit on my future, I bought the groceries I needed for the dinner I'd planned for my grandfather: *chili con carne.*

"It looks wonderful, but not too spicy, please," he warned, hovering at my elbow as I crumbled the ground beef into the saucepan. "Spice doesn't agree with me so well. Despite what I told you the other night. I hope you know to ignore me when I get talking that way. I can take a little spice, mind you. But not too much."

"You remember Arabella Wiseman?"

"Who?"

"The cryonics woman?"

"Oh? Yes. Interesting lady."

I stirred the sizzling meat, mixing it in with the onions and garlic as he stood there at my shoulder, watching.

"We've been invited to a party at her place tomorrow night."

"We? She invited me? I suppose you know I agreed to her proposal? I don't really believe in their ridiculous science, but what do I have to lose? They promised they wouldn't use me to promote their services until after I'm gone. If I'm not coming back, what difference does it make to me? If I am coming back…? If she's inviting me over, she probably wants to up-sell me. And I've already bought, so what's left to explore in the relationship?"

I had not known for sure, Mary Abraham. That was the first I knew. I was not really involved, except tangentially. I had arranged the introduction, but nothing else.

"She's dying. She's saying goodbye." Philip Bentley did not respond. "They're freezing her body the day after tomorrow and she hopes to come back. So she wants to have a few people over to wish her well. On her journey. And I guess they thought that since you're a client …"

"I didn't realize she was that close. So we're invited to the last supper?"

"Cocktails and *hors d'oeuvre.*"

I poured the hamburger fat down the sink, running the hot water to make sure it washed through.

"Is that legal? Don't clog my pipes!"

"I'll get some liquid plumber the next time I'm shopping."

"Good idea. Who else is coming?"

I opened a can of tomatoes and mixed that in with beef and onions.

"I'm not sure. Her doctor. Other friends. Not too many."

"A dozen or so," my grandfather said.

I opened a can of kidney beans. "It's not legal. We might be seen as accomplices to murder if we go."

"Really? That does sound exciting. In that case, maybe I will tag along. Don't get much excitement anymore." He crossed into the living room and stood looking out the glass patio door at his tiny balcony. "I never go out there. Even my balcony's too much excitement. Did I ever tell you the story of when I went to see Ezra Pound at St. Elizabeths asylum in Washington, DC? Drove down there from Montreal in the spring of 1955. I'm not sure why. Wanted to talk to the old man. Wanted to tell him I'd met his son. But he refused to see me. They told me he wasn't interested in talking to me. So I went away. Saw the cherry trees instead. Blossoms everywhere, like pink snow drifts."

I stabbed at the stewed tomatoes with my wooden spoon.

"I thought you said you didn't want to be famous for being frozen."

Philip Bentley shrugged. "Maybe it's better to be famous for something than to be forgotten completely. If people still hear my name, for whatever reason, maybe some of them will search out the paintings and look at them. I just want people to look at the paintings. Not only the old ones, but these too. Maybe cryonics will help me ring down the centuries. I mean, even if they can't really bring me back, at least I'll have that sort of immortality, and that would be more meaningful. In the long run."

"Maybe."

He turned from the glass door and stared hard at me, his chin quivering. I stirred in some chili powder.

"Not too much," he said. "Do you object? I thought you thought it was a good idea."

"It's really up to you," I said. "I don't like the idea of Arabella being frozen alive."

He came back into the kitchen to inspect my work. "No? I have to admit, the idea does not sound unappealing to me. What have I got left but long empty days watching these shaking limbs?" He held his right hand up before me. I shook my head.

"You have plenty to live for."

"Maybe I do now, with a grandson for a roommate. That's why I'm seeking your opinion on all my final arrangements."

"It's up to you," I repeated, spearing the meat with my spoon.

—

There were some tense miles, brief whiteouts, but after a while Tara prevailed and we broke through to hard clear sunshine. The Kenora radio station said it was thirty below. We spun on through the tunnel of trees, through the red rocks, the yellow lines guiding us. When we reached the Manitoba border I started to sing "Coming in on a Wing and a Prayer" and that started a singalong where each of us chose a song and the others joined in. Julia chose "Jingle Bells." Mom chose "Danny Boy." Sheena chose "Respect." You had to think for a while to come up with something we might all know, and finally chose "You Are My Sunshine."

By the time we reached Winnipeg, the car was quiet, Julia and Sheena both sleeping, their heads lolling onto your right shoulder and your left. When I looked in the mirror I was surprised to see you were watching me. You smiled, your eyes glowing in the gathering gloom. Mom was snoring, her mouth wide open, and every now and then she would bark something in her sleep, arguing with my father, the words almost, but not quite, decipherable.

Only six hours to The Beautiful Place.

January 4, 2013

I'm lying in the double bed I slept in as a teenager, in the bedroom I occupied all the years of my childhood until I went to Vancouver. Orange lath and plaster walls, the paint beginning to peel off the ceiling in places. Some moisture must be getting through. When I was a young boy, orange was my favourite colour. We had these Melmac plates and bowls—still have them downstairs in the kitchen cupboard—and at every meal I had to have the orange plate or the orange bowl or I would not eat. Frank always had to have the green ones. I have no idea what it was about orange that I desired. I suspect it was only because Frank liked green and I needed something that would clearly distinguish me from him. I needed my own colour.

Closet and cupboards custom-made by my father take up the entire north wall of the room, aside from the doorway. My father bought the bed frame at an auction sale for five dollars and added a new box spring and mattress. The same pulp paperbacks line the bookshelf in the headboard that were there when I was eighteen. I know where to find all the sex scenes. Not difficult. The books fall open to those pages.

All those miles covered to end up right back where I started.

—

Everyone had been anxious enough to get on the road that we got an early start from Winnipeg this morning. They could smell the barn, my father would have said. They were all in the car before nine, everyone in their places. It was the last day, but there was now a routine that made it feel possible we might keep right on going, on to the west coast and into the Pacific Ocean. Except we wanted it to be over, to reach our goals and destinies. I waited for the latest goddess to appear, but she remained hidden. Julia played with the three we already had protecting us. When we crossed the Saskatchewan border the anticipation increased, though everyone had slightly different anticipations: for Mom it really was the barn, and the house across the farmyard where she had spent the past fifty-something years. Julia too had fond memories of the farm, even if they were the shallower memories of a ten-year-old. Sheena and you, on the other hand, were both imagining your arrival at The Beautiful Place, Sheena's reasons a bit nebulous and perhaps superficial, yours far deeper.

Getting so close made me anxious. I began to imagine Sid waiting there for us. I knew I wouldn't be able to talk you out of going, but what sense did it make to take my mother and my daughters?

"I enjoy the landscape, but the cold would take a lot of getting used to," you said as you scanned your menu for something vegetarian at our mid-afternoon lunch in Regina. We were at a family restaurant near the highway. It was a somewhat upscale restaurant chain with a parrot for a logo, chosen because it had a range of vegetarian options.

"Just two-and-a-half more hours and we'll be on the farm," I said.

"When do we go to The Beautiful Place?" Sheena asked.

Your eyes were asking the same question.

"Well, I was thinking that maybe we'd go to the farm first, and leave Mom and Julia there, and maybe you should stay with them. Mary and I could drive back. We'll need the truck."

"Stay with them," Sheena said, her eyes beginning to take flame.

"You're going to The Beautiful Place?" Julia asked.

Mom sat listening, her head tilting slightly to each of us as we spoke.

"I was thinking it would probably be best if just Mary and I were to go."

Sheena pushed her chair back, got to her feet, yanked on her jacket, and marched out the door. At first I'd thought maybe she was going to the washroom, but when I saw her push open the door and walk out into the cold, I rushed after her, not even pausing to grab my jacket. The air hit me like a hard slap when I stepped outside. I called her name, but she didn't slow down, and having to negotiate the slippery sidewalk, I didn't catch up to her until she was half a block away. She still wouldn't stop, so I rushed past to block her. She turned and started walking the other direction. I grabbed her arm, and she flailed her limbs to extricate me.

"Where are you going?" I grabbed her arm again to make her stop, and she threw her fists at me, forcing me to step back.

"What difference does it make to you?"

"Of course, it makes a difference to me. You're my daughter. I love you."

I said this as much for a couple trudging by, listening, forced off the cleared path and into the snow in order to get around us, obviously wondering if they should intervene. It seemed to satisfy them at least, and they continued slowly on their way.

"You're such a liar! You bring me all the way here and then it turns out you just want me to look after Grandma and Julia."

"I'm worried it might be dangerous."

"Fuck dangerous! You're dangerous!"

Wild-eyed, she shrieked at me, her exposed ears glowing red in the brutal cold.

"Sheena! Please!"

"Fuck you," she said, and began to march away.

"Okay, okay. We'll go straight there. Come back inside and eat. Then we'll go." She stopped and stood for a moment, taking this in, turning back to look into my eyes, assessing my words. Our breaths plumed. It was so cold that I had started to shake. "Let's go and eat," I said, motioning for her to follow, and I walked back toward the restaurant. To my relief, she followed me inside.

We settled ourselves at the table and no one spoke for a few moments. Julia had been crying, and was being comforted by you. I touched her chin and said, "We're going to The Beautiful Place. All of us."

December 1986, Vancouver

The morning after I made chili con carne for my grandfather, we ate breakfast together, looking down through the patio windows that led to his balcony and into the damp green of Stanley Park. There were already the beginnings of a routine. He offered me "haggis or Cornflakes," chattered on to me about all his life's regrets, and followed me to the door as I was leaving, where he wished me a good day.

"I'll see you after work. We'll go to that party tonight. Should be interesting." He closed the door and turned the bolt. Those were the last words I ever heard him speak.

There was a plain white envelope, my name typed in capital letters, sitting on the messenger desk. "No personal deliveries for the brokers," Sparks said when I picked it up. "We don't want to set any precedent." Somehow he must have known it was from Denise. I waited until he went on his run to tear it open. Inside was the name of a basement restaurant not far from the Universal offices that served smoked meat sandwiches that were supposedly like the ones served in Montreal. The name and *3:00 p.m.* were scrawled in Denise's handwriting. I was puzzled by the location, a dreary fluorescent cavern I'd only once been to for lunch, but it was a place where it was unlikely that anyone from the office was going to show up.

The eternal rain misted down in waves, the mountains obscured behind a sheen of thin fog. People marched along, hunched under their umbrellas, thinking about tomorrow or yesterday or what might be happening in fifteen minutes or what they thought had happened fifteen minutes before. It made me think of the forty-below Januarys of Saskatchewan, the way the lethal cold made you focus right in on the here and now. I trudged along, thinking about tobogganing: the longest run of the day, when the body and the sleigh acted like water and traced the perfect route down the hill all the way to the creek.

I thought about Arabella, who was having herself frozen that evening.

When I entered, the restaurant looked empty, but I wandered around until I found Denise sitting at a table behind a partition in the back corner, writing something on a sheet of yellow, blue-lined paper. As I shimmied along the bench across from her, she did not speak or raise her eyes. I sat a while, watching her write, not wanting to be the one who made the first move. I wasn't yet sure of the rules of the game we were playing.

"I'm lost," she said, still without looking up from the paper.

"What are you writing?"

"Nothing. Shopping list."

For the moment I thought better to retreat and offered no response. She kept writing. A man came in and ordered a deluxe on rye with mustard and extra pickle. The electronic buzzer that had sounded when he entered also sounded when he left. Her pencil scratched on the table.

"You want me to get you a sandwich?"

She looked up at me. Her eyes steadied and focused on mine. She set the pencil down on the paper.

"No. Let's go home."

—

Four hours later I was lying in her bed, staring up at the white ceiling, Denise's head on my chest, her ear to the pounding of my heart.

I rotated my head sideways and saw that the clock said eight.

"Oh my god!"

"What is it?" Denise asked, not lifting her head from my chest so that I felt her words as much as I heard them.

"Nothing," I said, but I felt her body coiling and I knew I'd have to tell her something. "I just remembered I was supposed to take my grandfather to a party tonight."

"What sort of party?"

"Some friends of his. He doesn't get out much, so I thought I'd take him."

She was too still, rigor mortis setting in. A moment later she looked into my eyes.

"You want to go?"

"No."

"Go if you want. Good to let him know what's going on. Thank him. That was nice of him, to take you in. He probably doesn't like to stay out very late anyway."

She rested her head back onto my chest and I ran my fingers down the ridges of her spine, the way she liked.

"No. He won't mind. It's not that important to him. I don't think he even knows the people that well. I'll call him in the morning."

—

When I did call, after I'd made pancakes for Denise and done the dishes, the machine picked up and my grandfather's recorded voice, more than a little self-conscious and suspicious, asked me to leave a message. There was a long pause during which I could hear the old man breathing and struggling to find the right button before the beep finally came.

"Hi … It's me. I have good news. I had a long talk with Denise yesterday and everything's okay. So that's good. I won't need to steal your couch anymore. Thanks. Thanks a lot. I was going to call you last night but…. We were supposed to go to that party. Sorry. I figured you weren't that crazy about going. I'll stop by later and pick up my things. Thanks, Grandpa!"

Denise was vacuuming the carpet in the living room and I was putting up wallpaper, a fancy border just below the ceiling, a job I'd volunteered for ages ago and never got done, when someone buzzed the apartment. Denise answered and I heard mumbled voices and her buzzing someone in.

"The police would like to speak to you," she called.

There were two officers: a man and a woman. The man was middle-aged, paunchy, and the woman younger. The woman said my full name and I nodded. The man removed his sunglasses. There was glue on my right hand. I hid it behind my back.

"May we come in? We should sit down."

Denise took two steps back and motioned them inside. The man closed the door behind them and I directed the two officers to the loveseat. Denise and I sat ourselves on the couch across from them. Both officers looked me directly in the eye, and the woman spoke.

"Philip Bentley is your grandfather?"

I hesitated before confirming.

"I'm sorry to have to tell you that your grandfather died during the night."

They were watching my face for my reaction. I scratched my nose. "Died? How?"

"The circumstances were unusual, sir. Were you and your grandfather close?"

I nodded before I could make myself speak.

"I was just staying with him. For a few nights. Not last night, but for a few nights before that."

"You knew Arabella Wiseman?"

Denise took a deep breath. Both officers glanced at her.

"Yes. I've met her."

"Ms. Wiseman was your grandfather's companion?"

I nodded and then shook my head. "No, no. They were only acquaintances. Recent acquaintances."

"Acquaintances?"

"They have a professional relationship." Both officers waited for me to say more. "She is interested in his art. He was an artist. They were not a couple. My grandfather was gay."

The woman wrote something in her notebook.

"Ms. Wiseman also died last night. With your grandfather."

"With him?"

"Apparently it was a suicide pact."

"Suicide?"

"Apparently," the male officer spoke for the first time. "He left a note for you." He got up and carried the note to me and then returned to his spot on the couch. I looked at the note in my grandfather's spiky handwriting, but could not read a word.

"He's dead?"

The female officer nodded.

"We wanted to inform you as soon as possible. Ms. Wiseman, you probably know, is a public figure, like your grandfather, and we didn't want you to hear about it first in the news. There will be a lot of media attention, I'm afraid."

"Oh. Thank you."

"I'm sure this is a shock. You said you'd been staying with your grandfather?"

"That's right. I had. A few days. I was there yesterday."

"Yesterday?"

"No. Well, yes, but just in the morning, early, before I went to work. Last night I was here." I looked at Denise.

"He was here," she agreed, touching a hand to her stomach.

"This must be a shock," the female officer said.

I looked at the note again and made out my name at the top of the page. The glue on my hands stuck the paper to my fingers. When I looked up again I could see they were waiting for me to continue reading. I did.

The apartment is empty without you. I knew, of course, that you wouldn't stay forever, but now that I'm realizing you're gone I find I can no longer face the emptiness of my life, living with this disease. I trust you understand. I leave to you my service pistol and the abstract paintings hanging on my walls.

Love, your grandfather,
Philip Bentley

My breath caught, and I held it there for a moment.

"You're going to be okay?" the woman asked.

"Yes, I'm fine."

"Did your grandfather ever talk about taking his own life?"

I shook my head. "He talked a lot about dying. Well, actually, he did say something once about jumping off his balcony. But I never took it seriously. He didn't jump off his balcony?"

They both shook their heads.

"An overdose. Both of them. They were in Ms. Wiseman's home. Ms. Wiseman's physician discovered them and the sleeping pills and the notes. They'd made arrangements so that their bodies could be frozen immediately. You knew about that?"

I nodded. "He said he hoped to be brought back when they found a cure for his Parkinson's."

They looked at one another. "I'm sorry for your loss," the woman officer said.

We all sat silently for a few moments, imagining the old man's frozen body.

"We should be going," the woman finally said. I looked from her to the man, and got to my feet.

"Yes, thank you."

They stood too, and I walked them to the door. The woman handed me a card and I took it with my left hand, as it would have been awkward to take it with my right hand, the suicide note being stuck there.

"If you have any questions or if there's anything else you want to talk to us about, don't hesitate to call."

"Thank you," I said, the card already stuck to my left hand.

"Our condolences, sir," the male officer said before they turned and walked to the elevator. I pushed the door closed and turned the bolt. Denise was still sitting on the couch, staring at the floor at her feet.

"I'd better get this paper up," I said, looking up at my unfinished border.

—

I took the two right turns that got us onto the Trans-Canada Highway and set the cruise control. Julia started singing "Jingle Bells," repeating the verses endlessly until Sheena asked her to please stop. We drove in silence for a few miles before you said, "So this is home," indicating the almost perfectly flat landscape surrounding us. I glanced at Mom and she looked as if she were awaiting my response.

"I suppose. Haven't lived in this province in many years and where I'm from is not quite so flat. You'll see."

"I shall."

I couldn't help thinking about the gun packed in my suitcase between my shirts. My grandfather's gift. This visit to the Beautiful Place is what I had brought it for, and part of me felt it should be in the pocket of my parka, but I had my mother and my daughters with me. You with me.

"Can you tell us now where *it* is? Exactly," you asked.

"There's a Canadian Air Force base just south of Moose Jaw. Bushell Park. Where the Snowbirds train. There's a landing strip right beside the facility so that we can get the patients in quickly."

"Snowbirds? So there is military involvement?"

"Nothing beyond a monetary arrangement that benefits the Canadian taxpayer. Argyle rents the land. It's only half an hour from here."

Mom gave a slow nod.

Half an hour later I turned off the highway and drove a few miles along a paved road that took us past the gate to The Beautiful Place. White prairie rolled to the horizon beyond the high chain-link fence, three turbine windmills turning slowly in the frigid breeze. As we passed the gatehouse I checked to see if there was anyone there. It was empty.

"High security," you said.

I drove another half mile down the gravel road that led into the property. Traces of snow drifted across the road. In the distance the hulk of an old wooden aircraft hangar came into view.

"What's this?" you asked.

"The Beautiful Place."

"Really? And what about the spectacular Egyptian architecture from the film you showed Joseph?"

I glanced at you in the back seat and saw the reflection of your betrayal in both of my daughters' eyes.

"Arabella wanted to build, but after she died the funding for the facility never got off the ground. Sid felt that it was better to keep expenses manageable so that the cost of the infrastructure wouldn't cut into maintaining adequate care for the patients." I was attempting to sound ironic, but only ended up sounding like a rote Argyle apologist.

Smoke or vapour escaped from a vent and floated into the frozen sky. The snow had been plowed to the edge of the tarmac out front and on either side of the huge hangar door there was a smaller garage door and single red door. A beat-up Chevrolet and a new rental car were parked there beside an old Fargo pickup truck. I stopped the car and everyone got out, including Mom, who did not want to be left behind. I took her arm.

"Shall we knock?" you asked.

There was the sound of an engine and we turned to see another car approaching on the gravel road. When the car reached us, the window scrolled down and the driver, a young woman with bright orange lipstick, peered out.

"Can I help you? Are you here with Mr. Hedges?"

Perhaps she made the leap from our Ontario license plate.

"Yes," I said. You looked a little shocked at this lie, but Sheena nodded to support me.

"Well, it's bloody cold. You should get inside."

"Yes. We're not sure …"

"Is Arthur not there?" She rolled up the window and opened the door, got out of the car, and summoned us up the shovelled path to the red door, where she pressed a button. We stood waiting, stamping our feet to keep the circulation going, watching our breath, saying nothing. Julia started to sing "Jingle Bells," then stopped. At last the door opened and a man wearing a parka and aviator glasses peered out.

"They're here with Mr. Hedges," the woman said and the man nodded, stepping back to motion us inside. The woman led us through the doorway and Arthur closed the door.

The woman disappeared down a darkened corridor. The hangar loomed over our heads, machinery humming, lights blinking in the darkness. It was still cold, but not nearly so cold as outside. There was some large machinery, including a tractor, parked near us, and there was a smell of oil.

"Where are you coming from?" Arthur asked.

"Toronto," I said.

He nodded, scanning your face, my daughters' faces, my mother's bewildered expression, trying to make sense of this strange crew of visitors from Toronto. This bedraggled family. You stood looking around you at the cold aircraft hangar, more like a messy machine shop than something from the science fiction movie you were imagining you'd be walking into.

"How's the weather there?" Arthur asked with typical prairie politeness.

"Warmer than Saskatchewan," I said. "We're here for Joseph Abraham. One of the patients who came in a few months back."

Arthur blinked repeatedly behind his aviator glasses. "Uh huh. I remember. A neuro. What about him?"

"Where is he?"

He pondered the question.

"Right over here. The pod's still not full."

He led us across the hangar, through an aisle between piled boxes, and motioned at a cylindrical eight-foot-high metal pod at the front edge of two long rows of identical pods.

"He's right in here." He smacked the metal pod with the palm of his hand. "There's three full bodies and a couple neuros in with him so far. We can put six whole bodies in each dewar. That's the proper term for these vacuum containers ..." His words stopped and his expression changed to one of alarm.

I turned to see that you were weeping.

"I think Ms. Abraham would appreciate a moment with her husband," I said.

"Oh," Arthur said, glancing fearfully upwards. "I have some things I need to deal with…," and he scrambled away.

Sheena looked accusingly at me before embracing you. You returned her embrace, sobbing deeply.

"Mary's husband is in there?" Julia asked, pointing at the pod. I put my arm around Mom. Julia walked over and threw her arms around you and Sheena.

And then Sid appeared.

"Bentley? What the hell are you doing here?"

"Hi, Sid. You remember my mother. And Julia. Sheena and Mary Abraham. We've come for Joseph Abraham's head. And my grandfather's body."

"Hello, Sid. How's Arabella doing?" Sheena asked, smiling her most wicked grin.

"Arthur!" Sid called, and when there was no answer he called again. The little man finally appeared in the passageway, stopping abruptly when he saw the expression on Sid's face. "Arthur. Did you let Mr. Bentley and his family in?"

"Monica said they were with you."

"Monica said?"

"I'm sorry, sir. Should I call the police?"

Sid turned to me.

"What do you think? Should Arthur call the police?"

I stood contemplating the question.

"Police!" Julia said.

"I don't think there's any need to do that, Arthur," Sid said soothingly. "Apparently Ms. Abraham wants her husband's head, and Mr. Bentley wants his grandfather's body. Do you have any idea where Philip Bentley's body is, Arthur?"

Arthur wasn't getting enough oxygen and it took a few moments before he was able to speak. "One of the old original dewars. Near the back."

"That's great, Arthur. Let's find out exactly and get Mr. Bentley and his family on their way." Arthur nodded and hurried off.

Sid stretched, slouching slightly and reaching up to massage his right shoulder with his left hand.

"You just waltz right in here. Excellent plan. And bring the whole family. Excellent. Hello, Mrs. Bentley. Wonderful to see you again."

"Nice to see you, Sid," Mom said, looking very pleased to recognize a familiar face. "I remember you talking to Philip about the crops. You always thought we should have horses. Didn't you?"

"I did," Sid said wearily. "I like horses. Every farm should have horses."

"There's just one problem," I said. "We've only got the car. We can't get my grandfather in the car. Unless we strap him on the roof rack. Is there a truck we could borrow? I can bring it back in a few days."

"Excellent plan," Sid said, baring his gritted teeth.

Arthur and Monica came running, the expectation of blood and mayhem on their shocked faces.

"Do we have a truck the Bentley family could borrow?" Sid asked.

They looked at one another, taken aback. "I guess they could use the Fargo," Arthur said.

"Great. Let's get them on their way," Sid clapped his hands, all business, as if this were something he did every day: send corpses off to fend for themselves in the Saskatchewan winter.

Arthur went to work a little frenziedly, donning safety goggles and gloves, fetching a stepladder and climbing atop the pod to lift the lid. Vapours wisped off from the open portal. Arthur used a metal tool to fish around inside, finally pulled something out, something which he put into a burlap sack. He placed the sack into another sack.

"Got him," he raised it to show us. You gazed up at the offering, the shock showing in your blank expression. Arthur climbed down and handed your husband's head to you.

"Be very careful until he's warmed up some. He's so cold, he could burn you."

"Thank you," you said, hoisting the sacks slightly to test the weight.

—

The path to my grandfather twisted through a labyrinth snaking between the metal pods. Finally, Arthur knelt and pointed to the 4 painted at the base of one.

"How do we get him out?" Sid asked.

Arthur's forehead wrinkled. He was accustomed to putting bodies into storage dewars, but not removing them. "We'll have to roll the crane back here along this aisle."

It took them fifteen minutes to get the crane into position, towing it with a small Case tractor. Sid made a show of directing the progress. Arthur and Monica, and all of us except Mom, who sat resting on an old kitchen chair, helped to clear the aisle in spots where supplies had been stacked and were blocking the way. Julia was particularly enthusiastic. The work made us a team of sorts, each doing our task for the common goal. As we worked, lifting boxes from one spot and piling them in another, Sid was smiling, looking much like the man who sat across the table from me at so many lunches, or scarfed down muffins in the food court back in Vancouver.

Arthur, still wearing his PPE, lifted the lid of the pod and attached the hook to something inside. He climbed down and pulled one of the levers controlling the hydraulics. Philip Bentley, feet-first, a metal harness around his ankles, slowly emerged into the air above us, swaying slightly. No definite features were distinguishable, but we could see him dangling there above the cement floor. Arthur pivoted the crane and lowered him slowly into a burlap sack that Monica was holding, and onto the dolly. Sheena and I, wearing face-masks, our parkas and winter mitts, helped to ease him to rest horizontally.

Pushing the dolly together, we rolled Philip Bentley's body out of the hangar and up some planks into the back of the Fargo pickup. Night had descended, the world enveloped in darkness, though it wasn't yet five o'clock in the afternoon. Arthur and Sid stacked the planks against the east wall of The Beautiful Place and I slammed the tailgate closed.

"Where's Mary?" I asked Sheena, and she pointed to the Lexus. You were already behind the wheel, prepared to drive away, the burlap sack on the front seat between you and Mom. I opened your door and leaned close to you.

"He'd be better in the back of the truck with my grandfather. Cooler."

You looked accusingly into my eyes, then turned to my mother, who was examining the sack. Your face was rigid as you lifted it with both hands and passed it to me. I took the surprisingly heavy sack and placed it in the box of the pickup.

"Okay! That's everything you need, Bentley?" Sid asked, his ears a bright red, his bangs dishevelled by the wicked breeze. He clapped his hands to keep the circulation flowing.

"That's it, thanks. I'll bring back the truck … soon."

"Don't worry about it," he said. "You keep the truck. Consider it a gift from Argyle. Maybe you can sell it to pay for Sheena's education."

"Fuck you, Sid," Sheena said before stepping into the car and slamming the door.

"You're very welcome," Sid said. He turned his back, walked to the door of The Beautiful Place, and disappeared inside.

January 5, 2013

I led you home, driving the Argyle pickup truck with your husband's head, and my grandfather, in the box. I'd asked if anyone wanted to ride with me, but Sheena and Julia preferred to stay in the Lexus with you, and Mom looked at me blankly. Something made it clear that all the females should be in one vehicle and all the males in the other.

Our last turn was a left, south, off the Trans-Canada Highway (which had led us west, with only a few minor curves, from Moose Jaw to Broken Head) and onto the super grid, built to withstand the pounding of semi-trailers full of wheat. I was driving into my past, leading my ghosts home by the leash of this frozen road. There is not a road on earth I have travelled so often. So many trips to town with my father behind the wheel, or with my mother behind the wheel. Twelve years, Monday to Friday, morning and evening, on the school bus, and later nervous trips as I was learning to drive, Mom in the passenger seat stomping an imaginary brake. Later still, so many trips back and forth with Sheena and Denise. Once Denise went into a fishtail and ended up doing a one-eighty and dragging the side of the car along the barbed-wire fence before we came to rest. Sheena was sure we were all going to die, and told the story every time we passed the place where it happened. I'll bet she told it to you last night.

Negotiating gravel is like driving on ball bearings, and you, not having the knack, drove very slowly, so that I had to drive much slower than I normally would.

We reached our home grid, I signalled right, and you slowed to a crawl as you followed me around the corner. Despite what I'd said to you earlier, it is still home. When we had travelled another mile, we once again reached the lip of the creek valley we had already passed through a few miles earlier. We crossed what looked like an abandoned road but was actually the rail bed where the branch line ran until it was torn up in the eighties. I remember the cry of the trains as they sounded their whistles at the crossing to warn the non-existent traffic. I'd heard them at night as I was lying here in this bed. Both the trains and my father are gone.

Crossing the rail bed, we began our descent to the farm, which was marked by a bluff of trees I'd helped to plant. They are mostly deciduous—poplar, Siberian elm, box alder—but there is also Scotch pine, green in our headlights against the white of the snow. A sign, *Philip Bentley*, is posted at the drive-way. One of the neighbours had packed or plowed the snow so that the driveway was navigable. The trees badly need pruning, windfall lying thick in the groves where rusted hulks of ancient farm machinery hunch, waiting for yesterday. The paint on all the buildings, a strip of reddish brown over a strip of white to match the colour of our Hereford cattle, is badly peeling. The cattle were all sold last year, after Dad died.

I stopped in front of the house, you braked behind me, and a moment later we were all standing there in the yard, looking at the dark house looming over us, while I helped Mom out of the car. I was a bit taken aback by how pale she was, how frail she was, the way her hair stood in unruly tufts like a worn scrubbing pad.

"We're home, Mom," I said.

She looked around her, at the house, and then at you and Sheena and Julia, shuffling in the cold, waiting to be invited inside.

"So we are," she said. "Door's unlocked."

—

You did not want to leave Joseph Abraham in the box of the truck, for fear wild animals, coyotes perhaps, might find him there, and so we took the luggage out of the trunk and locked him up safely. My grandfather remained where he lay. Wearing my mitt, I touched him through the burlap, felt the solidity of an arm that had been constantly quivering when I knew him. Was he thanking me, or was he cursing me for betraying any chance he had at another few years in this cold world? His frozen body would not tell me.

Once inside, I turned up the furnace, which had been set quite low. Mom kept apologizing for the mess, but there was not much mess. There was a rather unpleasant odour that I couldn't identify, the intensity of the smell increasing near the fridge and stove. You settled at the kitchen table with Sheena and Julia, everyone awkwardly silent. Julia propped on her knees on her chair, looking out into the darkness, and began to sing "Silent Night." Mom placed the kettle on the largest burner and turned on the heat.

The scent was strongest by the microwave oven. When I pushed the button to open the microwave door a putrid sour-milk smell wafted out and I caught a glimpse of something growing before I pushed the door closed.

"Oh, I never use that anymore," Mom said.

I saw by the expression on your faces that the smell had reached you and Sheena and Julia, adding new textures to the various accusations I could read on your faces.

"Let's have our tea in the dining room," I suggested, picking up the teapot from the table.

"Oh? Sure. We could do that," Mom said. You all stood, and Mom gave you a shy smile. "We might like to use my good china too. It may be a good china sort of visit."

"Why not?" I said.

She led us to the dining room and busied herself opening the china cabinet and bringing out a fancier teapot and frilly bone china cups and saucers laced with flowers. We all settled ourselves around the table. The clock chimed, hanging there in its spot on the dining room wall, the hands pointing at metal studs that represented units of time in their perfectly analog way. Mom placed a cup and saucer for each of us, making sure that Julia was having tea too, then took the teapot back through the wide arched doorway into the kitchen and rinsed it at the sink with hot water, swishing the water around the pot. You leaned close to the window to look out at the garden under snow. How many hours did I spend planting and weeding and harvesting that garden? You saw only an acre of earth surrounded by trees, lying under snow.

A few ragged cornstalks and raspberry canes pushed up into the cold winter moonlight.

Mom took tea bags from the canister on the rack over the stove and put two in the pot, before walking into the dining room and sitting down with us to wait for the kettle to boil.

"Their souls had to be lighter than a feather in order to get into heaven," Mom said. "The Egyptians. I remember reading that."

"I have heard that too," you said.

"That's true!" Julia said. "Their heart was weighed against the feather and if their heart was heavier than the feather, Ammit would eat their soul! Ammit was a goddess who was part lion, part hippopotamus, and part crocodile."

"Really?" Sheena asked and Julia nodded emphatically. "Ammit," Sheena repeated the name. "Maybe I'll paint Ammit."

Everyone turned to me.

No one spoke again until the kettle began to whistle.

—

I cleaned out the microwave oven, holding my breath to stop myself from gagging (as best I could tell, it was once a bowl of mushroom soup). Julia tried calling her mother on my cellphone, but there was no reception. Sheena tried hers too, and got the same result. I knew this from past visits, having to drive up out of the valley to the open prairie before I could make a call, but every time I returned I expected the relentless march of technological progress would have solved the problem. Julia used Mom's landline and got no answer and so left a message.

"We're here safe at Grandma's, Mom! Love you!"

My mother struggled to her feet. "I'm sorry, but I'm going to need to go and lie down. I didn't sleep at all well last night. The beds are all made. Julia and Sheena can take Frank's room and Mary can take Alice's," she told me. The guest room had taken on that name because Mom's friend Alice used to visit every weekend. I assured Mom that I would show everyone their room. Mom wrapped her arms around you and gave you a long Bentley hug. She did the same with both girls and then fluttered her hand at me.

"Night, night," she said.

I helped her up the stairs, worrying about how she had managed the climb when she was here alone.

When I came back down, you, Sheena and Julia were in the living room, staring into Dad's diorama of stuffed birds. I sat in Dad's chair, which you'd left unoccupied. There are twenty-eight birds, including the dead partridge that is being eaten by the great horned owl, but it is the golden eagle in flight and its pheasant victim that are the focus of the scene. The pheasant's pain, the eagle's claws in its back, its head thrown back and its bill open in a silent scream, have a certain eerie power: a death in action as portrayed by two dead birds.

"Your father did this?" you asked.

"Yeah. The painting too. The background. The landscape. The coulee."

"The coulee," you echoed.

"Grandpa painted that?" Sheena asked and I said that he had. "I didn't know Grandpa painted. I thought he hated artists."

"He hated his father, not you," I said, and thought of Philip Bentley out there in the back of the truck, finally come to the home his son had built for him.

"People sometimes have trouble seeing the good in themselves," you said. "But he makes you see the good in that eagle.
Not hatred. Not anger. Not fear. It's hard to see the compassion, but it's there."

I looked once more, for the millionth time, at the eagle
and that dying pheasant.

"A baby jumping into its mother's lap," I said.

You turned from the eagle and pheasant and gave me a
puzzled look. Julia, sitting next to you, still watching the
eagle, huddled closer to you, and you draped your arm
around her.

We continued to stare at the diorama, our eyes moving
on to study the other birds: sparrowhawk, snowy owl, great
horned owl (in the process of consuming its prey, so men-
acing that it used to traumatize our house cat when it was
displayed on the china cabinet, before Dad completed the
diorama), barn owl, bluebird, cardinal, Baltimore oriole,
meadowlark, brown thrasher. Most of them were found
dead, thrown in the freezer, or brought by neighbours who
had found them dead and froze them for my father. But not
the bantam rooster.

When I was three the bantam rooster attacked me. It had
strutted about the place like it ruled the world, and had tried
attacking me a few times before, so that I was afraid to go
outside. Dad's solution was to take me out and hold me in
front of the rooster, telling me there was nothing to fear.
Years later he explained that his plan was to bat the rooster
away when it displayed any aggression, thus teaching it not
to attack. Instead, the rooster sprang so quickly that its claws
were in my face before Dad could react, its wings flailing the

air around me like Zeus raping Leda. The bird drew blood. Dad dropped me, grabbed the rooster, and wrung his neck with one quick twist. I watched that rooster die and carried the trace of his claw above my left eyebrow for many years, but the physical scar has long since faded completely.

"Your mother needs you," you said.

"Yes. Maybe I need her."

"Maybe?" You didn't look at me, focused as you were on the diorama. "Would it be acceptable for me to spread his ashes here? Joseph. In the coulee from your dream?"

"That's it," I said, pointing to the background of the diorama.

"Yes. I thought that was the one."

"When would you bring his ashes?"

"I have them here. In my bag. What are you planning on doing with your grandfather?"

I looked at Sheena, who was listening intently.

"I'm not sure."

"What about cremation?"

"I was thinking that. We used to burn the dead animals in our pasture."

"I don't like the way you say it. *Burn the dead animals.*"

"Sorry."

"Joseph wanted to be *one*. He told me. All in one place. He didn't say where, but he was there in the coulee in your dream."

I glanced again at Sheena, who lifted her eyebrows but did not speak. Julia had curled up on the couch and her eyes were closed. You stood, apparently wanting a closer look at something in the diorama.

"What's that one," you asked, your finger indicating the bird with the brilliant red spot on its head that was boring a hole into the tree, only a foot or so below the branch where the great horned owl ate its partridge.

"Flicker. A sort of woodpecker."

You nodded. "It's beautiful. I wonder what it's thinking."

—

I carried Julia up to Frank's room, tucked her in, brought up Sheena's bag with hers, and showed you Alice's room. You said goodnight as you closed the door, not meeting my eyes. I left Sheena still reading in the living room. I'd intended to sit there with her and talk, but when I attempted an approach, asking how she was doing, she just grunted. I went off to my room.

I woke to find Frank standing at the foot of my bed.

"There's two girls in my room," he said indignantly

"My daughters," I said, before I realized he could not be there and woke myself to find the room empty.

I sneaked down the hall and found the girls both sleeping soundly.

—

This morning I came down the stairs to find you and Mom sitting at the kitchen table, drinking tea, gazing out at the sun coming up over the garden. The reflection off the snow was blinding, a brilliant golden halo.

"Good morning," Mom said. "Did you sleep well?"

"Not too bad," I said.

"You grew up waking up to this?" you asked.

"I did," I said, thinking of rushing through breakfast, trying to be ready when the school bus arrived. I'd certainly never recognized any beauty in the view. It was just there. I poured myself a cup of tea. We sat in silence for more than five minutes.

"How old are you?" my mother suddenly asked you.

You looked from her to me.

"Forty-nine."

Mom shook her head. "You can't be. You look twenty-nine."

Thirty-nine at most, I thought, but did not say. You are almost my age.

"Meditation must keep you young," I said.

"That's sweet. Thank you for having me here. For bringing me here."

"You're welcome."

"I knew it as soon as you told me. That you and your wife were separated."

You reached out and took my hand. I sat there looking at your brown hand holding my hand, the blue veins showing through my pale skin.

"You knew? What did you know?"

"That we'd be together," you said.

"Together?"

"Yes. For the rest of our lives."

Smiling with that spectacular warmth of yours, you took a sip of your tea.

"For the rest of our lives," Mom said.

I sipped my tca, considering this statement. What were you saying? I had been out of my marriage for one brief week, and you seemed to be proposing that I leap back into the fray. Did I not need a rest? You were even suggesting that I was already in, somehow, without even noticing. An arrangement that I had agreed to, presumably. It was such a natural state for me that I could not escape it if I tried.

"You knew right away?" I asked.

"Instantly. I've never known anything more clearly."

I sipped my tea. You sipped your tea. Mom sipped her tea. The sun rose higher.

—

In the afternoon we drove out—Sheena, you and me—in my father's four-wheel drive to look for the right place for the ceremony. You wanted to see the coulee from my dream, and so we went up there, in our north pasture, even though I told you I didn't think it would work. Grandpa's body was heavy, and there was no safe way we could drive down into the coulee. It was quite deep and steep sided, which is why the Cree had used it for the buffalo hunt. Bison. It was the kind of place that Frank might have driven, but he was not here to help us. We did not want his sort of help, which only led to disaster.

Perhaps we could put the body on a toboggan. But what about the fuel?

We found a spot at the end of the coulee, where it meets the valley, right beside the creek. There's a hollow there next to the trail, making it easy enough to reach.

"Perfect," you said, and Sheena agreed.

"I think I'm going to spend some time here, on the farm, if that's okay," Sheena said, as we were driving back through the north pasture toward the house. I had to speed up at a low spot to ram the truck through a deep drift, you clutching my wrist to brace yourself, all of us swaying as the vehicle lurched ahead.

"Sure, that's fine."

"I'd like to do some painting. There's an art supplies store in Broken Head?"

Back at the house we started pruning the trees along the driveway for fuel. Julia came out to help load the wood into the back of the four-wheel drive and Mom came out to watch. When we had the box full, we drove up to our chosen spot in the pasture and unloaded, heaping the branches into a funeral pyre.

—

I found the winch out in the shop where my father always kept it. Blue metal. A simple mechanical device that worked without computers or electricity. It holds a place in my memory because of that night I ran afoul of Mr. Whiteman, the English teacher, and lost my high school education. She was a good heifer, but she was small, and the bull calf was so large my father could do nothing to get him out even though he was coming the right way. He had me pulling too, both of our bodies heaving back on the chains that were attached to the calf's front feet. We could see the nose appearing between its front legs, but we did not have the strength to drag him into the world. So Dad went and got the winch, hooked that to the chains on one end and to a metal bracket on the wall of the barn on the other. He cranked the lever back and forth, pulling it up so tight that it began to lift the heifer's hind quarters off the ground and drag her across the floor.

He ordered me to stand on the chain to try to force it to a lower angle, and I balanced up there like a tightrope walker.

We did finally manage to force the bull calf through that tiny passage and into the world but both calf and mother died. We cremated them later, up in the Big Pasture, in what we called the burn hole.

You directed me as I backed the Argyle pickup against the box of Dad's pickup and winched my grandfather from one truck to the other. It will be better to take him there in the four-wheel drive. Tomorrow. We don't want to get stuck. Tomorrow.

—

Mom roasted a chicken with carrots and potatoes, and boiled beets and green beans she canned last summer. I worried that there's wasn't enough protein for you and Sheena, but you waved me off, saying we could go for groceries tomorrow. After the cremation. We'll do the ceremony in the morning. You are planning to say a few words.

"And I'm going to sing," Julia said. "Not Christmas carols," she assured Sheena. "I'm going to sing something else. What's a good song for a cremation?"

"Is That All There Is?" I suggested, but no one else knew the song except Mom, who looked at me and smiled when I prompted her with the first few notes.

"It's so strange," you said, eating the beans you must have found bland and the roasted carrots and potatoes. "We could easily have never met. I might so easily not be here. But I am here. And we are so very happy. All of us together."

Sheena smiled, just a little ironically, and no one disagreed.

—

After dinner, you, Julia and Sheena started a meditation session in front of Dad's diorama. Julia and you had set up the goddesses—Guanyin, Mary, Tara—in a homemade shrine on the end table beside the couch.

I helped Mom up to her room, went to my own room, and closed the door. Lay there contemplating the orangeness.

For the rest of our lives.

I took the gun from my bag and examined it. Put it back.

Tomorrow I will return it to my grandfather.

I took my journal and stepped into the hallway. Mom lay on her bed, reading. I had noticed her reading earlier and realized she must have recovered from her double vision. When I asked about it, she did not seem to know what I was talking about.

I lay down next to her and she turned to me, not looking particularly surprised to see me there.

"Mom. Would you read to me? From this?"

I handed her the journal. She took it and turned to the opening page. I lay back on the pillow and looked up at the ceiling above my parents' bed. This was probably where I was conceived.

"November 1st," Mom read. "I address this to you, Mary Abraham, because you told me how you had met Jesus in a dream…."

She paused and turned the journal over to check the cover.

"What is this?"

"I'm not sure. Something. Keep reading."

ACKNOWLEDGEMENTS

The epigraph from Rilke's *Duino Elegies* is from the translation by David Young and Bentley quotes a line of Wallace Stevens on page 159.

In the only recorded interview he ever gave, Sinclair Ross was asked if he felt that neglect of his work had destroyed him as an artist. His answer was that a writer needs to be careful where he chooses to be born.

I was careless enough to be born less than one hundred kilometres from Abbey, Saskatchewan, the small town where Sinclair Ross held his first job at the Royal Bank, and the place he said was closest to his model for Horizon, the prairie town at the centre of his seminal novel *As For Me and My House*. By the time I decided I was going to be a writer, on November 7, 1980, four days after my nineteenth birthday, Sinclair Ross had already spawned a whole generation of prairie writers who influenced me (including Margaret Laurence, Robert Kroetsch, Lorna Crozier, Fred Wah, and Ed Dyck, to name just a few) but he, along with Wallace Stegner, was definitely my literary grandfather.

When I went off to University, I found myself defending his work to more than one student who had been forced to read it in an English or creative writing class, and insisted that it was dusty, boring and irrelevant. One English PhD student at the University of Victoria told me that Canadian literature was an oxymoron. I sensed that if there was no place for Ross's writing, there would be no place for mine.

In April of 1985, I moved into an apartment on Comox Street in the West End of Vancouver, but it wasn't until almost twenty-five years later that I discovered I had, for a short time at least, settled just four blocks from literary icon Sinclair Ross, who also lived at that time in an apartment on Comox Street. I made the discovery by reading Keath Fraser's *As For Me and My Body: A Memoir of Sinclair Ross*. I'd searched out this wonderful little book as part of my research for the novel I'd just begun writing. In its early stages I was calling my manuscript *Something*, because I had no idea what it was and I hoped it wasn't nothing. Its protagonist was a man who had gone through one difficult marriage only to find himself in another: not so surprising, which is perhaps the reason I'd decided to make the man the sales manager for a cryonics firm. Then one day Ed Carson, my boss and mentor at the School of Continuing Studies, University of Toronto, suggested I should write a sequel to *As For Me and My House*. It was only then that I realized I already was.

Thank you to Keath Fraser, whose portrait of Sinclair Ross was the inspiration for my Philip Bentley. Thanks to Ed Carson for reading my early drafts and encouraging my admittedly bizarre response to his challenge.

Thanks also to John O'Neill, Elizabeth Mulley, Linda Rui Feng, Diane Terrana, Lorne Kulak, Sherri Kulak, Dennis Bock,

Chris Gudgeon, Riley Gowan, and my agent Sam Hiyate who all offered feedback on the manuscript along the way. Thanks to Alison Hahn for the beautiful cover.

Special thanks to Kim Echlin for helping me to finish the puzzle of the penultimate draft, and to my incredible editor Elizabeth Philips at Thistledown Press for pointing the way to a final draft that makes me feel I've managed to achieve something I'd begun to think was impossible.

Finally, I am eternally grateful to Ranjini George for all of her insightful comments on the manuscript, her love and support at every turn along the twisting path to publication, and for her undying faith in the impossible.

Lee Gowan grew up on a farm near Swift Current, Saskatchewan, and studied at the University of British Columbia, where he earned an MFA in creative writing. He is the author of three previous novels: *Confession*, *The Last Cowboy*, and *Make Believe Love*, which was shortlisted for the Trillium Award for Best Book in Ontario. He is also an award-winning screenwriter, and was nominated for a Gemini Award for his screenplay *Paris or Somewhere*. He is currently Program Director, Creative Writing and Business Communications, at the University of Toronto School of Continuing Studies.